THE DESERT BEHIND ME

SHANNON BAKER

Severn River

Severn River Publishing
www.SevernRiverPublishing.com

This is a work of fiction. Names, characters, businesses, places, events and incidents are either the products of the author's imagination or used in a fictitious manner. Any resemblance to actual persons, living or dead, or actual events is purely coincidental.

ISBN: 978-1-951249-10-6 (Paperback)

ALSO BY SHANNON BAKER

The Desert Behind Me

Echoes in the Sand

The Nora Abbott Series

Height of Deception

Skies of Fire

Canyon of Lies

The Kate Fox Series

Stripped Bare

Dark Signal

Bitter Rain

Never miss a new release! Sign up to receive exclusive updates from author Shannon Baker and the SRP Mystery & Thriller Team.

Shannon-Baker.com/Newsletter

For Dave.
The voice I'm always happy to hear.

PROLOGUE

With all the evil people in the world, why did she target him? People murder children, beat them, neglect them. Terrorists drive trucks into families. Lone snipers open fire in crowds. Instead, she attacked him. He wasn't hurting anyone. He gave them money and gifts. They loved him. Why else would they come to him whenever he asked?

But she stuck her nose into it.

She ruined it.

She'll pay.

His family is destroyed. Emily and Tabitha are robbed of a father. Their mother will never afford the lifestyle he provided. Unless she remarries. Oh God, what if his beautiful wife remarries and his daughters call another man Daddy?

The cloying scent of lilacs mixes with the musty smell of damp earth. Through the new leaves and purple blossoms, the blonde hunkers over a textbook, nibbling on candy under the garish light of a cheap chandelier. She's pretty, but a little older than he prefers. Doesn't matter. This time it's not about desire.

He'd been waiting for this opportunity. Almost given up, deciding to take her from school or a track meet. She's careful, this little one. She's watched over closely by a loving and attentive family. Still, there's usually a breach, if one is patient.

He's patient.

And smart.

And justified.

He grins at the thought of her pain. Both the daughter and mother. The one will be over in a matter of days. The other will suffer agony forever. Guilt, despair, horror. His one regret is that she'll never know why. She should understand it's all because she interfered where she had no business.

If she'd have stuck to traffic tickets, DUIs, and burglaries, her daughter would live.

Silent footsteps carry him from under the window to the front porch. This is the part he hates but there's no other way. The knife is sharp because he hates his own pain. With a quick flick, he slashes above his hairline. A head wound bleeds so gratifyingly.

Holding the knife behind his back, he opens his throat and howls. He bangs on the door. "Help me! Please! Car wreck! My daughter!"

The sound of feet scampering through thin walls. She's probably thrown down that gnawed pencil into her open book. The porch light has already been turned on to welcome her mother later. She peers through the peephole, taught caution so well. Too bad it won't help her tonight.

The Academy Award should go to him, but again, no one will ever know. Except this child, and she's never talking to anyone else again.

1

Look at me. Maybe I'm not cracking jokes or bantering, but I'm not hidden behind my front door. Or surrounded by white walls, people with white shoes squeaking on white floors. I count this as a good day and promise myself better days ahead.

The exuberant energy of the Kino Elementary School fifth grade class rose from the playground. Hot desert sun sank through my black uniform and heat absorbed into my cap and beat on my bare neck where I'd tucked my ponytail under my hat.

It smelled of hot pavement, sweaty kids, and the sage of the desert on the breeze.

"It's good to learn how to fight back if you're attacked, but self-defense is more about preventing danger. Especially for us girls, who might not be as big as boys." These children thought of the lesson as a game. I hoped they'd never learn what I carried in every breath.

My partner, Patricia, fist bumped a chubby boy in baggy shorts. "You got it, Jose. Way to go!" Kids swarmed her, catching her enthusiasm like the flu.

Though they were polite and attentive when I spoke or

demonstrated a move, their affection gravitated toward Patricia. The kids might not warm to me as they once would have, but this afternoon marked real progress.

Tara worried that being around the kids and teaching basic self-defense, especially this week, might be too hard on me. Mom did her best to persuade me not to take the assignment. So far, I'd maintained control, even if they'd never think of me as the fun one.

We'd been assigned one of the volunteer student aides from the high school. A leggy blonde with a sweet smile. I couldn't help but steal glances at her, even though each time was like a knife to my heart. She helped out two little girls in rumpled shorts and messy hair. Obviously not the most popular girls in the fifth grade, the young volunteer's attention made them glow. The giggles from the three of them eased my discomfort a little.

Across the playground a Pima County sheriff's deputy worked with the younger group. Like Patricia, he seemed easy with the kids and they loved him. A Latino man, he was tall, broad shouldered, and had a teasing, confident attitude.

"Officer Jamie?" The four-and-one-half-foot-tall, tow-headed girl, all arms and legs, tapped me on my arm.

My muscles contracted, jaw clamping down for a split second before I registered the touch was no threat. "I'm an Arizona Ranger. You don't have to call me officer." I'd sounded stern and she hesitated.

Patricia caught my eye. Vivacious and magnetic, Patricia was everything I wasn't. We'd worked together often, as members of the all-volunteer Pima County Arizona Rangers unit. She'd been open and friendly, and I'd supplied her with the most basic details about me. She didn't seem to care if I responded with less transparency.

With conscious deliberation, I smiled at the girl in front of me and lifted my voice. "Officer is fine, too."

She met my smile, her teeth covered in braces, with bright pink bands. "I'm not sure I'm doing it right."

Swishing blonde ponytail, gangly limbs, a posture of such confidence she'll conquer the world. Someone else's pride and joy. Another mother's child. Not mine.

I waited for the tide to rise up and carry me off. Sadness pierced a hole into the warmth of the day, then faded to a dull ache. But I held together, no washing away.

With a breath to clear my head, I softened my face. "Show me your moves."

I placed my hands softly around her neck and she brought her arms up, knocking me free. "Like this?"

"Exactly." I raised my hand for a high-five. She slapped my hand in triumph, then ran back to her friends. The spontaneous gesture felt foreign, but good.

A real smile hit my face as I watched her practice with her friends. Movement caught my attention. My smile disappeared.

Across the playground, on the other side of the chain-link pocked with blue and red Solo cups outlining KES, a man watched the group.

Something about him. He wore pressed slacks, a blue golf shirt, a beige ball cap pulled low. More formal than usual Tucson attire, but not crazy. Nothing to alert me, except maybe the way he thrust his chest out, or the intense focus of his gaze, even if I couldn't really see it from the hundred yards that separated us. Still, the hairs on the back of my neck flagged and an electric shock jolted me.

The blonde helper with the two messy girls followed my attention. I must have looked alarmed, because her eyebrows cocked in curiosity. The man lifted his hand and waved, his white teeth flashed in a smile that sent a chill ricocheting down my back like a pinball.

I couldn't place the memory that hovered in my peripheral vision and I didn't pull it any closer.

I feel the darkness. See the moment of shock in his eyes when they focus on me. Then the smile in the night. Like a ghoul.

My handcuffs brand my palms with cold, and the orange glow of a street light casts telephone poles in black shadow. Frosty air stings my face.

Disgust clogs my mouth and tastes like ashes I want to spit onto the cracked pavement.

All I can do is haul him in. I hope they lock him away for a long time.

The memory dissipated and left me feeling sick. Where had I seen that smile? I couldn't go after him because of the children surrounding me. Had Patricia spotted him, too?

She stood in a crowd of children, all clamoring for her dazzling smile. Patricia wasn't watching the man on the sidewalk. She seemed disconnected to the children crowding her. Her lopsided grin and unfocused eyes on the school building surprised me. She swayed, acting like Dad on those long-ago Saturday nights, before Mom ordered him to bed.

Drinking on the job? That made no sense. One glance spared for the grinning man while I rushed toward Patricia. His shoulders pulled back and his chin raised in a stance like a hero. He tipped the brim of the ball cap. That's all the time I had for him as Patricia wobbled to the right, stumbled and staggered to the left.

The kids around her laughed, as if she clowned for them.

"Patricia!" I raced into the sea of little bodies and latched onto Patricia's shoulders as she tilted, just in time to break her fall to the concrete. Her eyes closed and she mumbled unintelligibly.

With only a flick of my head and a shout to alert the teacher's aide, I yelled over my shoulder. "Call 9-1-1."

I patted Patricia's black uniform pockets. "Where is it?"

She swatted at me with feeble effort; her words sounded like she spoke through mud.

"Come on," I mumbled. "You always have it."

A body squeezed in next to me. The Pima County deputy leaned toward her. He grabbed her chin. "Pete. Hey, look at me."

My fingers tapped a bulge in her pants pocket and I fished out a plastic pouch the size of a man's thumb. I bit the top off and a drop of sweet berry paste colored my tongue. With the pouch aimed at her lips, I directed the officer holding onto her chin. "Open her mouth."

He kept talking to her. "Pete. Hey."

The blare of an ambulance siren grew louder. "Open her mouth," I shouted again.

He turned dark eyes to me, noticing me for the first time. He looked confused as he scanned my face and then the plastic pouch. Finally, he seemed to understand. He pulled Patricia's chin down. I thrust the opening of the pouch between her lips and squeezed.

She wagged her head and spit out the goop.

The kids ewwwed at the slobbery pink paste dribbling down her chin.

I swiveled around to make eye contact with the aide. It only took a second for her to read my meaning and she grabbed hands of the two closest kids. "Let's back up and give them room."

With my face close to Patricia's, I clamped her mouth shut. "Swallow it."

Fingers gripped my shoulder and yanked. I resisted and wrenched free, then realized the EMTs were trying to get me out of the way. I scooted back so the EMT could do his job. "She's diabetic. I think she's in insulin shock."

The county deputy shot me a puzzled look before he too moved aside for the second EMT to get to work.

The teacher appeared, a young woman probably a year or two out of college. She stood hands to her mouth, eyes bright and teary. Maybe next time something like this happened, she'd be better equipped to handle it, but today, she needed help. The kids clumped around her, creating confusion. The blonde aide tried to assert authority, but her soft voice and lack of experience were no match for a panicky teacher. Some of the kids started to cry.

I clapped my hands. "Okay, let's line up by the swings so the emergency responders can help Ranger Sanchez."

Only a couple of the kids turned their heads toward me. The teacher stared at Patricia.

The young aide spread her arms and corralled several youngsters. "Listen to the Ranger. She wants us to go over here."

Patricia's eyes closed and she lay still. The first EMT spoke in a loud, commanding voice. "Ms. Sanchez. We're going to help you."

The deputy must have told them Patricia's name. I hadn't been aware they knew each other. Patricia and I had arrived much earlier than the deputy for this law enforcement appreciation day at the grade school. Our two-hour stint involved speaking about the Arizona Rangers, a civilian auxiliary that assists law enforcement. We talked about stranger danger and self-defense training to get the kids involved and interested. The deputy's session had something to do with an investigation where he'd staged a burglary scene on the playground.

The deputy, with a friendly face and a commanding presence, stood up, and with calm authority said, "You're all under arrest. March single file to the swings."

He hadn't raised his voice. In fact, he spoke much quieter

than I had. The kids scrambled away from Patricia and hurried to the swings.

The aide scurried behind them, her voice high-pitched, on the verge of laughter, and it worked to distract the kids into feeling like they played a game. "Hurry, hurry!"

Even the young teacher snapped out of her paralysis and made a stab at establishing order. "Let's go."

The deputy caught up to me. "Call Deon. I'll get the kids settled."

"Deon?"

He shook his head, puzzled. "Pete's husband."

I knew Patricia was married but not his name. She had kids, but I hadn't asked for details. In another lifetime, I'd have known their names and ages. We'd have shared babysitting and pool days. I was getting better, but I hadn't yet made the leap to friendship. "I don't have his number."

He reached for his phone. "Got it."

By now, the kids were stretched out at the edge of the pavement as if in a pint-sized police lineup. The teacher stood in front, right arm raised and hand flat. A signal, I assumed, for the kids to be silent and still.

Movement on the other side of the chain-link raised the hairs on my neck again. The guy in the blue golf shirt watched me. From this distance the details of his eyes and smile should be impossible to see. Yet, familiarity sliced at me with an edge so sharp I slapped a hand over my chest at the pain.

The deputy stuffed his phone into his pocket. "Deon is on his way to Tucson Med Center. Go with Pete. I'll talk to the kids about emergency responders. A real object lesson here."

The guy on the other side of the fence watched me, another ghoul from a hidden memory. I said, "We should get the kids back inside."

The EMTs had Patricia on a stretcher, still talking to her. They wheeled her toward the gate into the parking lot.

Without raising his voice, the deputy said, "Okay, kids. Ranger Sanchez is going to be fine. The Emergency Medical Technicians are doing their job. Police, fire, ambulance... we all work hard to make sure you stay safe."

Patricia on the stretcher, the deputy with the kids. The man watching me. I couldn't help seeking out the plucky girl with the blonde ponytail. She focused on the deputy with rapt attention, and a warm drop of relief spread through my chest. The helpful aide knelt next to a crying boy and hugged him.

Maybe it was wrong for me to focus on these two girls. They shared the soft blonde hair, long legs, and a certain kindness. So familiar. So painful.

A six-foot fence kept the man and the rest of the world away from the children. The deputy and the teacher wouldn't let them out of sight.

One more glance at the man before running to the ambulance. He tipped his head back and laughed.

2

The county deputy knew Patricia well enough to have her husband's phone number, so he should be riding with her, not me. But, since he already had the kids engaged, and someone should be with Patricia, I reluctantly climbed into the ambulance.

"Helps knowing she's diabetic," the EMT said to me. He inserted a PICC line into the back of Patricia's hand.

I'd done one thing right today. Steeling myself, I reached for Patricia's free hand and squeezed. "It's okay. Deon is on his way."

I had nothing else to offer so I kept hold of her hand until we pulled up to the emergency entrance and they rushed her through the glass doors. A handsome man with dark skin and black hair rushed from the hall. He wore a suit and tie. "Pete!"

Assuming it was Deon, I stopped and watched them move down the hall. There was no reason for me to hang around, but I did. They'd give her something to stabilize her blood sugar and she'd be fine in a couple of hours. At most, overnight.

The cool of the air conditioning made me jumpy and the hospital antiseptic smell kicked at my nerves.

Nothing waited for me at home, so I perched on the vinyl

seats in the lobby of the ER. Early afternoon on a weekday, the staff seemed capable of dealing with the few emergencies and I sat with only the voices in my head.

After a time, the sliding doors to the outside opened and the deputy rushed inside. He spotted me and hurried over. "How is she?"

"Deon is with her. I'm sure she's fine." I glanced at my watch. An hour had passed. It had felt like a couple of minutes.

An hour. Gone. Missing chunks of time unsettled me.

He sank onto the orange chair next to me. "I'm Rafe."

The name badge on his breast pocket said Grijalva.

By now, I'd mastered the art of meeting people again, most of the time even able to shake hands without snatching mine away. "Jamie Butler."

He watched the corridor where they'd taken Patricia. "You've known Pete for a long time?"

My answer came after the smallest of delays. Maybe he didn't notice. "We've worked together for a year or so. A couple of times a month, I'd guess."

"You must be pretty good friends."

I had hoped Patricia and I would become friends, but the constant fear she'd hate me if she knew my secret kept me at a distance. "Not really, just work."

His face remained passive but I felt scrutinized. "You know she's diabetic. Pete and I have been friends for a long time; our kids even play ball together. I never knew about her diabetes. But she told you, even though you aren't close?"

The industrial tile floor suddenly seemed fascinating. "She didn't tell me. I noticed her taking one of those glucose packs a few months ago."

He seemed curious. "You ask her about it?"

"Nope." Everyone is entitled to their secrets. I had enough of my own to protect.

Deon appeared from down the corridor and Officer Grijalva jumped up to meet him. "How's she doing?"

Deon slapped Grijalva's back. "They're talking about keeping her overnight but she's got them convinced she's fine and won't miss her assignment patrolling a high school baseball tournament tomorrow. I was looking for soda or something."

Grijalva directed him in another direction. Cops know the lay of the land in their city's ERs. Information gleaned from unhappy circumstances. He tipped a chin my way. "Can I get you something?"

I'd already risen and headed for the door. They didn't need me hanging around. "I should get going."

Deon hurried away, probably anxious to get his drink and return to Patricia. Grijalva started to say something, stopped and started again. "Isn't your car at the grade school?"

I'd already thought of that. "I'll call an Uber."

"Wait." He trotted after Deon and exchanged a few words. In seconds he was back at my side. "I'll take you."

Sure. Natural. No problem climbing into a cop car and making small talk with a stranger. I'd practiced in front of my bathroom mirror responding to invitations and introductions. My script and rehearsed facial expressions pulled from memories of Before. "Thanks."

We stepped into the blazing spring sunshine reflecting on the hospital parking lot, and Grijalva led the way to his Charger. He unlocked it and I braced myself. It had been three years since I'd been in a cop car. The light bar decorating the roof and the county logo on the side of the door pricked like a heat rash. The radio secured to the dash and the heft of the door, the controls for the siren and the unforgettable smell of coffee, old food, boredom, and adrenaline made me squirm.

I climbed in and reminded myself to draw the seatbelt across my chest, though Grijalva wouldn't. A cop on duty might need to dash out of a car, but that wasn't my job anymore. We maneuvered through the lot and onto busy Grant Road. He flicked his eyes toward me, then back at traffic. "Are you new to Tucson?"

Again with the questions. Of course this is how people get acquainted, but I was out of practice. "I've been here about two years."

"Where did you move from?" Friendly. Interested. Normal.

"Buffalo, New York." I answered before thinking of lying.

He didn't laugh or even chuckle, but his eyes somehow gave me that impression. "I can see where moving to the desert would be a big change. Were you a cop in Buffalo?"

I blurted, "How did you know?"

"You took charge when Pete went down. You didn't hesitate. Looked like you've had experience in emergency situations."

"Yeah. I was a cop."

"How long?"

"Twenty-three years. I'm retired."

His eyebrows shot up. "You don't look old enough to be retired."

A cold wave smacked my forehead. I'd said the wrong thing. Always. "I started young."

"My misspent youth will keep me working for a long time, I'm afraid." He didn't seem suspicious. Maybe I'd be okay.

"I liked being a cop." That was the truth, even though it had surprised me then.

"I do, too, I suppose. The brotherhood." His lips turned up in a hint of a smile. "Camaraderie is the better term."

Exactly. Friendships deeper than family ties. My chest contracted with a labored breath. Long, lost friends. "What about you? Been in Tucson long?"

He seemed to smile, though his face barely moved. "Born here. Three sisters, one brother. Sometimes they drive me crazy, you know? But it's family and you gotta love 'em. Don't see myself living anywhere else."

What must it be like to be part of such a large clan? Surrounded by so much love and acceptance?

We flowed through afternoon traffic to the school. Dismissal time clogged the street and parents lined up to take their turn in the circular drive to pick up their kids. In a well-choreographed dance, the cars moved through until school monitors placed their precious cargo into the safety of their vehicles. These parents probably believed their children were safe.

In the melee of children, teachers, helpers, and parents, I picked out one of the messy little girls from my earlier group. My heart beat quicker until she climbed into the back of a shiny SUV and the adult helper strapped a seatbelt around her before shutting the door.

Grijalva pulled into the lot to the west of the front doors and I directed him to my car. "You've been in Tucson for a couple of years, have you been to happy hour at the Hotel Congress?"

My chest tightened. He was steering me toward social waters. "I don't go out much."

He stopped beside my car. "I get you. When you're young, going to school or hanging with your group of friends, it's easy to meet people. Everyone is going out and having fun. Then you start to pair off and pretty soon you're having kids and just trying to keep up. Then, if you move or life changes, it's not so easy to meet people and make friends."

In another time, his easy conversation would have prompted me to join in. "I like being alone." *Liar.*

Not that Grijalva boiled over with exuberance earlier, but my words, or maybe the dull tone of my voice, seemed to shut him down. "Sure. Solitude is good. If you feel like you want to have some social interaction, though, feel free to give me a call."

Isn't this what I wanted, to make a connection? Maybe not

best buddies, but someone to talk to besides Tara and Mom? I hadn't prepared for it to happen today. I needed more time to get used to the risk of someone getting to know me.

He fished in his shirt pocket and brought out his Pima County Sheriff's Deputy card. "I hike a lot on my days off. If you haven't been up to Seven Falls in Sabino Canyon, we could plan a day."

This whole encounter threw me. Privacy kept me safe. Being alone made my secrets easier to hide. Still, I couldn't stop from spouting, "That's one of my favorite hikes. I did it a couple of months ago and the stream was running so high I had to take my boots off to cross."

This time he smiled wide enough to see his teeth. "That's the best time of year."

"I even saw a couple of big horned sheep." It seemed almost easy to carry on.

"That's rare. I've never seen them up there."

"In Buffalo we mostly had deer and squirrels. There's a lot more wildlife here. I've come across javalinas and bobcats in the desert behind my house. Lots of lizards and jackrabbits, of course. I even heard a mountain lion in Madera Canyon."

That nearly passive face somehow showed excitement. "Have you been to the Huachucas?"

"I was stationed there when I was in the Army a long time ago." The crack in my armor surprised me.

This time it didn't feel so much like interrogation. "You were in the Army?"

"Right out of high school. Like lots of kids, it was my rebellious phase. Kind of a 'screw you' to my mother. I grew out of it, went home, and became a cop."

"Me becoming a cop was my rebellion. My family hates it."

"I loved Arizona when I was in the Army, so when I retired, it seemed like the place to come." Not to mention the distance between Buffalo and the desert, which could never be enough.

He glanced at his watch. "Hey, I'm off duty in another hour. Would you like to catch a drink or coffee?"

Whoa. My pulse ratcheted up and heat scalded my cheeks. *Far enough.* "I'm. I. There's something I need to do." *Lame, lame, lame.*

He narrowed his eyes, seeing through my bluster, but he let it go. "Sure."

I opened my door and climbed out. "Thanks for the ride."

Most of the congestion from after school student pickup had cleared. One of the kids from our demonstration, the plump boy in baggy shorts, held the hand of another boy who couldn't be more than six or seven years old. They walked away from the school. No adult.

Rafe leaned down to look up at me from the open door. "You've got my card. Let's do a hike sometime. Or a drink. Or dinner. I like to eat."

I tried my best to smile and hide the fear throbbing through me. When the confident blonde fifth-grader with the gangly legs skipped out of the school and down the sidewalk, I quit even trying to smile. She headed off away from us, waving and shouting to friends, before she disappeared around the corner of the school.

Rafe lowered his chin in resignation. "I'm not as desperate as I sound. Sorry to come on so strong."

"It's fine. You're... it's good. Thanks for the ride." I swung the door closed before it got any worse.

I was so distracted tracking where the girl went I almost missed seeing the blonde teacher's aide exit the front doors. She scanned the street, then her face lit up. A generic gray sedan with the typical tinted windows of the desert crept into the pick-up lane. When it lined up with her, the girl leaned over and spoke into the passenger side window. She stepped back, swung open the door and slipped inside. I wanted to shout at her to stop, but couldn't pinpoint why. The driver was probably someone she knew.

Something pushed at my brain. It lay buried inside my head. But I wasn't in any shape to go looking for it.

Thankfully Grijalva drove away and didn't wait for me because as soon as he was out of sight, I started my car and drove slowly through the neighborhood surrounding the school.

I drove the route I'd seen the little blonde girl take. Around the corner of the school. She skipped and sang, her backpack flopping with her movements. We could teach them all about stranger danger and even some self-defense, but this girl paid no attention to anything, not even my red car idling past her.

The two boys, I assumed brothers, took their time, throwing rocks at a stop sign and petting someone's friendly Pitbull through a fence, not in any hurry to get to the house a few blocks away from the school.

I didn't think I encountered the car that had picked up the aide, but there are a million gray sedans in Tucson. It could have been just about anyone.

The boys didn't notice me and by the time they unlocked the door of a tiny slump-block bungalow, my uniform was slick with sweat and my hands shook.

Today, they'd made it home safely. But I couldn't be here to protect them every day. I backtracked to find the little blonde. She wasn't on the street where I'd last seen her, of course, and I drove in ever widening circles. They wouldn't let her walk home if she didn't live close, so logic said she was safely munching cookies telling her mother about Patricia's seizure.

Probably.

3

Patricia's collapse and meeting Rafe had been more excitement than I'd had for a while. When I pulled into my garage, shut the door, and retreated to the solitude of my house, I realized another couple of hours had slipped by. Had I been driving around? I hated that blank, though it happened less and less often. Worn down with worrying about toeing closer to making friends, and concerned about the aide getting into the gray car, I had a tough time sleeping and ended up taking a half a pill.

I jerked awake in the middle of the night, sure I'd heard my front door lock click. After checking it, my mind wound itself tight for the rest of the night, playing and replaying scenes that hadn't seemed disturbing during the day.

I woke groggy and took a quick swim to liven up. Driving through Tucson on my way to the ball park I had time to think about the day before.

The man in the blue golf shirt kept appearing in my vision. Royal blue against the dull browns and sages of the desert. I couldn't shake the feeling that I knew something important, but the memory lay buried with so many others.

I felt as though I'd been climbing a mountain, the summit in sight, and I'd slid halfway down. I probably should get through this assignment and hurry home to my solitude.

On such a beautiful spring day, the ballpark was crowded. People squeezed in the bleachers, jostled at the concession stand, and mill about waiting for their teams to play.

I met Patricia by the parking lot, where her husband dropped her. We said hi and not much else before walking through the ball park. I waited for Patricia to bring up her seizure. When she didn't, I thought I should at least show my concern. "How are you feeling?"

She acted as if nothing unusual had happened. "Fine. Great." Nothing more.

I understood not wanting to share everything so I turned my head to the concession stand.

The crowd shifted and I saw a poster plastered several places on the concrete structure. A locomotive slammed into me and I couldn't catch my breath.

The smile, fearless and full of mischief, reached out to me. She grinned at the camera, her blonde hair lit by sunshine. Above her impish face in bold black letters: HAVE YOU SEEN ME?

Patricia walked several steps before realizing I wasn't next to her. She followed my shocked focus and gasped. "Oh my God! She was in our class yesterday." Patricia sounded as sick as I felt.

I couldn't move, could only stare at that happy face, so full of life.

Patricia leaned toward the poster. "Zoey Clark. It says she didn't come home from school yesterday." She shook her head as if wanting to rid herself of the thought. "That's my worst nightmare. Losing one of my kids."

My throat was too dry to answer.

Patricia sounded close to tears as she continued to talk,

ending with, "I can't imagine what her mother must be going through."

I didn't have to imagine.

We patrolled together for a while without talking, then wandered apart.

These people filled the stands and ordered nachos and Cokes. So much laughter. A thousand smiles. Their daughters were safe. Life hadn't ripped apart the fabric of these lives. Yet.

Shaken and edgy, I pulled out my phone in case I felt the need to talk.

Two-years-old, maybe three, red-striped T-shirt and red shorts, diaper peeking out of the elastic waistband. Only interested in pushing his matchbook cars in his private bit of sand under the bleachers. Alone.

I held my phone to my face, my fingers tingling, and watched the boy.

Frank hissed into my ear. Whether I pretended his voice came through my phone or not, no one else ever heard Frank. *"Are you going to stand there and let someone steal him, too?"*

A tidal wave of voices rose and fell as I scanned the crowd for the toddler's parents.

Frank yelled at me. *"You let him take that girl."*

I didn't need my phone to hear Frank, but I used it in public when I felt I needed to answer him out loud. I spoke with as much calm authority as I could muster. "I've got my eye on him. He's not in any danger."

Only slightly mollified, Frank fumed. *"Like you protected her yesterday?"*

A young woman in a blousy tank top, with an improbable array of spaghetti straps crisscrossing her back, appeared and scooped up the little boy. He giggled and the mother collected the tiny cars, toting toys and boy toward the stands.

I slid the phone into my uniform pocket, tugged the bill of my cap to shield the glare of the sun and continued to patrol.

Three girls and one boy about eight-years-old, in shorts and tennis shoes, hair dark with sweat, and grime rubbed into faces, zipped through the beams of the stands in a frenzy of tag. A cluster of teenaged girls strutted past me on their way to the concession stand, their Daisy Dukes too short to hide the half-smiles of underage cheeks, tight tank tops creeping up their bellies. They seemed wrapped up in each other, but I'd bet they knew the location and level of interest of every potential boyfriend. They didn't spare a glance for a middle-aged woman in a uniform and badge.

All of these children. Vulnerable, stupid, asking for the world to do its worst and not even aware of their danger. Like Zoey Clark. Parents had no clue how fast little Johnny or Becky could be snatched. I watched the children of others, but I hadn't paid enough attention. And now she was gone.

Patricia stood thirty yards away, talking with a couple in their early forties. Someone in her neighborhood with kids in the same grade school as her own. Their serious faces told me they were probably talking about Zoey Clark, and Patricia's gaze traveled beyond the couple, quickly scanning the concession stand and alighting for a fraction of a second on me. If I were the envious type, I might be jealous of her blonde attractiveness, robust energy, and abundant friends that she ran into whenever we drew an assignment together. I didn't have the room to waste on those kinds of feelings anymore.

Apparently satisfied that everything remained orderly, she turned back to her friends.

I swept the area behind the bleachers, noting the knots of parents in red and blue. People meandered to and from the stands and I scrutinized each one, concentrating on not hearing specific conversations.

This was my least favorite tournament site in Tucson. The two diamonds were well manicured and facilities maintained, but the location concerned me. Only a chain-link fence separated the playing fields from a large park, with well-spaced palm trees providing puddles of shade, and scrubby grass rubbed bare in places. Not much of a park by my northeastern standards, without leafy trees and thick lawn, but by desert measure it afforded reasonable comfort for a large homeless population.

I suspected most of them were harmless, and more than one talked to invisible companions. Sometimes those voices told people to do things they wouldn't normally do. Bad things. Those voices could be clever and seductive and quite convincing. So, I kept a nervous vigil.

Three girls in tight yellow and black cheerleader uniforms and skirts lingered by the fence, showing no interest in the ball game. Even though they were dressed the same, down to the oversized bow in their ponytails, the sight of the tall blonde jolted me and I braced for shock waves.

The bright bow constructed of polyester ribbon encasing the silky blonde hair caused me to lose my breath.

I closed my eyes and saw our kitchen, the table littered with her geometry homework. She'd strung red ribbon across the kitchen counter and plugged in the glue gun. With one eye on the clock so I'd have enough time to get ready for my evening, I pinched and held while she glued the loops of red to create a ridiculous concoction for team pictures. I told her that hideous monstrosity will never stay on the barrette she'd glued it to. She laughed until tears flowed and offered to let me wear it for my date. She left it on the counter amid snippets of ribbon and the abandoned glue gun. She anticipated wearing it the next day.

These bows were yellow and black. Not red. Zoey's disappearance had me rattled. I reminded myself this is now. Not then.

After I felt sure I wouldn't crumble, I looked closer. I did recognize her. She was the teacher's aide from Kino Elementary. The girl who stepped into the gray car. Alive and safe, no need to worry about her.

Less than two feet from the others, she seemed outside the circle. She joined in with a forced giggle. The other two girls rolled their eyes and turned from her, they raised voices too excited by nearness of adulthood to hint at caution.

My job was to make sure they didn't have to learn the truths I knew. If I could, I'd tell their mothers to grab the girls' delicate wrists, shroud their fragile limbs in thick canvas, lock them behind steel doors. Keep them safe. Dear mothers, keep them safe.

I sauntered toward the group, expecting that one glance at my crisp uniform would scare their laughter from lips slathered in bubble-gum flavored lip gloss. They'd lower their eyes and turn away, barely noting a forty-something woman, brown hair in a neat ponytail, face that was slowly learning to smile again. They'd only register authority. Even though they weren't breaking any rules, I'd bet they'd created mischief too often to be purely innocent. So, they'd whisper until I paced away.

The blonde spotted me, then looked to the ground. Her slender neck stretched as if she placed it on the guillotine. Her straight blonde hair clasped in the oversized bow with wisps straining to escape in the hot breeze. She glanced up again, her face registered recognition. She started toward me.

The other two girls didn't notice me. Both with fawn-brown hair, the face of one was marred with acne and she seemed to take the lead from the shorter, obviously more confident of the trio. Stout and compact, the leader thrust a hip and tossed her head, like a filly straining to run. Her eyes sparkled and she laughed up at a dark-haired man on the other side of the chain-link.

The guy talking to the girls wasn't the high school quarterback, not even a frat boy. Maybe early thirties, almost six feet tall, straight shoulders, Levi's slung on narrow hips below a flat belly, blue golf shirt, dark hair. A young girl's ideal of suave and handsome.

Red flags flapped in a gust of suspicion. Blue golf shirt. Like the man at Kino Elementary. Except this man was taller, younger, and didn't have the arrogant tilt of his head. Nothing about him, save the blue shirt, should bring to mind the man from the grade school. Yet, there it was, throbbing inside my head. Someone said, "*Remember.*" The word evaporated on the wind.

The blonde took a few steps in my direction. The others huddled close, vying for the man's attention. The scent of budding desire wafted around them like the odor from a dead mouse in a basement.

My fingers started to tingle and an unseen fist squeezed my brain. The guy raised his arm and rested it on the fence, leaning into it. A pose like a centerfold.

"*Stop him! You can do it right this time.*" Frank's voice echoed mine.

I shouldn't have taken today's assignment. I'd probably stretched myself too far and the most dreaded day of the year was close. But my intuition triggered a warning about this guy. I couldn't risk ignoring that tingle, even if my inner struggles had thrown off that cop's sixth sense.

"Um, hi." The blonde girl approached me. "You were at the grade school yesterday, right?"

I shifted my attention to her, trying to keep an eye on the other girls. "Good to see you again."

A brief smile slid on her face and disappeared. "How's your partner? It looked like she was really having trouble."

The girls at the fence giggled and flirted. At least this girl was safe with me. "Thanks for asking. She's fine. In fact, she's here today."

Her face brightened. "That's great. Well, I'd better get back."

Not sure how to caution her about the man at the fence and my strange feeling that whomever she got into the car with yesterday was bad news, I hesitated. For all I knew, the driver was perfectly safe.

"*You know he wasn't.*"

"When you left the school yesterday—" Before I could form the words, I was interrupted.

"Hey. Hey, you." The voice behind me slipped off as soon as I heard it. I struggled to articulate my fear for the girl.

She backed up and waved. "Glad she's okay. Bye."

"Wait." What was I going to say to her?

The same voice sounded more urgent: "Will you help me?" I needed to address the guy at the fence. The girls didn't know how close they were to stepping on a land mine.

The man in the blue shirt called to the pretty blonde and she smiled shyly. She appeared not to question why a man, more than a decade her senior, would be fascinated by her. Girls on the cusp of becoming women assumed their position in the center of the universe. That could get them killed.

The short, confident one must have said something mean because the blonde colored and frowned. Both of the other girls laughed.

I needed to send that guy on his way. Whatever his game, I'd bet one look at my uniform and gun would drive him away. Unfortunately, like a wasp, he'd probably return when danger passed.

"Please, she's all I have. I—"

The hand on my shoulder made me twirl around and grab for my gun, heart jumping up my throat, eyes taking in every-thing at once. Several clusters of people standing around, more meandering to and from the concession stand, the group of teens behind me, kids under the bleachers, fans watching the game. The crowd of voices raised in confusion.

A man in a battered cap, with bad teeth and skin weathered to jerky by the sun, jumped back and held both hands up as if afraid I'd pull my gun. He shrieked and a few people stared at us. "Don't kill me. Please."

One deep breath to still my nerves and get my bearings. "It's okay." I used the calm voice I'd perfected by talking to Frank. "What is it?" The girls at the fence needed my full attention but this guy seemed on the edge, and if I looked away, he might go berserk.

Dirt covered his face like a mask. Once, he might have been as handsome as the creep coming on to the teens. Living on the street took a toll.

His eyes flicked around, absorbing as much of our surroundings as I'd done. Maybe he felt out of place on this side of the fence. "I lost my Petunia."

The high-pitched giggles of the girls rose above the noisy crowd. I held up a finger to the ratty guy, already turning away. "I'll help you in just a—"

He grabbed my arm and a chorus of shouts burst, drowning him out. His lips moved but I heard roaring and cheering. I pulled my arm away and the sounds faded enough I made out his voice. "She's my baby. My little girl."

My stomach lurched and bile swirled. "A child is missing?"

He grimaced, his mouth a mess of yellowed teeth, black lines against too-red gums, outlining each single tooth. "Not my daughter. My pup. Petunia."

Because of the anguish in his voice, I wanted to help. But the girls. "Okay, just give me a sec— "

"Please help me. I always watch over her. But this once I left her alone. Only for a little while. Now she's gone."

"I'll help you as soon as I—"

Tears overflowed his eyes and left streaks in his dirty cheeks. "You see, I'm always with her. But this one time I went out with a friend. And someone took her. What if they hurt her? What if she's dead? At the end of the day, she's all I've got."

He couldn't know how he dug at a scab that would never heal.

Once again, he reached to touch me, but I jerked away before his grungy fingers landed. The crowd roared again. I focused on the guy. "My partner will be here in a second."

I whirled around, striding away before I realized the group of girls no longer stood behind me.

A rush of people surged from the bleachers, making their way to the concession stand, bathrooms, and toward where the girls had been, with the parking lot beyond the park. One game over and the stands spilled, creating chaos.

Even though I fought to stop it, my heart kicked in and the tingling increased in my hands. My head whipped as I scanned the crowd, searching for the yellow and black uniforms.

Patricia's cheery greeting kept me from panic. "Look at this crowd! I'm sorry I wasn't patrolling with you. I couldn't get away from them. They're trying to get a teacher fired—hey, are you okay?"

People dodged around us, intent on their business. The voices rose and fell like waves, and I concentrated on Patricia, on her calm and normal appearance. "There's a guy with a lost dog. Can you talk to him?"

Patricia cocked her head and studied me. Her questioning expression wasn't anything new to me. "Of course. Where're you heading?"

I tipped my head toward the opening to the bleachers. "I want to check on something."

She snapped to. "What cha' got?"

I could tell her the truth, that I saw a guy yesterday who gave me the willies and—for some reason—think it's related to a girl who got in a car and probably has nothing to do with the same girl and a creep by the fence here. It swirled in a partial memory, and that made it smell bad. Instead, I hoped she'd give me the benefit of the doubt. "Probably nothing. Just icky hairs, you know?"

She knew what I meant by icky hairs. "I'll come with you."

I waved her off. Those neck hairs, what most cops rely on, had betrayed me before, and since then, even I questioned their truth. I didn't want others to witness my bad intuition if I'd really lost my instincts. I pointed to the homeless man. "That guy is worried about his dog."

Patricia's frown deepened. Clearly, she didn't want me running off on my own, leaving her with a homeless—probably disturbed and confused—man.

I only needed a second or two to prove to myself that I was overreacting, then we'd all quiet down. I hurried away before Patricia could stop me.

The buzz of conversation swirled around me, growing louder with the frantic beat of my pulse. The girls couldn't have gone far. I sprinted up the stands, hoping an elevated view would help.

There, that flick of the yellow and black hair bow and toss of brunette pony tails. The girls swayed and strutted away from the ball park along the sidewalk on the far side of the stands. The dark-haired man wasn't with them.

A voice in my head shouted at me. *Count them! There were three girls talking to him.*

I looked again. The third girl. The blonde was missing.

4

The acne-faced girl and the confident short girl, who couldn't pull off the tiny cheerleading skirt, sauntered away from the park. The shy blonde might be the most vulnerable to a man's attention, and she'd fallen for his compliments.

One small voice wished it had been either of the other girls, not the blonde.

I lunged down the bleachers, bumping and shoving my way through spectators, some arriving for the next game, most making slow progress toward the parking lot.

"Move it."

"Hey!"

"Excuse me."

Words bounced through my head and out again and I wasn't sure they were mine. It created a constant stream of static.

"Jamie!" Patricia's voice came through clearly.

I fought the urge to run after the girls and waited for Patricia to catch up. Trying not to sound breathless, I asked, "Did you find the guy's dog?"

Patricia held her palms out, unconcerned about anything. "I didn't see a guy with a lost dog."

My answer didn't sound as frantic as I felt. "Must have found his pooch and left." If I didn't hurry the girls would disappear and I'd never find the missing one. Except I had no good reason to think anything was wrong.

"You have a very good reason."

I fought my imagination that presented itself as a memory. One that didn't belong to me.

The junkyard is quiet—no one to hear her screams. She has no protection from the evil, the pain. Cold rain and icy wind shake the trees with branches sharp as bones, damp leaves and mud rubbed into her soft skin, stinging and raw. Skin her mother had lovingly sponged in her first bath the day she'd come home from the hospital.

I shook my head to stop it. Tucson, spring, blinding sun on a late afternoon. No musty leaves. Only saguaro and mesquite.

I couldn't ignore my icky hairs, even if they lied.

"A kidnapping." That's all the explanation I spared for Patricia before I took off.

Through the hubbub Patricia called me. She was as easy to ignore as all the others.

Heavy with my utility belt, awkward in polished black boots, I plowed through the people wearing tank tops, shorts, jeans, and sundresses. I nudged aside slow-movers in T-shirts, flip-flops, and ball caps. The smell of sun-ripened bodies and sunscreen twinned with hints of hot dogs and nacho cheese, overlaid by the desert-rare scent of freshly mowed grass.

The bright slash of yellow and black slapped against bare smooth leg. "Hey!" My voice sounded scratchy with fear.

Fifty yards out of the entrance the globs of fans had dropped off to a few people and the girls directly ahead. "Arizona Ranger. Stop!"

A young couple in front of me spun around and the woman reached for the man. Two grandma-types with sun visors gawped. But the girls, intent on their own hilarious conversation, bounced away from me, slapping each other and throwing back their heads in laughter.

I whipped by the people who'd stopped to stare, the sound of the crowd mixing with Patricia's light-footed race hitting the sidewalk behind me.

A few steps before I reached the girls, the taller one with acne twisted around and startled when she saw me. "Wha—?"

The other girl jumped back, eyes wide. They reached for each other instinctively, as if between them they'd find protection. One more lie they told themselves.

I struggled for composure. "Where's your friend? Where's the guy you were talking to?"

Patricia caught up to us, questioning me with her eyes.

"Did she leave with him? Did he give you his name? Say where they're going?" I was scaring the taller girl, though the shorter one showed signs of recovering. She hardened her face, narrowed her eyes, and shut her mouth. One corner of her lips rose in a sign of contempt.

I gave her my cop tone. "This is serious."

A slow smile built on her face. "What's crawled up your butt?"

Patricia stiffened and pulled up a tone she, no doubt, used with her children. "Can the attitude. One little girl has already gone missing."

I reached out and closed hard fingers on the short girl's wrist. The blood pumped under my hold, young, alive. "This isn't a joke."

As if she'd waited all her life for her starring role, she flicked her hair with a shake of her head. "You have no right to touch me. I'm a minor and this is harassment."

I squeezed her wrist. "Tell me. Where is she?"

Patricia laid a gentle hand on mine, signaling me to let go of the girl.

A woman's sharp-toned voice interrupted us. "What's going on here?"

The taller one shrunk into herself and cast a hopeful look at the confident girl.

The ringleader's eyes rounded; her whole posture changed to one of contrition. "Ms. Turner, this officer came after us. I don't know what she wants but we didn't do anything wrong. We were just at the game."

Ms. Turner looked to be in her thirties, decked out in yellow and black booster gear, complete with sequined ball cap. She frowned at me. "I'm squad sponsor. What's the problem?"

Patricia introduced us as politely as if we attended a reception, and added, "Arizona Rangers, patrolling the tournament."

I couldn't match her elegance of style. "They were talking to a man. One of the girls left with him. He's a lot older and I...."

Patricia's surprised expression didn't mask irritation that I hadn't told her about this.

Blood drained from Ms. Turner's face. She turned to the shorter girl. "Megan, is this true?"

Megan's faked look of shock shouldn't fool a seasoned teacher. "Absolutely not! I mean, I wasn't. I got a Coke at the concession stand, then Jen and I left the ball park. You said to be back at school right after the game."

Ms. Turner still didn't acknowledge the blonde. "Was Cali with you the whole time?"

Megan's look of guilt stunk. "Um, well...."

Right now, I wasn't interested in Ms. Turner and her investigation. I butted in. "Is Cali the blonde? Where is she?"

Jen, the girl with acne, opened her mouth. "You think Cali's in trouble?"

I barely kept my voice steady. "Do you know where she was going?"

Megan pulled Jen close to shut her up. Her focused jumped

between me and Ms. Turner. "Cali's not in any trouble. And we didn't do anything wrong."

Ms. Turner's eyebrows v'd; she let out a long exhale. "You three have pushed me far enough. Between showing up at practice late and disappearing midway through the last inning—"

"Jen started her period and she didn't have any tampons and Cali said she had some in her car."

I wasn't concerned with these girls earning demerits. I broke in again. "Cali. Did she say where they were going?"

Ms. Turner glanced back at the ball park, maybe looking for reinforcements, or giving herself a moment to contain her temper.

Megan took the opportunity to shoot me a derisive sneer.

I fisted my hands and bit my lip. A rusted white Honda Civic pulled up to the curb. The tinted window of the driver's side slid down, revealing a blonde ponytail held in a yellow and black bow, then worried blue eyes. Cali asked sheepishly, "Are we in trouble?"

Megan smirked at us. She whipped her hair from her face, stupidly confident. "No. But Officer Butthead will be if she doesn't stop harassing us."

Jen looked uncertain. Megan brushed past me and sashayed to the passenger side, hips swinging.

Ms. Turner rested a hand on Cali's window. "Okay. I'm not sure what all went on here, whether there was some guy flirting with you. I suspect Officer Butler is right. But no proof. I do know you ditched the game. For that, and for your disrespect of the officers, you're all on suspension for the rest of the tournament."

Megan's protests erupted. Cali immediately broke into sobs. Jen's mouth dropped open.

"I expect you to be at practice this evening, as usual." Ms.

Turner nodded at Patricia and me and stomped back to the ball park.

Jen slid into the backseat of the Honda and Cali's window started its smooth rise. Blinker on, slow and careful U-turn, the Civic joined the procession away from the ball park.

From the passenger side, Megan's hand slithered up, middle finger raised.

My stomach soured at the warning in my head.

"You're a moron. What happens now is your fault."

5

I trudged toward the park. The girls were safe for now, but my icky hairs stayed on alert. Recriminations rang in my head. Clearly my intuition was faulty.

Patricia fell in beside me.

I couldn't help defending myself. "The guy nosing up their skirts had to have been in his thirties. It could have gone wrong."

I heard Frank again. *"It is going wrong, moron."*

She nodded and kept her eyes on the sidewalk. "Always good to trust your gut. I only served on the force a few years before I quit when I got pregnant, but even then, I developed that sixth sense. How long were you on the force in Buffalo?"

First Grijalva, now more probing. I considered what to reveal. "Went into the Army straight from high school and to the academy when I was discharged."

"Your whole life, sounds like."

She had no idea.

She shook her head, pony tail wagging from the back of her Ranger's cap. As a teen, she'd probably looked similar to Cali. The image stabbed at me.

Patricia chattered as we walked. "I like taking shifts with you. Some people want to talk and don't let me keep an eye out. But, honestly, after the other day, I feel like you know me way more than I know you. So, you were military. What else?"

Possible replies, everything from a polite "not much to tell" to "get screwed" flew past me. They always ran the gamut, challenging me to pick appropriately. I chose a reasonable reaction. "Good thing about starting with the force early is getting to retire young enough to enjoy life."

"I agree. That was going to be my plan until I got the baby urge. Now volunteering for the Rangers is the closest I'll get to a law enforcement career. But I love being a mother."

My throat closed and I couldn't answer. My feet kept pounding on the sidewalk, taking us closer to the field.

Patricia seemed determined to be friendly. "I'm guessing you're happy about your move to Tucson." Her comment sounded winded and I realized I'd been striding out. I slowed.

"Desert's nice after the winters in Buffalo." I used to be good at small talk. The details of others' lives created curiosity. I could talk easily about how my daughter's teething kept me up for three days straight and I fell asleep standing up. Or how she'd organized her kindergarten class for a parade one afternoon when her teacher had taken a student to the nurse's office. Now, I struggled for anything to say to keep a conversation light. I could only fantasize about finding a sense of humor again.

"I wouldn't know. I've been a desert rat all my life." She kept at it. "What prompted you to volunteer for the Rangers?"

The last hope of salvation. An effort at redemption, though it was impossible. "Seemed a good way to help out."

She agreed. "I understand. On the force, we served and protected. Saved lives. Now, we wander around in uniform as glorified crowd control. Scan folks at the courthouse, play sit and fetch for the real law."

I stopped and quieted the roar in my head. "Maybe I overreacted with those girls. But something felt off and I'd rather be safe than sorry."

Patricia held up her hands. "Whoa. I'm not saying anything about that. I wasn't there. I know this whole thing with Zoey Clark has me jumpy. Maybe you are hyper-vigilant, too."

"Yeah. Maybe." First my icky hairs sent false signals, then I bristled up and got defensive. I couldn't blame Patricia if she quit trying to know me.

We made it back to the ball field. "The next shift is due about now. Let's go wait by the parking lot. Deon is supposed to pick me up there."

We wove through the crowd. Pete surveyed the area without looking directly at me. "Thanks for being there. Deon said you rode with me and told the EMTs about my diabetes. How did you know?"

She'd probably think I was a stalker or weirdo. "You drink juice or soda at regular intervals, or you suck on hard candy. I saw you down one of those pouches a few months ago."

She frowned. "I'm usually careful about anyone seeing me do that."

I shrugged. She didn't need to know how closely I observed everything around me now. She glanced at me. "I'd appreciate it if you wouldn't tell anyone else about it."

I didn't tell anyone more than they needed. "Sure."

"If the guys know about it, they'll think I'm not up to the job, you know? And I need this gig for my sanity."

I understood her desperation to keep her position with the Rangers. With her confidence and diligence, no one would doubt her. "I won't say anything."

A tall, broad-shouldered Latino in a khaki deputy uniform rounded the corner of the concession stand. My heart thumped.

Patricia broke into a grin. "Rafe, twice in two days! You're like stink on a dead cat."

He raised his eyebrows at her greeting, then turned his gaze to me, a smile growing in his eyes. "That's a hell of a welcome."

She slapped his shoulder. "Don't be so sensitive. What are you doing here?"

"Deon said you were patrolling the game and I wanted to check up and see if you're okay. Now I'm rethinking that courtesy."

Patricia lowered her voice. "We saw the posters for Zoey Clark. She was in our class at Kino yesterday. Do you have any word?"

Though he didn't have a change of expression, his eyes conveyed deep concern. "Not yet. Department's got all hands trying to figure out what happened. She was supposed to go to a neighbor's house after school but never showed up."

I inhaled, pulling myself closer, trying to keep from flying apart.

Patricia blinked and swallowed, then bent to type a text.

Rafe turned to me. "Jamie. How're you doing?"

"Damn it." Patricia stuffed her phone into her pocket. "Deon's meeting is running late."

"I can take you home." It popped out before I thought about it.

"Really? You wouldn't mind?" She whipped her phone out. "Deon thanks you. I thank you, too, because now I won't have to listen to him bitch about it."

While she thumbed a text, Grijalva shook his head. "Deon does not bitch. He dotes on you like a lovesick teen."

She waved Grijalva off. "He never says anything but I know he's got more important things to do than wait on me."

A reply beeped from her phone and she set about typing again.

Grijalva stepped toward me. "I'm glad to see you again." He held his phone up. "I found some pictures from a hike I did three years ago in the White Mountains. Thought you might be interested."

I leaned closer to the small screen. His scent of soap and warm skin didn't make me want to pull away.

The first shot showed a broad valley floor. "This is the drive up there, leaving the desert and heading into the mountains." Sun-speckled leaves and sandy soil along a trail featured in the next. My stomach tightened. Grijalva pointed a finger with a clean, trimmed nail. "See that guy? A collared lizard."

I focused on the rainbow colors of the lizard. "He's gorgeous."

The next picture was of a small clearing surrounded by leafy trees, branches on muddy ground. The area looked trampled but empty. Remote. Cool. Dank. The memory slinked past my defenses before I could stop it.

The musty smell of damp earth mingles with the sweet scent of lilac. Clouds hang heavy with rain that had fallen off and on for three days. Carcasses of vehicles crowd around us, leaving a narrow path. Their hoods gaping, engines picked over by mechanic carrion. The light is dim even though it is probably the middle of the day. Time stopped meaning anything in that impossible interim. Hope that started bright has faded. My feet gather mud, growing heavier as I search deeper in the gloom.

The picture on Grijalva's phone was the in White Mountains. It only took seconds to ground myself at the ball park. Neither Patricia nor Grijalva seemed to notice my hesitation. "That's pretty." My voice sounded steady. Surprisingly, I didn't have the strong urge to bury myself under the bleachers.

"That was a good trip. I've really been wanting to go back." Grijalva slipped the phone into his shirt pocket.

"I'd like to get up to the Grand Canyon before it gets too hot." Planning something in the future, even a short backpack trip, was something Tara and I thought would be good for me. I didn't tell Patricia and Grijalva I'd also tried to get up there before the snows fell on the rim last fall. That hadn't happened.

"You can do the North Rim all summer long," he said. "It's a great trip. Fewer people and more trees than the South Rim. Have you done Picacho Peak?"

"Not yet."

He sounded excited. "You should do it soon. But start at daybreak so it's not so hot. It's a challenge—there are cables you use to pull yourself up. I'd be happy to go with you anytime."

Patricia cleared her throat. "Hello. I thought you came to see me."

My face flamed, probably turning as red as Grijalva's did. He stepped away from me. "You look fine. I'd better get back on the mean streets."

She scoffed. "Not all the taco trucks along Valencia need inspected."

He walked toward the parking lot. "That's harsh, Sanchez."

"Thanks for checking up on me, Rafe," she said to his back and he waved. She winked at me and murmured, "Even though I think he was here to see someone else."

That wasn't good. Or was it? It might be pushing myself too fast. Or it could be what I needed.

Our replacements arrived and Patricia bantered with them.

"I'll bring the car." I skirted them and hurried to the lot. Nervous about driving across town, trapped in the car with Patricia, and maybe running out of conversation, I needed to talk to someone.

I pulled out my phone but Frank didn't have a number and I didn't need to dial. I spoke into the device, and Frank's reply sounded as if he stood next to me—a solid, weighty voice with no physical body.

He didn't want to talk about Grijalva and Patricia and making new friends. Uncharacteristically short winded, he only said, *"If you weren't such a moron, you could have stopped it. Just like last time."*

6

The trip across town went by quickly. Patricia chatted about her two daughters and the conflict between the teacher and some parents. Typical life for a woman with kids. It didn't set off any stomach clenching. My thoughts swirled around Cali. Too kind and soft to be hanging around with Megan and Jen. She singled out the misfits at the school yesterday and showed concern for Patricia when she'd had her seizure. I couldn't help worry, especially after Frank's mystic messages. I knew the good and kind were the most vulnerable. And I couldn't save them.

Patricia invited me in for iced tea but I turned her down. I didn't tell her that taking her home was no inconvenience for me. It took me closer to my next stop.

Tara's office occupied a suite in a collection of whitewashed adobe office buildings with red tile roofs, surrounded by a sea of palm trees. The whole scene soothed in a quiet, upscale way.

I liked my seedier south side of town, way more Mexico than suburbia, though my house was in a neighborhood aspiringly called Sonoran Ranch Estates. Drive five miles and the stores' intercom made announcements in Spanish, roadside vendors popped up with everything from oranges and honey to garage sale items. No well-tended landscaping in the shopping centers and medians. Taco trucks far outnumbered fine dining restaurants.

In north Tucson, everything felt like a resort. Mom wanted me to live here, close to Tara's office.

The outer lobby, with its tasteful southwestern art, water cooler, and comfortable chairs, made for a pleasant place to wait. A light, located by the door and behind whomever sat on the couch inside her office, would alert Tara of my presence. In no time Tara appeared, inviting me inside.

"Glad you didn't have to miss today's appointment. I know you like the Rangers assignments, but I don't like when you cancel appointments." she held the door open for me. "Especially now."

Most of the time I didn't mind that Tara kept the leash tight. "Sorry about missing yesterday, but I handled the school assignment well. The job tomorrow is in the afternoon so I'll see you in the morning."

"I'm glad you seem to be dealing with this time of year much better than last year. The Rangers might be good for you."

I wish Mom felt that hopeful about it. "It keeps me busy."

All soft femininity, Tara wore a pastel, gauzy dress and strappy sandals. She settled herself in her usual stuffed chair, tucked her dark hair behind her ear, and reached for her notepad, all the while holding me with a welcoming and open face. "That's a good thing?"

More comfortable on her couch than I'd been two years ago, I still felt that tug-of-war between total honesty and wanting to appear strong. "Getting out of the house is helpful, I think. Though Mom thinks maybe I'm overdoing it."

She nodded. "Why would she think that? Are you tired or upset?"

"Not really. No. I think maybe she's worried I'm not ready for a normal life. You know? Like when you have a baby, you introduce foods one at a time and make sure they tolerate those before you add something in."

Tara always took a moment to consider what I said. It didn't bother me, since it often took me time to process a response. "Do you think you're adding too much, too quickly?"

"Maybe."

We both knew her job was to ask me the questions until we dug down to the meat. "Why do you think that?"

I told her about Patricia's seizure.

Tara listened, of course. "Because of you, she got the help she needed right away. You were able to give the responders vital information. And you kept the kids calm."

"That's all standard."

She drilled me with her eyes. "Stop minimizing. You handled yourself in an unexpected situation and you helped people."

That's part of the life I used to take for granted. "Okay."

She wasn't done convincing me. "Why do you volunteer for the Rangers?"

"I volunteered because I have all this training I didn't want to go to waste."

She clucked. "Because you like to help people and you're good at it."

I couldn't help the one person I should have.

She gave me a stern pronouncement. "We've talked about this. You can't save everyone."

More to distract her than anything, I brought up the drive with Grijalva and letting down my walls to talk about hiking. "When he asked me for coffee, I panicked. It took me all evening to calm down."

Grijalva asking you for coffee is not what upset you.

"But you did calm down."

"Yes."

"Without meds?"

"Yes." Tara hadn't been convinced cutting my meds was a good idea, but I'd argued and eventually won.

"That's progress. Would you like to go out with him?"

My face warmed. "Maybe. But what if I get so nervous I can't talk? What if I make a fool of myself?" *What if going out with a man ends up like last time?*

Her kind face relaxed me. "What if?"

"Then he'll never want to see me again." Or worse.

"Then what?"

"It. Well." We were playing her game. One I knew well but fell for every time.

She tapped her pen. "Exactly. Then you won't see him again and that will change your life, how?"

I shared her smile. "I won't be any worse off than I am now."

"Except you will have gained experience to help you next time."

She scribbled on her notepad and looked up at me. "What did Frank and Maggie have to say about Grijalva? What's his first name, by the way?"

"Rafe." Maggie had been with me as long as I could remember. Until four years ago, she'd been the strongest of only a few voices. Now, more urgent and insistent voices often drowned her out.

"Short for Raphael?"

"I don't know. Maybe."

"Frank and Maggie, you talked to them last night?"

"Frank, as usual, thought I was a moron and should have told Grijalva—"

"Try calling him Rafe," Tara interrupted.

That sounded like what a friend would call him. I tried it out. "Frank wants me to tell Rafe to take a hike. Only in Frank's less polite vocabulary. I'm kind of worried Frank will make me say or do something I don't want to in front of Rafe."

"Frank is a voice. He can encourage or cajole, but he can't make you do anything as long as you remember you're in charge of him. It's not like split personalities, where they take over and your main identity is overrun."

I nodded and reiterated mostly for myself. "I have voices, not split personalities."

"Right." Tara nodded approval. "And Maggie? What did she say?"

I looked at my hands fisted in my lap. "Maggie likes R-Rafe. She thinks he's smart, kind, and safe."

Tara watched me as if I'd said something fascinating. "What's wrong with listening to Maggie?"

"She isn't discerning. She likes everyone. She even likes me."

Tara took that as a joke and chuckled. "I like you, too." She rested her pen on her pad and leaned back. "Did you tell your mother about Rafe?"

My silence was her answer. She took up her pen and jotted on the pad. "You think she'd disapprove?"

Disapprove sounded so negative. "She worries I'm not ready to make friends. She wants me to get a dog, maybe take up agility training. She thinks that will keep me busy."

"But you just told me you are busy." She held my gaze a beat. "So, how do you feel about a dog?"

"She never let me get one as a kid. Said they were too much work."

"But she wants you to get one now. Why, I wonder?"

"She got the idea when we were talking about the Arizona Rangers and a woman I partner with quite a bit."

"What's the woman's name?"

"Patricia Sanchez."

"Is she a friend of yours?"

Friends teased and joked, shared confidences and details of their lives. "Not really."

"Would you like her to be?"

Coffee and lunch. Movies, shopping, hikes. Laughter, tears. "Yeah, I think so."

"But your mother thinks a dog is better?"

"She doesn't want me to get hurt."

"And a friend would do that?"

The conversation felt like shots fired from foxholes across the battle line. "Point taken. Can we move on?"

She scribbled something then sat back. "Are you ready to start the memory work?"

My stomach flipped. The last thing I wanted was this journey. Moving forward without going back first wasn't possible. I swallowed around an island of dread in my throat.

I closed my eyes and Tara's quiet voice directed me back to a place before it happened. "Remember the difference between then and now. If this gets too much for you, come away from then and return to now."

"Okay."

She paused for a beat to let that settle in. "What do you see?"

"We're at Walgreens on Tuesday, right after track practice. We'd argued because she wanted McDonalds and I said we'd eat stir fry I made when we got home."

My voice sounded flat, almost sleepy, but inside, electricity shot through my veins. It was always like this when Tara guided me back and I saw *her* again.

"She pulls a box of blue hair dye from the shelf and begs me to let her get it. Her blonde hair is so smooth and beautiful. Nothing like my mousy mane. I hate the idea of hiding it. I laugh and tell her about the time I dyed my hair deep auburn without telling Mom. When she saw it, Mom made me cut off two feet of my hair to a pixie so the color would grow out quicker."

Tears fell hot on my cheeks but this memory made me happy. "When I say yes, she gives me a wet, sloppy kiss on my cheek in the aisle and an elderly man glares at us."

My heart beat faster. "Before we leave, she takes me to the hobby aisle. She and her friends decided to make matching obnoxious hair bows for the track team pictures and she needs red ribbon and a glue gun. I give her a lecture on spending too much money, but end up buying it for her anyway."

Pressure threatened to explode behind my eyes. "I have the key in the ignition when she squeals and dashes back into Walgreens. She comes out with a big box of Hot Tamales, like the kind you get at the movie theater. 'I can't do geometry without my tools.' I roll my eyes."

For a moment I stayed in the dark car with her beside me. Then Tara intruded. "What's next, Jamie?"

I wanted to turn away from the scene before my closed eyes. "The porch light is on and I'm thinking about how much fun I've had tonight. She was right, now that she's growing up, it won't be long before she's off to a life of her own. It's time for me to start going out."

My chest feels as though a house landed on it. "I call hello as I enter the front door. No answer. Her geometry book is open on the table. Pages scribbled with theorems and calculations are scattered across the table. The snippets of ribbon and hot glue gun are on the counter but the hair ribbon is gone. Hot Tamales litter the floor and dribble across her book. I run to her bedroom, to the living room, I'm probably screaming but I can't remember."

My words started shooting out on hot breath and I knotted my hands. "She's not in bed. Not watching TV. She's not in my room. To the guest room. Kitchen. Garage. Back yard. I know

I'm screaming and running down the sidewalk. I've seen this from the other side, the cop angle. I know what's happening and I'm panicking, even as I can't believe she's missing. There's an explanation. There has to be. Any second she's going to call and say she is at a friend's house. She's going to walk through the door. I'm fighting it, hoping, praying, as I call her friends, knowing with each phone call my worst nightmare is forming my new reality."

By then, I was sobbing, hardly able to draw a breath. I hiccupped and eventually brought it down to a sniffle. The storm subsided and I drew in a deep breath.

I opened my eyes to the tissue Tara held for me. "Thank you for your hard work."

By the end of our session, I felt drained.

She walked me to the door. "I know this was difficult for you. But think about the progress you're making with your new friends and the good work you're doing with the Rangers. Don't be surprised if you feel especially stressed for the next few days. Maybe experience some relapse. Be gentle with yourself. It's okay to take your meds if you feel particularly vulnerable."

I assured her I felt stronger than I had for some time. But her worry nagged at me. Maybe she saw something I wasn't aware of.

I'd somehow not got around to telling her about Zoey Clark and that I'd followed her away from the school, allowed something terrible to happen to her. I might have been the last one to see her before she disappeared.

Never even mentioned seeing the man, probably completely innocent, staring at me across the playground.

"Not innocent," Frank said.

7

The multi-use path along the Rillito River opened before me. My habit was to walk several miles after my appointments with Tara. It gave me a chance to talk to Frank, or anyone else I might need to debrief about the session. Since most desert dwellers used the path in the morning or evening to avoid the heat, in late afternoon, I had the path mostly to myself.

The first mile I set a brisk pace and tried to clear my mind. After that, with my phone pressed to my ear, I let Frank have his rein.

"*You're a moron.*" He launched in. "*Why in hell would Grijalva want to spend time with you? Think about it.*"

I'd been mulling that over since yesterday. "Maybe he wants to be friends."

Frank cackled in derision. "*Right. Because you're so fascinating and inviting.*"

I'd learned, just because Frank said something, didn't make it true. "People used to like me. It's not so strange they might again."

"*Dream on, cupcake.*" Before I shut down this line, Frank changed the subject on his own. "*You saw that guy at the school.*"

An alarm erupted inside my brain. Is this what Frank meant when he told me I missed something? The man at the school was not the same man as the ball park, but something told me there was a connection. "Who is he?"

"Maybe he's no one. Maybe someone. You figure it out."

The smile, with those even white teeth. The arrogant stride. "Do I know him?"

Frank taunted me. *"Isn't that why you spend so Goddamned much time on that couch? So you can answer your own stupid questions?"*

Frank's belligerence didn't penetrate my first skin layer. I gave him another mile before I turned back. Some days we marched ten miles before I felt steady enough to drive home. Tara didn't know about the walks and Mom certainly didn't. They might think a three-mile trek to ground myself was cause for alarm. Today, I counted it a victory that I hadn't walked ten miles.

My phone buzzed, interrupting Frank mid-rant. "Time's up, buddy."

"I'm not done. There's more you need to hear."

I checked the caller ID and punched to connect. "Hi, Mom."

"How was your meeting with Tara?"

In Buffalo, the sun would be starting down, her office would be glaring with overhead industrial lighting. If today was like most from my childhood, she'd still be at that desk for another two to three hours. "Sun is shining here. It's in the eighties. Lovely day."

She sighed.

"That's how small talk is done," I teased.

A smile crept into her voice. "Retired people have time for small talk."

"You could be retired. Stay up as late as you want, sleep in, read by the pool." If I made it seem wonderful, maybe she'd believe I was happy. Maybe I would, too.

"I'll retire soon enough. So, how did it go with Tara today?"

My footsteps kept a steady beat on the pavement and I passed under a mesquite tree. "About like yesterday and the day before." Except I'd skipped yesterday because of the school assignment. Mom didn't need to know that.

Mom would be shuffling reports on her desk, scanning the highlights and talking to me at the same time. "Stick with it. It's obviously doing you good."

An agave spread spiked leaves in the pea-gravel along the path. Like most living things in the desert, it protected itself against everything, not distinguishing between benevolent and evil intruders.

"What did Tara think about you getting a dog?"

I braced myself. She wouldn't take rejection of her idea lightly. "I think I'll hold off. Right now, I like having the flexibility to take assignments with the Rangers."

"Did Tara think that's a good idea? The Rangers holds a huge risk of stress. Whereas a puppy would give you the responsibility of caring for someone else, assuage your loneliness, and let you practice a relationship."

"I'm not lonely." *Liar.* "And if I were, the Rangers helps me get out socially, I take care of people, and I'm making friends."

"But are you really making friends? And are they the right kind? Law enforcement people tend to be cynical with a hard shell."

We both paused and then cracked up at the same time. She recovered first. "It's good to laugh with you again."

The path curved around a saguaro, its arms raised like a bandit in surrender. "Come for a visit. We'll laugh more then."

She answered predictably. "I'd love to. But I've got so much to do. Maybe next month, if I can keep everything from blowing up here."

"Sure." Was I more relieved or disappointed? That teeter-totter remained unchanged for forty-five years.

"I wish I'd made plans to be there for you this weekend."

It surprised me she'd thought of that. "I'm doing fine. No need for that."

"You thought you were good last year, too. And look what happened."

I didn't want to look at what happened but there it was. The pain had overwhelmed me and I'd let Frank have too much power. By then, I'd known not to give in to him, but it hurt too much and he seemed to have a solution. With him directing me, I'd gathered the photos, the albums, and loose prints. So far removed, I'd watched my fingers light a match, mesmerized by Frank's demands and the flickering yellow flame. I held up an 8 X 10 school photo. Her pink bodice disappeared and the flames lapped at her snaggle-toothed, seven-year-old grin. Frank wanted me to hold the photo and let the flames snap at my fingers, but I dropped it in the sink and grabbed another. And another. A whole album. Burned it all.

"I've worked hard this year. I'm okay."

"It's probably a good thing I didn't fly out there. It's a general cluster here."

A bench nestled in a nook of the trail surrounded by lush bougainvillea bushes. This signaled the end of my march, where I'd leave the path, wander through the well-kept office park, and make my way to my car.

Mom and I said our I-love-yous and goodbyes. Phone off and slipped into my back pocket, mind on Rafe Grijalva. Frank wondered what Grijalva wanted from me? Was it naïve to believe in simple friendship?

The magenta of the bougainvillea drew my attention and I

stopped dead. As if a cluster bomb blew up in my gut, every-thing in me shut down. The man in the ball cap and blue shirt, dress trousers, those polished teeth. He sat on the bench amid the blooms, scrolling on his phone.

Maybe I made a shocked noise. Maybe he sensed my frozen figure staring at him. He glanced up, registered me, then slowly rose and walked away. He didn't seem alarmed, didn't seem to recognize me.

I stood rooted to the path and watched.

Was it the same man? Had I imagined a stranger on a bench looked like another stranger outside a playground? Did either really exist?

I'd felt so confident of my progress, sure that in a matter of time, I'd be like any other person. Maybe I'd inch toward happi-ness, or at least not constant bleakness.

The man disappeared around a bend in the trail, dragging my hope with him.

8

Forty-five minutes on the path instead of the two hours she used to walk. He chuckled to himself. She thinks she's getting better. Putting it all behind her, moving on.

He'd show her how much progress she was making. The anniversary was approaching and she believed she could handle it. He'd make sure she'd self-destruct. And he'd be there to watch it.

He was already chipping away at her. Bit by bit. He'd seen her pick out the little girl at the school. And the older girl, too. He had to admit to a certain resemblance. Both skinny with blonde hair, they'd naturally make Jamie remember.

That made them perfect for him.

She'd followed that little girl, worried for her safety. Jamie had practically served the girl to him on a silver platter. The older girl would take a little more effort, but he was up to the task.

Jamie needed to be punished and he intended to make her suffer.

He laughed out loud, no crazier than anyone else around. Wait until Jamie realized it was all her fault.

He'd be there to watch that, too.

9

I craved silence. So rare I couldn't remember the last time.

Not that long ago I wouldn't have been in crowds. Wearing a uniform again had seemed nearly impossible. But I'd pushed myself beyond wanting to end it all , toward creating a new life. I don't know what primal instinct drove me to keep putting one foot in front of the other. I'd stretched myself further these last couple of days and everything jangled loose inside.

Zoey Clark. I closed my eyes and fought against the feel of damp air, the clammy touch of mud beneath my fingers, the sickening smell of lilacs. I tried to hope for the best, but in the deep tissue of my body, I knew the probabilities.

The best thing to do was race across town to my home that backed to the desert. Mom had called it the edge of the known universe and wondered if it was a good idea to live so far from a hospital.

I didn't tell her, because I didn't want her to think I needed help, that the desert healed more effectively than any doctor.

It took fewer than ten minutes from the moment I pushed the garage door button for me to park, dash into the house, tear off my uniform, and pull on running shorts. I tied a faded red bandana around my wrist to use when the desert sun caused me to rain with sweat. I needed to stop the images of young blonde girls, trusting, beginning their lives, brash and bold. Frank's vague warnings of disaster bouncing inside my skull—harsh, blaming, wailing, hopeless.

I sprinted out my front door, making my way toward the vacant lot next to my stucco one-story. I planned to slip into the desert behind my house and run until the demons stopped tormenting me.

"*Watch out!*"

I averted my step just before plunging it down on two tiny birds huddled together near an oleander bush at the corner of my yard. A desert dove shrieked and fluttered a few feet away, trying to draw me away by acting injured. As if all the mother's squawking could make up for leaving her babies laying in the open.

The sun beat on my shoulders while I hesitated. Let nature take its course? Which meant sure and violent death for the chicks. Or do what little I could to give them a chance?

"*What if the Universe is giving you an opportunity to start evening the score?*"

It took very little time to rummage in the garage for a bit of fencing the previous owners had around a small garden in back. I tossed the tools on the ground and worked at bending the wire. A slow-moving shadow shaded the tree from a gray sedan with tinted windows. Most cars drove too fast on this curved neighborhood road, so I should appreciate the driver's caution. But the dark windows made me feel under surveillance and an involuntary shudder erupted from tingling hairs on my neck. The ultimate icky hairs. With so many generic gray sedans in Tucson, it seemed nuts to think this was the same car as the one at the grade school. Obviously, my overworked nervous system at play.

Using a pair of pliers, I fashioned a play pen and dropped it over the chicks, protecting them from neighborhood dogs, hopefully also from coyotes who patrolled after dark. It wasn't much and I already mourned the loss of the chicks, even though the dove population didn't need my help to thrive.

Twitchy with thoughts of children in danger, I sprinted away from the neighborhood. Someone had fired a charcoal grill and the smell faded as I ran further toward the sweet bloom of creosote and mesquite. The powdery utility road behind the subdivision cut a trail through the brush and cactus, worn from weekend ATVs. It made an easy path for the start of my run.

The sun glared at me, throwing off the burning rays that battled, only to give in to another glorious sunset of brilliant oranges, pinks, indigo, and gold. I ran fast to leave everything behind me.

Today was no different from every other day. I couldn't outrun it. I never would.

About a mile from the house I dropped into a sandy wash lined with ironwood and desert willow, barrel cactus the size of whisky casks, yellow buds ready to burst in bloom.

The distinct maracas sound of a rattler made me leap and race from the wash, following the narrow trail through the sand. Brush, saguaro, and scrawny Palo Verde trees closed in on me. Lizards the size of my pinky, tails longer than my hand, zipped and zagged. Still, the voices egged me on, tried to convince me to return to the wash and offer myself as sacrifice to the rattler.

Anything would be better than this. Better than remembering. But I doubted a bite from that old snake would end me.

Nine hot miles later, mopping my face with the damp red bandana, I jogged into my driveway, the recriminations worn to the normal murmur. My breath puffed in short bursts as I walked in circles, letting the sweat catch up to me and start cascading down the sides of my face. Dry air scraped my raw throat.

"Hello! Hi!"

Facing my closed garage door, I waited to see if she'd speak again. It wasn't a voice I recognized and I panicked at meeting someone new. There was no room, not even for one more.

A baby screeched and started to cry. A smallish voice spoke quickly. "It wasn't me. I think it was a bee."

The woman said, "There was no bee."

The child's voice, now very matter-of-fact, stated with certainty. "Jackson wanted me to pinch him."

I had braced for blowback from the last couple of days, from the memories scratched raw by the blonde's appearance. But this was too much. My hands shook and I squeezed my eyes closed.

The tap on my shoulder couldn't have shocked me any more than a bullet in my back. I yelped and spun around.

A woman, probably ten to fifteen years younger than me, stood in my driveway, a huge grin across her face. She balanced a crying bald baby on her slim hip, held a tow-headed child by the hand, and flicked her gaze to a little girl with two messy braids a few steps off to the side. The braided tyke stood akimbo, assessing me.

Four flesh and blood people in my driveway. For the first time, I noticed the moving van across the street, back open, ramps sticking out the cavity.

Today had challenged me, grabbing me hard and twisting me like a wet dish cloth, squeezing until I dripped dry. My years of experience observing everything, from people to surroundings, had shifted into an internal struggle to keep myself together, and I hadn't even seen a truck the size of an ocean barge parked practically in my front yard.

I stepped back to pull my focus from inside my head.

The woman, in a strappy lime green top and cut offs, thankfully longer than the yellow cheerleading skirts, wore thin flip-flops, her mud-colored hair scraped into a scruffy ball in the back of her head. She hoisted the baby higher on her hip. "I'm Sherilyn." She tipped her head to the bossy child in the spotless sundress. "That's Cheyenne." She tugged the hand of the toddler. "This is Kaycee." She planted a kiss on the pink nose of the baby and he quieted. "And Jackson."

My ears roared. One small voice reached me like a pin prick of light through a closed curtain.

Say hello.

My throat, too dry from my run, managed to creak out, "I'm Jamie." The smallest of small talk that I hoped would buy me time to focus.

Cheyenne took her hands off her hips and pointed across the street. "We're moving in here because Daddy got a job on the railroad and we can't stay in Oklahoma because Grandmother is a demanding bitch."

"Cheyenne! What have we told you about using those words and about repeating our family talk?"

The memory struck with the force of a blow.

Mom's Thanksgiving table is full with too much food she'd had catered from a local grocery store. Mom sits at one end, Dad, quiet and morose as usual, sits at the other. Various county officials line the sides, with me and Larry feeling like odd balls. Our glasses are full of wine. She's only three and I've been cutting her turkey and trying to keep her entertained but she wants to be part of the conversation, only everyone is ignoring her. She's tired of being seen and not heard.

She's fidgeting and impatient for pie when a sudden lull drops in the conversation. "Mommy and Daddy play World Federation Wrestling on their bed at night." She struggles to pronounce the words, but leaves no question to their meaning. I want to hide, but join the laughter and forgive her. She's adorable.

I fought the memories and eased toward the closed garage door.

Sherilyn gazed up at me, her 5'5" height needed to elevate four inches to make direct eye contact. "She's right, though. My mother-in-law is a piece of work. But that's a story for a Friday night and a cold beer."

Cheyenne's quick mind jumped ahead. "What's in the little yard?"

My head pounded and the tingling in my fingers increased. "A pair of doves left their chicks on the ground and I put a fence around them for protection."

Cheyenne marched to the oleander with its dark green leaves and deadly pink blossoms. She squatted, folding her legs without effort, a position that always amazed me.

Sherilyn pulled Kaycee to the side of the driveway to get a better look. "Cheyenne has a mind of her own, and doesn't mind telling you about it." She ruffled the dandelion wisps on Kaycee's head. "This one, hardly says a word, and only to Cheyenne. She's our little shy baby."

The soft purr of an expensive car barely interrupted. The gray sedan with the tinted windows trolled by again. This time I noticed the plate number and hoped a part of me would commit it to memory.

"You're not supposed to touch them," Cheyenne said with authority. "The mother will smell you and then she won't feed them."

These girls forced bittersweet flashes of memory and I didn't know if I was grateful or not.

She folds down next to me. Branches heavy with new leaves sway overhead, sending shadows dancing. It smells like spring and life and happiness. The deep green grass rises up to her bare knees. I whisper, "Birds can't smell."

We pick up the chicks and put them back in their nest. Her fat little hands scoop the babies with such care and she settles them into the bed of sticks and grass. I place it back on to the branch from where the wind had flung it.

Another thunderstorm tears the nest apart the next day. We find one chick dead in the grass. The other is gone.

I forced my focus back to Cheyenne. Words tipped out of my mouth, though I hadn't known they would. "Doves raise their chicks in pairs, both mother and father feeding them. These probably got kicked out of their nest early because the parents hatched another clutch."

Sherilyn patted Cheyenne's head in a way meant to get her to move on. "That's fascinating. We'll watch these little guys grow up and fly away, huh?"

Disappear, more likely. But Sherilyn could lie to them, tell her kids the doves sitting on their back fence are these. "Nice to meet you."

Whatever scary-neighbor vibes I might have given off didn't hit Sherilyn. She kept that sunny shine. "We're really looking forward to getting to know you." With Kaycee in tow, she started down the driveway.

Looking forward. Sherilyn made it sound like it was something to anticipate with excitement. For me, looking forward meant something I did with grim determination. Maybe it would be good to get to know this family. Or it could kill me.

Cheyenne straightened. She assessed me and somehow found me lacking. Perceptive kid.

Kaycee suddenly jerked her hand away from Sherilyn. Her two-foot-long legs tottered in what must have been a sprint for her. She covered the few yards between us and latched on to my legs, her plump arms circling just above my knees, her grasp imprisoning me.

Screaming shot through my brain, stabbing pain. I closed my eyes against it. But couldn't stop myself from prying them open to squint down at the white-blonde head, face buried in my thighs, arms hugging me tighter than anyone had for years.

I watched my arm twitch as if it belonged to another woman. Someone buried long ago, rising impossibly from the grave. My hand opened from a clenched fist, spreading out, moving slowly as I fought against it, knowing this touch could undo me.

I let my palm rest softly, barely daring to touch the fine down of the child's head. My throat ached, my breath dammed behind the pain.

"Huh." Sherilyn said. "I've never, ever seen her do that."

10

I don't know if Sherilyn noticed my paralysis or if she simply needed to get back to unpacking, but she pried Kaycee from my legs and I breathed again. I managed to say the appropriate words to welcome Sherilyn to the neighborhood. At least, I tried.

My fingers fumbled to punch in the lock code on my front door. I kicked my shoes off, dropped the sweaty bandana on them, and peeled damp socks to allow my feet to cool on the Saltillo tile of my entryway. The safety of solitude—with pulled blinds darkening the house—usually helped to still my mind.

The abstract painting above the fireplace swirled with blues and pinks which always made me think of an ocean and encouraged me to hear the crashing of waves against the shore. I'd found the painting at a street fair and imagined some force of the universe put it there specifically for me. Mom hadn't been here since I'd hung it, and I worried she wouldn't like it and insist I move it.

Anyone stepping through the front door would see an open area, furnished comfortably with padded wicker furniture, an expensive Navajo rug over the Saltillo tile, flowing into an airy kitchen. A rustic wood dining table continued on the mission theme. French doors opened out to a small backyard and patio lined with desert plants in colorful Mexican pots. Aside from the location away from town, with the quiet desert stretching behind me, the reason I'd chosen this house was the pool. When I submerged myself, even the commotion in my head faded away. I only wished I could grow gills.

Not homey, but tasteful. Mom's taste, who had spent two weeks with me when I'd first moved from Buffalo, helping me furnish the house and get the lay of the land. I'd allowed her to place three photos in the living room because she thought it would be good for me. I never looked at them, but I felt their weight every day.

As soon as I'd convinced Mom I knew how to navigate to the nearest gas station and Safeway, and I could reliably drive across town for my sessions with Tara, she'd boarded the plane back to Buffalo, where she'd already been gone too long. I promised her I'd decorate the rest of the house, a promise two years later I had yet to fulfill.

Aside from the open communal space, the house had three small bedrooms, one with unpacked boxes, one empty except for a perfectly made bed, waiting for an inhabitant who would never arrive, and the room where I slept more and more often— blank walls, no family photos, little indication a living, breathing woman occupied it. One polished malachite sphere about the size of a grapefruit rested on a wood base on the dresser. I had bought it at Tucson's famous gem and mineral show a couple of months earlier. Something about it made me feel hopeful and I thought it would be a good start toward decorating. I intended to add more but the room looked Spartan.

From the front door, my home looked normal, if not remarkable. Anything more than white walls and bars on the windows was progress.

Lilacs. The smell crept up my nose. Impossible. There were no lilacs in Tucson, at least not in my southern neighborhood. I couldn't be smelling their sickening sweetness. My footsteps echoed on the tile as I traipsed through the bedrooms and back to the kitchen. No flowers, of course. Still the smell seemed real, not something I dreamed up.

"Ha." I laughed in the empty house. "And I ought to know about the senses and imagination."

Sheer determination allowed me to ignore what my brain had obviously conjured up. There were no lilacs here. Wouldn't it be dandy if I started having phantom smells to contend with on top of everything else.

After a shower and a carefully prepared chop salad, my nerves still jangled. When my phone rang, I nearly choked on lettuce.

I cleared my throat and sat up straighter. "Hi, Mom. Twice in one day, it must have been a hard one for you." She'd be winding down at home.

Her voice sounded tight. "The usual, plus some."

I pushed boiled egg around my plate and noticed the death grip on my fork. Deliberately, I set the fork down and shook out my hand. "You sound tired."

"It's nothing. Just that little prick, John Overton. The election is still six months away and he's playing hardball."

"Is he running ads already?"

"Not that I've seen. But he's got a special investigator digging around."

"He can't do that, can he? I thought only the governor could investigate a county sheriff. Overton's a private attorney, right?" Mom's career demanded so much she didn't have many friends and fewer confidantes. The least I could do was let her vent.

It sounded like she could chew glass. "It's not officially Overton's call. But he's got that limp-dick governor in his pocket. His father went to Harvard a few years ahead of the governor. Same good ol' boys crap I've been dealing with my whole career."

"As sheriff, you don't have a say in this?"

"It's always best to cooperate so they don't think you've got anything to hide. This time, they hired a woman investigator so it won't look sexist."

The election always brought tension into our lives. "You've been investigated before. It never amounts to much."

Something slammed, maybe a cupboard door. Mom liked to bang things to ease her anger. "Annual audits and checks and balances, sure. But this bitch is bringing in a shovel."

"Let her dig. You're clean."

Another bang. "Obviously, I'm clean. But she can leak a perfect record and an opposing campaign can turn it ugly."

It's not often I got the chance to comfort her. "You've been through campaigns before. You've got this."

"Of course, but that was before you...well, things were different last time."

My finger quit moving and fisted into my hand. Breath trapped in my lungs.

"Honey, I'm sorry. I didn't mean to upset you."

I flattened my hand on the cool stone of granite countertops. Not relaxed, but better. "I'm sorry if I've made it difficult for you. It's true. But families face tragedies."

Mom didn't bang anything now. "Everything I did, I'd do again. You're my first priority. But it wouldn't do me any good if this investigator figures out how you retired with full bennies."

The fog of guilt smelled foul around me. I waded through Frank's burning assessment of Mom's words. "I'm sorry."

"What's done is done." She sounded brisk. "Tell me about your day."

"It was good. I took an assignment patrolling a high school

baseball tourney. My partner, Patricia talked about hiking next week."

She hesitated. "Huh." I waited and she began again. "If you aren't ready for a dog, have you given any more thought to volunteering at the animal shelter?"

"The Rangers keeps me busy enough."

"Well, yes. But maybe try something less challenging. Being a Ranger is too close to being a cop. It might trigger bad memories."

"A new family is moving in across the street. They seem nice. Have some small kids."

The lilac odor lingered in my nose and a wave of nausea roiled through me.

Sigh. "Just be careful, Honey."

I lost my appetite for the salad. "What do you mean?"

Her voice now was nothing like her Erie County Sheriff one. More like a kindergarten teacher explaining why we need to share the red crayon. "You've always gravitated to the misfits and those who have issues. But now, you need to protect yourself. I want you to be cautious in making new friends."

A knife of Frank's indignation surfaced. "I'm not a bad judge of character."

"You tend to only see the good in people and haven't learned that not everyone is trustworthy."

I ground my teeth hoping she wouldn't bring up Larry and Sue. She blamed them for betraying me. Or had I betrayed them?

Her fatigue weighted her voice. "I'm sorry, Honey. I don't want to hurt you. I just worry about you. And this time of year...." She sighed again. "I hate that I'm not there to be with you."

"You could be. Forget about the election. Retire and move to Tucson. Sunshine. No snow to shovel. You'd love it."

"It sounds heavenly. But I'm not ready to quit, yet."

I'd quit already. But some sliver of survival instinct was forcing a feeble comeback.

We said good night, with our usual promise to talk tomorrow. With my phone turned to silent I scraped my plate into the trash and carefully washed, dried, and put away my dishes.

I filled a tall glass with ice water and dropped in a thick slice of lemon, turned off all the lights. I pulled a faded red hoodie off of the armrest of the couch and pulled it close to my cheek, the worn fabric soft. The scent had long since evaporated but that didn't prevent me from knowing the smell in the tissues of my body. I settled into a comfortable wicker chair and called Frank.

He was angry, as usual. I'd learned it's always best to let him go first and burn off most of it. *"I've said it before and I'll say it until you grow a brain. Being a Ranger is bullshit."*

"Mom doesn't like it either."

That lit him up. He called Mom obscene names that made me cringe and want to block my ears. I let him go on. This was his time. If I censored him, he'd escalate until I lost all control.

When he'd expelled the worst, I said, "And I've got the experience."

"Experience!" Frank shouted and I winced. *"Experience in failing, maybe."*

I redirected him to the ball park incident. "Those girls were in trouble. I had to do something."

Frank exploded. *"As if you can help anyone."*

The red sweatshirt weighed a million pounds. "I understand you feel I let you down." My voice sounded calm. "But I need to do what I can to make sure no one else suffers."

"Hey, cupcake, you didn't stop anything, only you're too stupid to know it."

Frank and I went back and forth for another hour, him accusing me of monstrous evils, including colluding with the smarmy guy from the ball park to harm those girls. I met him with calm disclaimers until he finally quit talking.

Eventually, my world quieted. Seconds before I drifted to sleep curled into the wicker saucer chair, clutching the red sweatshirt, my eyes popped open.

What had Frank said?

"If you weren't such a moron you wouldn't have missed the real danger."

I'd chalked it up to his constant paranoia on my behalf.

Frank was crude, often violent, and needed a lot of careful attention, but I'd learned his main goal was to keep me safe.

Not thinking it amounted to much, I said, "What is the danger?"

He growled at me. *"Ask Peanut."*

But he knew. They all knew. I would never ask Peanut anything.

Never.

11

The sun infiltrated the slats of the blinds and sneaked into the house, waking me. I unwound from the round wicker chair where I'd slept in a knot and padded to the kitchen. It was nearly ten, and that left me only enough time for a cup of coffee and toast before I needed to leave.

The office was a forty-minute drive, closer to an hour in the frequently heavy traffic. It annoyed Tara if I arrived late so I made a point of punctuality. Giving Tara a reason to think anything but good about me was the last thing I wanted.

I took care with my appearance. Fresh T-shirt, crisp jeans, hair in a neat ponytail. Clean teeth, straight shoulders, clear eyes. The smile I practiced in the mirror looked convincing. Cup rinsed, nothing out of place in the living room except the red hoodie, back on the arm rest of the sofa. Yesterday had taken care of itself. Today would be better.

I stepped out my front door. An unexpected sight smacked me in the face when I spun around. Frank couldn't beat me to the curses fighting to escape my lips. Hands on hips, I stared at the mess, waiting for my rage to cool.

Strung from the top of my mesquite tree, wound around the

Texas sage, strangling the fragrant purple blossoms, stuck in the tines of the prickly pear, roll after roll of toilet paper flickered in the scant desert breeze.

The heat from the morning sun sizzled my skin while I talked my way out of the murderous temper. A teenaged prank didn't require a blood feud.

Next door, Mr. and Mrs. Dempsey would be at their Friday morning Silver Sneakers class. I hadn't asked, but Mrs. Dempsey caught me outside fixing my rain gutter one day and filled me in on details of their lives, from their retirement fifteen years ago in Omaha to how Mr. Dempsey's stomach didn't tolerate raspberry preserves. All her words had made it easy to not talk about myself.

The U-Haul in front of Sherilyn's clunked and spewed a tall man with corn-tassel hair and beard out its back. He balanced a washing machine on a dolly and maneuvered it down the ramps. Cheyenne popped out of the truck behind him, carrying a table lamp nearly as big as her little brother. I didn't catch her words, but from her tone, it was clear she directed the operation.

Sherilyn scurried from the front door, propping it open for the washer. She glanced over and spotted me. "Morning!" Her shout bounded up my front walk and I wanted to duck before it hit me.

I raised my hand in a half-hearted wave, then diverted my attention back to my front yard. The noise swirling in my head urged me to punch the side of my house. At least I recognized that wouldn't help and would only injure my hand. Nothing to do but grab some gloves and a trash bag and take my frustration out on the toilet paper.

"Hey, good morning."

I blinked away the internal confusion. Sherilyn stood in front of me, Kaycee by her side. Kaycee's little hand wrapped protectively in Sherilyn's, her upper lip stained with red juice. "Looks like you're either super popular or you pissed off some high schoolers."

Relax your jaw. "The second one."

She clicked in a *what are you gonna do?* way. "Can I ask your advice?"

My mouth was too dry to answer.

Sherilyn squinted at me. "Are you okay? You look peaked. Maybe sit down?" She motioned me to a decorative wrought iron bench Mom bought at one of those Mexican pottery places. Mom said it brightened the plain stucco house. I'd had a fantasy of sitting with neighbors on a cool evening, laughing and telling stories. It might happen. Someday.

Sherilyn advanced to back me onto the bench. "I swear, it's only May and not even noon, but that sun will melt you."

I worked up what I hoped passed for a friendly face.

Kaycee smiled at me. Her wispy white hair stirred in the slight puff of air. Bright blue eyes sliced with a surgeon's precision, releasing a surge of longing so strong it took my breath. I might have crumpled on the patio if Kaycee hadn't shyly raised her hand and wiggled her fingers in a wave.

Sherilyn studied me. "Think you'll be okay?"

'Okay' was a level I aspired to on my best days. "Sure. Like you said, it's hot. And I'm surprised by this."

That seemed to satisfy her. "Donnie, that's my hubs, is about to starve. Is that taco truck about a half mile back any good?"

Taco truck? "I haven't tried it."

She pursed her lips, probably disappointed with my lack of knowledge. "Got any other good ideas for lunch? This neighborhood is so far out of town I'm afraid we made a mistake settling out here. You know, Donnie is gone a lot on the railroad."

I clenched and unclenched my hands to stop the tingling.

Why was I feeling so freaked out by this? It was only a good old-fashioned TPing. I'd done it as a teen.

Someone whispered to me with sinister intent. "*There's more.*"

Kaycee puckered up and blew me a kiss, her fat little fingers flinging it.

I stood up, making Sherilyn step back. "It's a quiet neighborhood. Safe. I don't eat out much. Sorry."

Couldn't seem to insult Sherilyn. "Guess we'll try to the taco truck and let you know." She started home, then turned abruptly. "Cheyenne bolted out of the house first thing and was across the street before I got on enough clothes to chase her down."

I tried to sound normal, but there was an edge to my tone. "Is she okay?"

Sherilyn laughed. "She complained about the rocks in your yard being hard on her feet but she's fine. And the little birds made it through the night."

The birds. I'd forgotten.

"Cheyenne says Kaycee named them Frank and Maggie." Sherilyn laughed. "Don't know where she comes up with these things."

While I struggled to breathe again, Sherilyn tugged Kaycee gently away. When they made it across the street, she dropped the little hand and picked up a box. With a casual glance over her shoulder, she said, "Let's go inside." She didn't watch to make sure Kaycee followed. But I did.

A dot of red drew my attention to the rocks by the side of my driveway. My ears rang and my fingers fizzled with a thousand pricks. Once I spotted the one, more and more splashes of red dotted my yard leading up to the bird enclosure.

A Hot Tamales candy box lay crushed by the fence.

My head rang and pounded like a half dozen hammers beat

inside my brain. What pulled me back was the sight of the gray sedan cruising by. I watched it round the curve twenty yards away.

Inside my house, I punched Patricia's number. It rang several times. Maybe she debated answering. I couldn't remember calling her before. Our few exchanges outside of working together were done via text.

"Jamie!" She sounded happy. "What's up?"

No time for small talk. "Did anyone vandalize your house last night?"

She stammered, "Vandal? What? No."

The French doors to my backyard locked with a bolt and I struggled one handed, finally flinging them open. "My front yard was TPed. I'm thinking it was those girls from the ball park."

"How would they even know where you live?"

My ankles crossed and I flopped cross-legged on the deck, sinking my hand into the blue ripples. "Don't know. Maybe they followed me. But it has to be them. No one else would do this." The candy had looked like red bullets. I flicked my fingers in the cool water, letting it soothe me.

She still didn't sound convinced. "Maybe. Girls can be mean like that and we did get them suspended from the squad."

"As soon as I get this cleaned up, I'm going to go to the high school to talk to them."

"Whoa. It's a harmless prank. You shouldn't make a big deal out of it."

With effort, I softened my tone and slowed my words. "I know this is going to sound crazy..." Ironic for me to use that word. "But I have a feeling there's more to this than a prank. I would feel a lot better if I could check on those girls and make sure they're okay."

She laughed. "I'd say if they're fine enough to trash your house, they're probably all okay."

"Maybe it wasn't all of them. I don't know. I'm worried they might be into trouble."

She hesitated. "Like you think they met up with that guy from the ball park?"

Was I really trusting my intuition again? "Yeah. Maybe."

"But there was nothing to that yesterday. Are you sure you're not just upset about Zoey Clark and seeing danger everywhere?"

"Yeah. That's not it." As long as I was digging my hole, I might as well make it deep. "It felt off to me. And this TPing thing." The Hot Tamales. I couldn't tell her about that. "I don't know."

She sounded skeptical. "Why not call Mitch? As company commander, he can probably talk to the principal at the school. They can call them into the office and talk about vandalism. Leave you out of it."

She made sense. I thanked her but couldn't help thinking of my old partner. Kari would have thrown in with me even if she thought I was nuts. That was a long time ago. Before she disappeared from my life like so many others. I dialed again.

Mitch picked up on the second ring. "Company Commander, Tucson Arizona Rangers." He took his position seriously.

I tensed. Sixty, if a day, Mitch preferred a traditional black cowboy hat with his uniform, making him look a little like John Wayne in his later years. I hated his fringe of gray hair that inched below his hat, usually darkened by sweat. Too much like Dad's.

I explained our encounter with the girls yesterday and the mischief at my house.

He sounded like warm milk. Mitch had a grandpa quality he'd probably cultivated for forty years. It didn't fool me. He'd retired as police chief in some east coast jurisdiction and now served as Commander of the Tucson Company of the Arizona Rangers. "Um hm. I understand you're upset. That toilet paper's gotta be a bear to get off cactus. But we don't want to go making a mountain out of this itty-bitty mole hill. We're here to protect the public and we value our positive image. Let's not get all boiled up over nothing."

I had nothing credible to make my case, so I agreed and hung up.

On my way to the garage for my gloves I stabbed another number into my phone. My eyes focused on the crushed candy box.

When her machine picked up, I cleared my throat to be sure I sounded normal. "Tara. Something's come up and I won't make it in today. I know that inconveniences you and I'm sorry. But I'll be there Monday, as usual."

Tara would not like this one bit. She couldn't hate it more than I did.

12

The sporty red Nissan didn't have the kick it should and the drive across town to the high school felt like a funeral procession. I bought the car because Mom liked it and by then, I'd learned the quickest way to relieve her worry was to act cheerful and optimistic about the future. Now that I was left alone with a Nissan Juke, I was free to my indifference.

Friday mid-morning traffic in Tucson trapped me between stop lights. In another couple of months, getting around would get easier as U of A students fled the blaze of summer, and the snow-birds returned to their grandchildren, bragging about their sunny winters. For now, I stuttered my way up Oracle Road to suburbs more established, with property values considerably higher than mine, taller cactus and agave in the gravel-covered yards.

The man at the school and the one on the trail looked the same to me. Were they the same man? Was he following me? What rattled me to my bones was wondering if either of them had been real.

Maybe Mom and Tara were right; I should retreat for a couple of days.

Another problem nudged at me. The faint scent of lilacs lingered in my car on my drive here. Maybe I didn't feel completely undone, but obviously the smell was some new sort of game my mind wanted to play.

It hadn't taken long to Google Tucson high schools and find Ventana High, the yellow and black Hornets. I planned to hang around and watch until I saw the girls. Once I knew they were safe, I'd deal with my over-reaction to the guy at the park, the smell of lilacs, the Hot Tamales spilled in my yard, and the toilet paper mess.

The honest truth, might as well admit it to myself, was that I worried about the guy at the park. Everything should be fine, but my icky hairs zinged and Frank fussed. Even if all the alarms rang false, I had to check it out.

While I waited, images of the man with the girls made my gut feel like a washer full of rocks, tumbling and bruising. He might do what bad guys do, like a coyote on the desert, born to scavenge and take advantage. It was our job—parents, cops, decent people—to protect the young and innocent. We couldn't build the nests on the ground, or kick fledglings out too soon, wings flapping but not knowing how to use them, feeling the exhilaration of flight only to be easy dinner for a passing predator.

The parking lot stretched across acres, filled with the shiny foreign cars affluent parents gift their image-conscious teens. The Mitsubishi Eclipse I parked behind afforded some cover but left me space to view the front walk to the Taj Mahal of high schools.

The argument ping-ponged in my head about the remote chance of seeing any of the girls. Frank's derision was like Chinese water torture, drip, drip, dripping with annoying consistency through the two hours I sat in my car. During that time, no security patrolled the parking lot. Twice, a mother pulled in a visitor spot, hurried into the palace, then returned to her luxury sedan and drove away.

The last high school I interacted with in Buffalo had a uniformed officer patrolling during school hours. Few windows graced the old stone building on its prison-like façade, the small front yard of crabgrass shaded by old-growth oaks and maples.

She's suddenly there in my memory.

I get a panicked call. Her forgotten geometry homework is on the kitchen table and could I please, please please get it for her? I'm on patrol and it wouldn't be a problem to swing by home, collect the work and save her. But she needs to learn responsibility. It hurts to say no but I am proud of myself for staying firm. My concern is for her character, so she learns self-reliance and the consequences of her actions.

But I can't stand the thought of those hours she'd spent bent over her geometry going to waste. Mom would say my weakness wouldn't be any favor to her, but I can't help myself.

Her gratitude carries forward to her home-cooked spaghetti dinner and spotless room for at least a week.

If I'd known how few times I could save her, I'd have gladly ruined her character every opportunity I got.

I pulled myself back to Tucson and the school.

The solitude of the parking lot was interrupted with a trickle of cars and SUVs, this generation's version of the family station wagon. They lined up orderly along the front walk, waiting for their princes and princesses. I perked up like a sheep dog guarding her flock.

A flood burst through the school doors. Rivers of kids spilled toward the parking lot, splitting and flowing in all directions. Doors slammed, engines fired, the line of waiting parents moved away, only to be replaced with more. Cars pulled out all around me. I should have found solace in so many of our children safe, full of life.

Finally, I spotted them. The short girl, Megan, and the acne-faced one. Jen? No tall blonde. No Cali. Jen and Megan stormed across the parking lot, heads together, clearly annoyed. No more aware of their surroundings than a toddler drifting off for a nap.

I jumped out of my Juke and intercepted them as Megan extended her key to a white CRV. "Megan?"

With a slow swivel of her head, she focused on me. A vague welcome bloomed on her face, habit from a lifetime of friends and family.

Jen looked puzzled, but wore a welcoming expression, the default of those who never considered their world could fall apart in an instant.

Using my firm mother voice I said, "I need to talk to you."

Megan's smile slipped and she narrowed her eyes, mouth diving into a frown. If she lived to middle age, Megan would probably develop that permanent sour expression.

When she finally recognized me, Megan colored. "You're the cop who stopped us. We didn't do anything wrong and you got us suspended from cheerleading."

Jen stepped back and looked around as if hoping for rescue.

"I could make it permanent if I tell Ms. Turner about your escapade last night at my house."

Megan thrust her hip out. "I don't know what you're talking about."

"Malicious mischief is nothing to laugh about." I sounded tough and expected them to cower. "But that's not really why I—."

Megan threw back her shoulders. "Your word against mine. Try it." A beat. "Bitch."

Jen bit her lips and stared at the pavement.

I hadn't expected that level of belligerence and I went full-on cop mode out of habit. "That's the way you want to play it?"

She twitched her finger on the key fob and her car blipped unlocked. "I'm outta here. Get in, Jen."

Without waiting, Jen shot around the CRV and jerked the door open.

Damn. I'd blown it. "Wait." Wrong. Stupidly, I reached out to stop her.

She yipped and jerked away, wrenching open her car door and diving inside. Jen hunkered in the passenger seat of the CRV.

I was already on my way back to my car as Megan slammed her door and locked it, then fired up and peeled away.

With the parking lot congestion, Megan didn't get much of a jump on me and I was able to follow. Her lack of self-preservation skills made trailing her easy. In a matter of five miles, I followed them into a quiet neighborhood with mature desert plantings, next to a golf course shaded by eucalyptus and several species of palm trees.

They pulled into the driveway and stopped in front of the closed garage door at a typical stucco two-story with a tiled roof. A chintz covered outdoor wicker love seat and a feathery palm greeted visitors on the front porch.

Their heads moved with angry animation, probably cursing me for my audacity to talk to them. They gave me ample time to park and walk up the driveway behind Megan's door. Without glancing around, she opened it and stepped out.

She startled when she finally spotted me. "Leave me alone!" She ran around the front of her CRV toward the front door.

Jen huddled next to her. They wasted their fear on me, but welcomed the real threat of people like the guy from the ball park.

"I'm not going to hurt you." I'd practiced keeping my voice slow and quiet. "I want to talk to you."

Megan pulled Jen toward the front walk, looking over her

shoulder at me. "We weren't at your house and I don't know what you're talking about."

My worry made me sound sterner than I intended. "How about your friend, Cali? Did you see her today?"

Megan's eyes flicked to Jen. "Yeah. She was at school."

With more effort than it ought to take, I quieted. "I need to know she's okay."

"Are you some kind of perv?"

The front door opened and a woman lumbered out. Her khaki capris and pink collared T-shirt stretched tight over a figure that probably sampled the three square meals along with desserts and snacks she prepared for her family. "Who are you?"

I focused on Megan. "Officer Jamie Butler from the Arizona Rangers."

She offered me a curious but pleasant expression. Remnants of Megan's youth lingered in her face, but a double chin made its debut and faint wrinkles hovering around her mouth more than hinted at frown lines. "I'm Megan's mother. Mrs. Thompson. What can we do for you?"

Mother to mother, at least we spoke the same language. "Your daughter and her friends TPed my house last night, but I'm more concerned—"

Mrs. Thompson threw her arm around Megan's shoulder. "It wasn't Megan. Whatever you believe. She was home last night. All night."

Megan smirked at me and cuddled under her mother's wing.

Jen shifted from foot to foot, not under Mrs. Thompson's protection.

"Okay. But that's not—"

Mrs. Thompson gave me her back and ushered Megan up the front walk. Jen trailed behind.

I followed them. "Cali. I'm worried about her."

Mrs. Thompson tossed the words over her shoulder as she

entered her house. "Cali is not my problem." She kept Megan tucked close and left the door ajar for Jen.

Jen hesitated, glanced inside the house, then whispered. "Cali wasn't at school today."

My heart hit my ribs. "Where was she?"

Jen's eyes shifted toward the house again and she said quickly. "Maybe at home?" She turned to leave.

I grabbed her arm, knowing I shouldn't but needing her answer. "Where does she live?"

Megan appeared in the doorway. "Jen! Come on!"

She turned her back to Megan and mumbled, hardly moving her lips. "Those apartments at Ina and First. The one with the dead lime tree in front."

"Now!" Megan's shrill voice commanded and Jen lurched toward her.

It took a long time to exit the neighborhood because I made a wrong turn and ended up in a maze of stucco and palms. Megan and Jen were safe behind walls with a mother who watched them closely. I had a bad feeling about Cali.

13

Each red light throbbed in my belly and my fingers tapped the wheel. The well-heeled neighborhoods faded into strip malls and multi-unit complexes until I located a two-story block of apartments where Jen had directed me. Six slump-block buildings of a half-dozen units upstairs and down clustered around a central area with a rusted swing set and metal picnic table. The roar of traffic on the busy intersection washed over the area of scabby bushes, concrete, and dead grass. A completely different world than Megan's sanctuary of landscaped homes.

The cracked sidewalk led me around the buildings as I looked for a dead tree to mark Cali's unit. So much felt abandoned here. Cali's bright smile from Kino Elementary flashed through my mind. She belonged someplace green and flowery, the sound of birds and a soft breeze.

The tree was little more than a brown twig thrusting from dry dirt in a chipped Talavera pot. The screen was ripped out, leaving a dented aluminum frame in front of a hollow plywood door. I rang the bell and waited.

Nothing.

The screen door protested with a squeal when I wrenched it open to bang on the door. Still nothing.

A potbellied man stepped out of the unit next door. He squinted, as if he'd been sleeping. A couple inches shorter than me, he rubbed black hair and spoke in a thick Latino accent. "You can quit the noise. Nobody's home."

An empty house. No one home. A memory sent an arrow through my skull.

Ringing in my head as I remembered checking her bed, moving quickly to my room, the dining room. Running, screaming, searching.

Breathe. *Then and now.* "When did you see them last?"

He shrugged and blinked. "I work nights. Try to sleep in the day. I usually see them when I get home. But that girl plays her music most of the time. I asked her to keep it quiet until five, when I get up. She's good about it. House was dark last night. Ain't heard them today."

"Do you have a pen and paper? I'd like to give you my number so you can call me if they show up."

He shook his head and reached to open his door. "I don't know them. Don't have time for this. Just wanted you to quit banging so I can sleep."

He disappeared inside, the click of his lock ending the conversation.

I stood on the concrete, staring at the door. Cali and her mother might have gone away for a couple of days. Nothing sinister about that.

Voices harangued me, telling me Cali was in danger and I was the only one who could help her. I repeated that Cali was probably off with her mother someplace. "Most of the time, the simplest explanation is the best." I looked around to see if anyone heard me talking to people they couldn't see.

A spot of faded red drew my attention to the ground next to

the pot. My fingers tingled and blood rushed through my ears. I stood for several seconds before I made myself bend down to retrieve it.

A tattered bit of an old red bandana, stiff, as if from dried sweat. My hand shook as I examined it. Just a bandana. Like a million of them. Like the one I'd used yesterday.

"Still think the simplest explanation is the best?" Frank cackled.

14

The moving van still hunkered in the street across from my house. More disturbing, the gray sedan was parked down the block. On impulse, I drove past my house and continued toward the car. I couldn't see through the tinted windows to tell if someone sat inside or not. The street curved, forming a giant loop through the neighborhood and I followed it around. When I made the circuit and returned to my house, the gray sedan was gone.

I pulled straight into the garage and closed the door before crawling out of the car. The scent of lilacs lingered in the garage. Another reminder of the awful anniversary, only a day away, and how tightly my nerves must be pulled. I felt more in control of myself than these strange happenings suggested.

When I entered the house, I took tentative steps to the front door, where I'd shed my shoes and socks after yesterday's run. The shoes lined up next to the wall in their orderly formation. The socks rested on top, as usual. No bandana.

Maybe I hadn't used it yesterday. I closed my eyes and concentrated. Standing in the driveway, Sherilyn walking over. Mopping my face. I knew I had it. But it wasn't here now.

I'd lost touch with the real world before. I knew what it felt like. This didn't feel the same. The Hot Tamales hadn't been a hallucination, my bandana was missing, and even though the gray sedan probably didn't pose danger, it was definitely real.

At Tara's suggestion, I'd started a mosaic project in the serenity of my backyard. A tabletop of one-inch Mexican tiles. The task distracted and the vivid blues, from cobalt to sky, soothed me. This afternoon its benefit was minimal. I paced, muttered, and argued. I finally heaped my clothes on the deck and dove into the pool.

Cool silence. Blessed relief for the forty seconds I held my breath and swam along the bottom. It was never long enough.

It wasn't my job to raise those girls. They had mothers. But Frank's warning circled around my head. If only I'd seen Cali myself.

Tara called and I managed to sound as chipper as ever. I told her I'd had a flat tire. If she didn't buy the lie, at least she didn't challenge it. "I don't usually work on Saturdays but I think you should come in before Sunday. How about eleven tomorrow?"

"Okay." I wanted to refuse, but that wouldn't look good to anyone.

Without warning, I remembered.

The second day. By then, I know she's not at a friend's house or out for a walk. She's gone and time is a demon that makes no sense. It's speeding too fast, she's been gone too long. It's slowed to a dull throb in meaningless space. People are talking. Different friends and cops I work with cycle into my awareness so there must be coming and going. I clutch her red hoodie. Occasionally someone forces a cup into my hand and I drink. I take a bite of flavorless food when it seems easier than fighting against whoever insists.

Unable to stand another minute of waiting, I push out of my front door to stand in the drizzle on the front porch. That's when I see the red of the ribbon under the lilac bush by the dining room window.

Weak legs take me down the steps and I fall to my knees in the cold mud.

The ribbon is marred with ground-in mud. The barrette she'd glued it to is missing. But my eyes focus on something else and I want to die. A drop of brown staining the red ribbon. Blood. Her blood.

Maybe I screamed. Maybe I'd simply been gone too long and she'd come to find me. All I know is that Kari has her arm around me.

She's leading me up to the front door and somehow managed to pry the ribbon from my hand. "Evidence," she says softly.

Exhausted by the battle waging in my brain, I finally gave in and took a pill. I'd been trying to wean myself from the meds and Tara had lowered the dose so there would be no worries about sleep walking.

Locked behind my own doors, I'd lost hours at a clip, coming back to awareness with no recollection of passing time. It happened less frequently now. I thought reducing meds was helping.

The evening slipped away as so many had in the last few years. It wasn't quite living, and even though I hated the way the clouds absorbed all emotion, it sure as hell wasn't dying. Some days, that counted for victory.

I woke Saturday morning to my door bell, the sound so foreign it took a moment to figure out what it was. In my two years here, I'd only heard it a smattering of times, Girl Scouts selling cookies or landscapers soliciting labor. Those times, I'd peeked out the slats in the shade of the window that opened onto the porch. I'd never answered.

This morning, when I spied through the blinds, the khaki of a cop's uniform greeted me.

My athletic shorts and t-shirt kept me decent. I unlocked the door and swung it open. I still hugged the red sweatshirt close to my chest, so I set it on a bench inside the door.

The officer, handsome Rafe Grijalva, watched the moving

progress across the street. He popped his attention to me and his eyes lit up. "Good morning."

He held a small spiral notebook and pen. It looked official.

I cleared the morning croak from my throat. "Hi. What are you doing here?"

Even though I'd pulled myself from the drugged sleep on the chair in the living room and had to look like a zombie, he didn't seem to mind. It had been a long time since I'd cared about male attention.

He raised an eyebrow and his mouth ticked up at my appearance. "Following up on a report."

It felt odd that I cared how he saw me. I squirmed under his scrutiny. "Report?"

"It came to the department and I recognized your name. Thought we could get it cleared up. Maybe I could come in and talk about it?"

I indicated Mom's decorative but uncomfortable bench on the porch. "Please, have a seat." I didn't have anything to hide and my house was more than tidy. My policy was never to leave a mess, nothing anyone else would have to clean up. But I felt too exposed to have anyone inside my home.

He didn't protest. I slipped into flip flops and joined him, perching myself on the end of the bench, two feet between us.

He read from his notebook. "A Mrs. Thompson says you were harassing her daughter at the high school baseball tournament on Thursday."

It took me a moment to work it out. "Oh. Arizona Rangers. The mother must have called Mitch Harris and got my name. She should be a detective."

The brown of Grijalva's eyes was so deep it looked almost black. He probably pulled more confessions with that gaze than others did with a stick. "Smarter than some with a badge. I saw you and Pete working the tournament."

Of course he had to get the official business taken care of. "Crowd control. I'll be there again this afternoon."

He scribbled in his notebook. "The Rangers have you busy. The elementary program and then the tournament, all back to back. Doesn't sound like retirement."

Friendly. Meaningless conversation. Small talk, like people do. "It's not like having a full time job, but it's plenty."

He raised his eyebrows, maybe teasing? "So, you were harassing Mrs. Thompson's daughter?"

Harassment is an exaggeration."

Grijalva nodded. "What would you call it?"

"There was a creepy guy hanging around the gate between the ball fields and the park. The girls obviously thought he was all that and a bag of chips."

Grijalva rested his back on the wall of the house. "So you broke it up."

I rubbed the pain starting in my temple. "I meant to, but a citizen distracted me. When I turned back around, they'd all disappeared." He seemed relaxed enough, the only thing missing was a beer. Maybe he'd be like Patricia and give me the benefit of the doubt. "A smarmy guy, way too old, panting after three cheerleaders. It tripped alarms."

Grijalva wrote in his book. "So you did what?"

"I searched for the girls and when I spotted them, there were only two."

He nodded and waited.

"So I went after them."

His face fell. "You chased them down?"

"I was worried the creep took off with the third girl."

"But he didn't?"

The cement of the porch under my feet looked as gray as my mood. "No. She'd gone to get her car."

Grijalva balanced his notebook on his knee. "So, why is Mrs. Thompson upset?"

I didn't look at him. "Maybe because when I was talking to them, the cheerleading sponsor came over and suspended them from the squad." I still stared at the cement. "Or, maybe because that night, they TPed my house." I paused. "It could be because as soon as I cleaned it up yesterday I went to the school to talk to the girls and Megan drove off." A beat. "But it's probably because after she blew me off, I followed her home."

Grijalva whistled. "Now we're getting somewhere."

I finally looked him in the eye. Dark, intelligent eyes that gave nothing away. Chasing the girls down because of harmless vandalism would seem crazy, but I didn't know how to tell him why I was worried. "Something about the whole thing didn't seem right so I wanted to make sure the girls were okay."

Grijalva's face remained expressionless. "What made you think it was off?"

The pain in my temple throbbed and my fingers started to tremble. Hot Tamales at the scene wouldn't make sense to him. "Does it matter? The fact is, I checked on the girls and one of them is missing."

"You checked on them?" Did he think I was a stalker?

Arguments raged inside me. I should shut up about my intuition, save myself embarrassment. But if I was right and Cali was in danger, I couldn't keep quiet. "I think maybe one of the girls might have hooked up with the guy later. You need to follow up."

Grijalva raised his eyebrows at my directive. "Because?"

"When I saw Megan Thompson at school yesterday, she was with only one of the girls. When I asked her if she'd seen Cali, she lied. Jen, the other girl, told me Cali hadn't been at school and when I went to Cali's house—"

He held up a hand. "Wait a minute. You went to Cali's house, too?"

I ignored his interruption. "She wasn't there. Her neighbor said she hadn't been home the night before."

He took that in, though I couldn't tell what he thought. "Tell me about the encounter with the guy and the cheerleaders."

I spared a second to close my eyes, knowing I would sound lame. With a dry tone, I related the whole incident, including a description of the guy, and as much information about the girls as possible, down to the Honda Civic.

He leaned his back on the house, impassive face. "Why do you think there's danger?"

I couldn't tell him about Frank's warning. I shrugged. "Intuition."

He seemed to accept that. "If it was those girls who TPed your house, how would they know where you live?"

"I can't answer that. Maybe the girls followed me home. Maybe they're smart enough to get my address from the Rangers, like Mrs. Thompson."

Obviously, I hadn't convinced him of my sanity. His smile was anything but sincere. "Sure."

I jumped up. "Forget it."

He didn't move but spoke with force. "Sit down. You didn't call me here, remember?" He said it quietly, no anger or violence behind it.

I sat.

He tapped his pen on the pad. "You've got no evidence or proof but you think this Cali might be in trouble with a smarmy guy you saw at the ball park?"

I watched him, not bothering to respond.

He stood up. "Okay."

Mouth dry, I croaked, "Okay?"

He flipped his notebook closed. "I'll look into it. The department is stretched thin because of Zoey Clark's disappearance, but I'll do some checking."

Even though I dreaded the answer, I had to ask. "Do you have any news on her?"

He tucked the notebook in his shirt pocket. "Afraid not." He didn't need to add that time was running out for good news.

Grateful not to be dismissed, I thanked him. "Don't expect to get any cooperation from Megan or her mother. They are pretty good at deflecting and lying."

He snickered. "They come by it naturally."

"What do you mean?"

He tucked the notebook into his shirt pocket. "Megan's daddy is Jim Thompson. You might have heard of him."

My blank stare didn't seem to put him off.

He explained, "Jim Thompson is the Pima County attorney. That's why the department is following up."

That was exactly the kind of favoritism Mom worked so hard to avoid. She'd always explained that she had to be extra tough on me so we couldn't be accused of nepotism. "But you'll check it out? I don't know Cali's last name but I know where she lives." I told him about the lime tree. Not the bandana.

He stood. "I'll check into it. Meanwhile, don't contact any of the girls again." He reached into his breast pocket and pulled out a card. This time, his face lit up. "Just in case you lost the last one I gave you."

He drove away and I stared at his card. What would happen if I called him to set up a hike? My heart lurched and sent flutters into my stomach. I'd better talk to Tara first. And definitely wait until I'd made it through tomorrow.

I plopped onto the bench as he climbed into his cruiser and drove off. The sun burst over Sherilyn's house, shooting arrows onto my covered porch. I closed my eyes, praying for the sunshine to sanitize me, to burn through my skin, straight into the shriveled bits inside me.

At some point, a cheerful tone broke through to me. "Hey, Jamie, the truck has amazing Sonoran hot dogs." Sherilyn intruding again. She stood in her cutoffs and tank top, holding silent Kaycee's hand.

Sherilyn had chased away the dire images so I owed her at least an effort. "Oh, yeah, the taco truck. How's the moving in coming along?"

She bounced with energy I only half-remembered having. "Everything's off the truck. Kitchen's all unpacked. I need to ask you if you can watch Jackson."

"I'm...I'm on my way out. Sorry."

Sherilyn wasn't easily put off. "He's sleeping and we have to return the moving truck. Won't be more than fifteen minutes. Jackson cried all night and just now fell asleep. If I move him, he'll wake up. The little guy really needs to sleep."

The U Haul roared to life. The man inside rolled down the window. "Babe, I've got Cheyenne. See you there."

Kaycee tugged free of Sherilyn's hand, took three steps to stand nearly touching me. She peered up at me and tilted her head, as if she could hear my thoughts. Her pudgy hand patted my knee.

I closed my eyes and the memories flipped in vivid color.

Two-years old and wispy blonde hair escapes from pigtails messed from too many tumbles.

Her face Kool-Aid stained, peanut butter on her breath, standing sweaty and triumphant in her soccer uniform.

So few years later posing for pictures in a party dress, too expensive and grown up for eighth grade graduation.

Later still, her geometry book open on the kitchen table, that last theorem left unsolved.

I was careful not to touch Kaycee when I stood. "Sorry. I can't."

Sherilyn ignored my protest. She shoved a baby monitor in my hand. "It'll work from here, just not in your house. If you want, go on over to our place. Help yourself to the Diet Cokes in the fridge. There's nothing else in there. We'll be right back."

Sherilyn snatched Kaycee in her arms and spun away. Making fast time with such short legs, she crossed the street to her well-used, mud-colored 4 Runner and strapped Kaycee in the back seat.

"It's only a sleeping baby safe in his home," I muttered.

I turned the volume up on the monitor as far as it would go and stared at the house across the street.

15

If Sherilyn knew about me, she'd build a fence around her house, string it with concertina wire, and rig it with sensor lights. The plastic monitor grew slippery with my sweat.

"She said the baby would sleep. A few minutes. They'll be right back." My own voice startled me.

I needed a few moments to breathe and process. An hour or two to write in my journal, talk to Maggie, get some perspective about Cali. Steel myself for tomorrow. I'd kept myself shrouded from life, and now it felt like it was rushing at me at breakneck speed. As soon as Sherilyn returned, I'd take some time to sit by the pool, then go see Tara. We'd be fine. It was time for me to take hold.

The phone in my back pocket erupted, the jangle so unnerved me I dropped the monitor. I checked the caller I.D. Phone pressed to one ear and retrieved monitor to the other, I steadied myself before pasting on a smile. The outward sign I hoped would transfer to my voice.

"Good morning." I sounded cheerful, perky almost. That should satisfy her.

I must not have been convincing because Mom's tight

concern pulled her words close. "I got your text last night that you'd taken a pill and turned off your phone. How are you today?"

I paused to listen to the monitor and kept working my way up Sherilyn's driveway. "Good. I slept great last night. Ate a big breakfast." My stomach clenched at that. I had to swallow the clutter in my brain before adding false vivacity. "Already hot here. How's the weather in Buffalo?"

Mom's silence stretched. "Jamie." The word studded with disappointment. "You know what Tara says. Face the sadness when it comes."

"Well. You know." Mom hated when I sounded unsure. "The new neighbors across the street have a little girl. She's got the softest white hair. Reminds me...."

"Oh, Jamie. You can't fall apart every time you see a blonde girl."

"I'm not falling apart."

I'd made it to Sherilyn's front porch, out of the blazing sun. I squinted into the front window, trying to see between the slats of the blinds. Boxes, a couch piled with toys and blankets and pillows, furniture and moving mess. Would the baby be in a bedroom, in a crib they'd set up first thing?

Keeping a high note in my voice, I said, "I've got some plans for today. Going to spray for weeds. Weird how they pop up in the gravel yards around here when it's so hard to get anything to grow in the desert."

Mom sighed. "You don't have to try so hard, Honey. It's a tough time. Not always the happiest for a lot of us, to be honest."

I slipped along the front of the house, checking windows. I'd probably missed part of the conversation since I concentrated so hard on hoping she wouldn't bring up tomorrow's date.

I knew it was coming. Talking about it only made it worse. Bright and cheerful. "Actually, I'm babysitting."

An edge of surprise shot back. "Babysitting? Honey, do you think that's a good idea?"

Frank said, *"Hell no it's not a good idea. You can't be trusted to watch a child."*

The baby grunted in his sleep and I froze. Distress? A gas bubble? Nothing. When I felt certain he was safe, I spoke. "He's sleeping. I'm outside with a monitor."

"You sound stressed."

"I'm good. Really. They'll be home in a couple of minutes."

After last year, I made a plan to get through. I would keep busy. Today I had the tournament and tomorrow I'd taken an assignment at the horse races at Rillito Race Track. But maybe Mom was right. Why tempt fate? I could stay home, work on my mosaic, take a pill if I needed.

The worry in her voice was the same as always. "I appreciate you trying to move on, but pushing this hard isn't good."

Despite feeling wobbly and a little overwhelmed today, I was a long way from falling apart. But Mom knew me so well she could see my cracks, maybe better than I did. The phantom lilac smell, the missing bandana, and the obsession with the gray sedan might be signs I was losing it again. "I'll see Tara later today."

"I'm proud of you, Jamie. Last year, you didn't handle this well at all."

I considered the monitor grasped in my hand and fought memories of last year. And the year before. And the worst one, four years ago. "Thanks."

Terrible things happened, but not every time. That's what Tara told me and what I wrote day after day in notebooks scribbled into and piled in the empty bedroom. Most of the time, things worked out.

Only sometimes, they didn't.

I made my way back to Sherilyn's front porch, to the sweet relief of the shade. "Thanks for calling."

"I'll be working all day tomorrow so don't worry about calling."

"Okay." Should I go back to my house or hang out here until they returned?

One more sigh for good measure. "I'll go ahead and wish you a happy Mother's Day now."

My knees buckled and I propped myself against the stucco of Sherilyn's house.

16

Mother's Day. I'd tried to prepare for it, but the words still hit me like bullets.

A memory exploded with full force.

Her braces give her face a different profile but she's still so pretty. Milk and flour make paste on her sleep shirt that hikes up well past her knees. We just bought that shirt a couple of weeks ago and will need to shop for new pajamas again already. She's growing so fast. Three big pancakes fill a platter usually reserved for Thanksgiving but it's probably the fanciest plate she could find. It sits on a cookie sheet decorated with dandelions because we had no bed tray and we hadn't planted our garden yet.

Her little face is nervous while I cut the syrupy mess, crisp on the outside, gooey on the inside. When I'm able to swallow and declare the breakfast delicious, she jumps on the bed, upsetting the tray. "Happy Mother's Day!" Beautiful, delicious, love.

I blinked away tears and recalled Tara's calm direction about then and now. Then was gone. Now I needed to live.

"Glad you didn't wish that bitch a happy day," Frank said.

"Stop it." The monitor burned in my hand. Jackson was a boy. Bald. Not a blonde girl.

"If that nitwit had half a brain she'd see you're not fit to keep a child safe."

I clutched my phone. Mom hadn't meant to explode a Molotov cocktail into my brain.

With help, I'd effectively blocked the images from the grocery store displays. I didn't watch much TV and never shopped the malls. My isolation helped buffer me. But it hadn't slipped my mind completely. It's why I got so worked up over girls I shouldn't care about.

Frank's voice pounded through to me. *"How stupid do you have to be to let this blindside you?"*

Maggie spoke in her comforting way. *"Don't listen to him, dear. You didn't deal with it well last year but you're better now."*

Frank again, *"If you call igniting a box of photos 'dealing with it' then no, she didn't deal so hot."*

My grip on the conversation loosened. I ground my teeth while Frank and Maggie escalated, along with the Chorus, who ratcheted from their usual whispers to muttering.

"Everyone. Stop it." I closed my eyes in the shocked lull and listened to the monitor. The voices hadn't awakened the baby.

"I know it's a bad day. Last year I wasn't strong enough but I'm better now," I said.

Frank's harsh laugh boxed my ears. *"You think so?"*

Concentrating on my right hand, I willed my fingers to relax around the monitor. I focused on hearing my breath enter my nose and exit my mouth. Finally, I answered Frank with confidence. "Better. Yes. Getting stronger."

"Then why are you talking to me?"

Frank knew what talking to him meant. "It's better than screaming," I said.

"Jamie?"

I whirled around and the monitor crashed into the gravel. Sherilyn stood on the walk, only fifteen feet away. Her husband climbed out of their 4 Runner. I hadn't heard them drive up.

Sherilyn eyed the front window I'd been peeking into and tilted her head to the side, sizing me up. "Who are you talking to?"

17

Frank shouted obscenities that made me cringe.

Sherilyn's husband bent into the backseat unlatching Kaycee. Cheyenne kicked the back door open on the passenger side and trundled out, apparently needing no help to free herself from restraints.

How much had Sherilyn heard? "No one. It's a bad habit of mine. From living alone."

She nodded, keeping her appraising stare. She bent to retrieve the monitor. "Slept right through it, huh?"

The man hoisted Kaycee to his shoulder. Cheyenne marched to me and put her hands on her hips. She gave me a disapproving stare.

Sherilyn pivoted sideways and shouted. "Donnie, this is Jamie."

His smile opened up as if nothing inside him needed hiding. He briefly waved.

Sherilyn tucked the monitor in a back pocket of her cutoffs. "Soon's we get organized, we'll have you over for a cookout. Give me a day or two." She acted as if I was any regular person.

Not a killer.

The Chorus of guttural chanting encouraged me to punch, shout, or even run.

I squeezed my eyes shut for a moment and slowly took control.

Sherilyn didn't interrupt.

When I opened my eyes the two of them studied me. Cheyenne spoke first. "Do you have invisible friends?"

Sherilyn planted a hand on the child's head. "Cheyenne. Some things you keep to yourself."

The voices rose in a whirl of sound. I swallowed hard, made eye contact with Cheyenne, and nodded.

Cheyenne raised her little shoulders with a giant inhale and let it out in satisfaction. She gave Sherilyn a knowing look. "I told you. Like Kaycee."

Sherilyn spun quickly and motioned to her husband. "Donnie, come say hi to Jamie."

With Kaycee riding on his neck, little hands clasped in his beard, Donnie lumbered over like a friendly grizzly bear. With one hand around Kaycee's back, he swooped down and snatched Cheyenne around her middle, lifting her like a sack of potatoes. Both girls squealed in delight. Donnie grinned and nodded at me. "Thanks a bunch for watching Jackson. Sure was a big help."

The girls giggled and struggled. Cheyenne admonished, "Daddy. Put me down before someone gets hurt."

Donnie winked at me. "I'm the daddy. You're always safe with me."

My heart stuttered at his words. I needed time alone to gather myself. "He only made one little mumble in his sleep."

Sherilyn reached out cool fingers to pat my arm. Just a quick touch that sent my nerves flaming and the Chorus erupted.

Sherilyn didn't hear them, of course. "Glad we lucked out with such a good neighbor."

I hurried home, the sun blazing and slapping my skin with reflective heat from the street. Safely behind my locked door, the words spilled from me. "I'm Jamie Butler. I'm Amanda's daughter. I'm a retired Buffalo cop. I am 46 years old. I can run a half marathon in less than two hours."

I continued listing facts about myself until the voices settled. Frank and Maggie kept their usual conversation going. They'd probably always be with me, but the three of us understood our boundaries better than we had for the last few years.

A tall glass of ice water, thick slice of lemon, soothing Chopin wafting through the house, and an hour with my notebook, the pages filling automatically, like ghost writing.

"You're a goddamned fool if you get involved with that hillbilly circus over there," Frank said.

"Not involved. Just being a good neighbor."

18

Frank chided me while I changed from running shorts and tank top to my uniform and boots. He didn't let up all the way across town, through light Saturday afternoon traffic. He knew the rules. I'd talk to him on my terms. But he liked to see if he could make me break, like any bully.

Living so far on the edge might seem inconvenient to most, but I loved the quiet. It seemed a reasonable tradeoff for having to drive across town for almost everything. Today, I used the time to calm down after letting Mom's casual comment about Mother's Day blindside me. I talked with Frank and Maggie and a few others chimed in on the half hour drive. By the time I reached Tara's office, I felt calm again.

We settled in and Tara asked how I'd been since we'd last met.

It took some time to explain about the cheerleaders and my concern for Cali. We discussed how Zoey Clark's disappearance might be translating into paranoia about Cali and I let it go without defending myself, even though I was certain it wasn't the case. I didn't delve into that the creepy feeling about the two men in blue shirts or the driver of the gray sedan. Having Tara think I was teetering wouldn't do me any good.

"Evidently I made enemies of the girls because they TP'ed my house."

Tara raised an eyebrow. "How did you deal with that?"

I didn't mention that confrontation, but came clean about talking to Frank in front of Sherilyn.

"Does your mother know you still talk to Maggie?"

I squirmed. "It would make her worry."

"And you feel as though you need to protect your mother's feelings?"

"Mom doesn't need protecting from anyone. She's the one doing the protecting."

"And yet, you won't tell her about Maggie to keep her from feeling worried."

Mostly. But if she didn't know, she couldn't fight me about it. "Only because she's never understood about Maggie or Frank. Or any of the others. She doesn't know how important they are to me."

Tara tilted her head as if intrigued. "What doesn't she understand?"

Everything. "She thinks they're damaging and are bad for me."

"Do you think that?"

We'd been over these questions many times. "If I did, I wouldn't spend so much time with them."

"Do you have a choice how much time you spend with them?"

"I have some control, yes. As long as I give them time of their own, I'm able to keep them in line."

Tara nodded and made notes. "Why can't you tell your mother that?"

Did Tara see the spike of fear I felt? "If she knew I spent time every day with Maggie and Frank, she'd be upset. Chances are she'd move me back to Buffalo where she could keep better track of me."

"You're an adult. You can make your own choices."

"We still have the DPOA."

She set her pen down. "Why do you feel you need the power of attorney? Aren't you confident making decisions for yourself?"

I'd never thought of rescinding the DPOA. "Do you think I'm ready?"

"It's not about what I think."

Circular dialogue to make me figure it out on my own. "Mom would be hurt if I asked to withdraw her authority."

"Back to protecting her?"

Frustration started to build and I took a deep breath. "What's wrong with being nice to people you love and who love you?"

"Is hiding your true feelings being nice?"

"It seems the least I can do. After everything happened, she took care of me. She's the only one who's been by my side my whole life."

Tara's mouth tightened but she didn't respond. "You're not telling her about Frank and Maggie and you won't revoke her DPOA. What else are you doing to mollify her?"

Typical Tara, push at my comfort. The logical part of me understood she wanted me to heal and be stronger. The other part wanted to walk out. "Not mollifying."

"You've had some stress lately. Maybe we should delay the memory work for a while."

It would be nice to drift and not have to confront the memories. But, as Mom would say, there is no progress without effort. I didn't want to spend five days of every week in a therapist's office. "Let's keep working."

"You're sure?"

I settled back on the couch and closed my eyes. "Ready."

It wasn't quite hypnosis. Tara spoke slow and quiet and directed me to a time or place, then asked me to see, smell, hear, touch, and remember.

"Remember, this is all in the past. It isn't happening now. Tell me where you are," she said, after she'd guided me.

It was frightening to be in another place and strange to be in Tara's office at the same time. I paused a moment to be grateful for that much distance between then and now. Then let myself sink into then.

"I'm in Mom's office, standing at the window. My palm is open on the glass and the cold seeping into my skin makes me want to scream. She's out there somewhere. Is she wet or cold? Or is she inside? It's drizzling again from heavy clouds. I haven't seen sun for three days, and feel as if I'll never see it again."

If I opened my eyes, I'd see the bright southwest décor of Tara's office.

"Mom's phone rings and I listen to her grunt to the caller, keeping her response neutral so I can't read any meaning in it. I shouldn't be here, but I can't help it. I've been hounding her, demanding she put more officers on the case. She told me she'd like nothing more than to pull every cop off whatever they're doing and set them on this. But she can't. She has to avoid any whiff of nepotism.

"The phone call is obviously about **her** but Mom won't tell me. She tells me to wait in her office and she'll be right back, but I know better. After she leaves, I convince another officer to take me with him.

"We drive through drizzle that mutes everything to look like an old movie. The windows of the cruiser fog over and I rock in the passenger seat. I can't sit still, can't talk. The car is abandoned outside the gates of an automobile junkyard."

My words beat out in huffs of hot breath. I wanted to stop but I needed this if I was ever going to heal. I took a moment to calm down.

"The overcast air is suffocating in the spring humidity. Trees shove and crowd everywhere and it feels like a fortress outlines the junkyard. Red and blue lights pulse against gray sky. I've been to a thousand crime scenes. But never like this. The chain-link gate, lined with barbed wire on top, is attached to a crumbling cinderblock garage at the entrance where the junkyard owner tinkers with old cars and collects the fees from those dissecting the wrecks in the yard. The Boneyard is spread in red paint, cracked and peeling across the front. An appropriate name for the cars who found it their final resting place. Mom is framed by the open garage. She's barking orders and asking questions. In charge. I try not to let her see me because I know she'll send me away."

I started to pant and fought the urge to open my eyes, transport myself back to Tara's office and safety. But I can't hide.

"A uniformed officer hands Mom a barrette with a bit of tattered red ribbon glued on and wispy blonde hairs attached."

"Jamie," Tara's voice called me back. "That's enough for today."

I squeezed my eyes closed and held myself tight. "I can go a little more."

"I really think—"

"Green weeds sprout from the hulks of Chevys and Fords rusted and ruined. Some of them have been there so long they're probably older than Mom. Officers shout through the yard, checking in. No one has found anything. The air fills with garbage smells of rotting upholstery and mice, along with the sickening sweet scent of lilacs. I know whose ponytail the barrette had been stripped from. The voices are thrumming in my head and sometimes I'm not sure if it's officers' talking to each other or within me. They're louder than they've ever been. Like clanging bells beating on my brain, taking over my head. Then I see it. The silver chain, with mud ground in, as if it had been placed in the exact spot for me to find. The tiny silver runner poised and proud."

"Jamie." Tara's calm voice is colored with urgency. "Come back now. You've had enough."

I blinked in the bright, cheery office. My cheeks felt hot and wet and I realized I'd been sobbing again.

She handed me the tissue box. After my breath returned to normal and I felt stable, we talked about the memories and Tara asked me to journal my thoughts as soon as possible.

I snapped up a dry tissue and patted my eyes and cheeks one last time. "I have a shift at the ball park now, but I'll write this evening."

She furrowed her brows. "Maybe you should cancel today's assignment."

I stood. "No. Part of this whole thing is learning how to deal with life again. I need to be responsible for my obligations."

She didn't respond, but in a swoosh of skirts, rose and walked me to the door. "We can explore farther next time. For now, you need to be good to yourself. Remember to hydrate and eat well."

19

The lot at the ball park was about half full. Mid May brought the temperature into the low 90's, not hot by Tucson standards. After the cold of my last years in Buffalo, when no matter how many layers I piled on or how high I set the furnace all that I felt was the chill of the grave, I embraced the desert heat.

My uniform clung to damp skin, the duty belt strapped heavily around my waist. I used to wear it and a Kevlar vest as thoughtlessly as shoes. And, like it felt to wear shoes in the desert now, the belt was unusual and confining.

Patricia and I met up by the concession stand where the poster for Zoey Clark hung wrinkled and sun faded already. *Please, Zoey, be surviving better than these fragile bits of paper and ink.*

We began our rounds. She seemed stiff, not as chatty as usual. I waited for her to bring up my call to her yesterday. Instead, she talked about getting her husband to take the kids while she volunteered for the Rangers. I let her chatter wash over me as my attention wandered the ball field, and over to the fence separating it from the rest of the park. Several knots of homeless dotted the sparse grass, huddled around picnic tables.

Various contraptions such as rusted grocery carts, grungy bikes, even a battered stroller, sat heaped with colorless belongings, the mobile homes of the drifters.

I didn't spot the flirting guy from Thursday. Maybe I'd scared him off. But guys like that could always find vulnerable girls flattered by his attention. I kept an eye out for the homeless guy with the missing dog. I felt bad about blowing him off. To someone so alone, who'd lost so much, his dog must be his world. I hoped he'd found her.

I suddenly realized Patricia's monologue wasn't playing. When I glanced at her, she dropped her gaze to the ground, as if nervous to speak. She met my eye. "So, hey, I got a call from Mitch."

She'd finally gotten around to it. "He said you'd gone to Megan Thompson's house and confronted her about TPing your house. If I'd known one of those girls was Jim Thompson's daughter, I'd have tied you up before letting you go there."

Normally, I wouldn't respond. Today I didn't feel at all normal. "Mrs. Thompson will lie to keep her kid out of trouble. The kind of mother who complains to the coach that her baby deserves more court time. She probably writes the term papers and completes the science projects."

My words flooded me with a memory.

She's tall enough to reach mid chest to me now. In that awkward stage of all arms and legs and teeth too big for her mouth. Tears are building and she's regretful for her procrastination. Pleading.

"Emily's mom signed off on the badges and her sash is totally full. I only have three. Can't you just sign this and I can finish the require-ments later? Come on. Please."

I want to do that, just to see her smile. But I resist.

Later at the ceremony, she keeps her eyes to the ground, embar-rassed because of her bare sash.

It takes a year before I know I've done the right thing. At that

ceremony, she beams with a sash filled with colorful badges. All right-
fully earned.

Patricia's eyes traveled over the ball field, taking in everything. "Well, she was upset enough to light a match under Jim.
He's a prick, but he's powerful."

We walked to the edge of the bleachers and sauntered back.
We both surveyed the grounds, not each other. She wasn't quite
done. "Mitch asked me to talk to you. Wants you to tone it
down."

I stopped. "What you're saying is that if I see something
wrong happening, ignore it so no one gets upset?"

"Not at all. I mean, if there's something legitimately going
on, by all means, that's why we're here. It's just...."

No matter how soft she couched it, she was asking me to
shirk my responsibility. "That guy was a predator. And those
girls, whether they knew it or not, were in danger."

Patricia looked pained. "Yeah, but hunting down a teenager
because she TPed your house is extreme."

I opened my mouth, not sure what I intended to say, but a
shadow blocked the sun and I closed it.

"Hi, Pete." Officer Grijalva stood in front of us.

Patricia blinked. Her O of a mouth morphed into a wide grin
and she punched him in the arm. "Rafe, what the hell are you
doing here...again?"

Grijalva smiled a greeting at me and I nodded, worried we'd
have a replay of my dressing down this morning. "Officer
Grijalva."

The corners of his mouth lifted in a slight grin. "Call me
Rafe. How are you?"

"Fine." Feeling the need to look anywhere but at Grijalva, I
shifted my attention to the bleachers behind his head. Megan
and Jen, in their shorts and low-cut shirts, held drink cups a few
yards from the concession stand. Instead of the brazen grin and

thrust out chest, today Megan wore a grim face and her shoulders hunched like the troll she'd probably turn into, just like her mother.

She caught my eye and sneered my way. In a quick movement, she lifted her hand and launched a bird in my direction. Obviously, she hadn't learned any lessons. Without thought, I headed in that direction.

A strong grip clasped my arm and my momentum swung me around.

Frank hissed and shoved forward in my head. I fisted my hand, but easily resisted bringing it up to throw a punch into Grijalva's calm face.

With a serene expression he spoke quietly. "You're not going over there. Save all of us some trouble and leave them alone."

I shook Grijalva off. "I'm not going to cause any problems."

Patricia looked skeptical. "Better stay here."

"I'll be right back." I expected them to try to stop me again, or at least follow along.

Megan scowled at me while I approached. "I need to speak to you." I could still drum up the authority of a cop.

Megan's head tilted to the side and her lip curled to the right. "I'm not supposed to speak to you."

Frank and The Chorus urged me to slap Megan. I kept my voice steady. "This isn't about you. It's Cali. You haven't seen her, have you? Did she go with the guy?"

The two girls exchanged a look that seemed to solidify their bond. Megan firmed her mouth, then said. "You got us suspended by saying we were talking to some guy. But there was no guy."

Dumb teenagers. Hiding and covering, sending their own into a dark forest of biting teeth and shredding claws. "I saw you talking to him."

Jen recited, as if rehearsed. "We weren't talking to anyone.

You just, like, came out of nowhere, accusing us of, whatever. I don't even know what."

I rubbed my temple and focused on the girls. "Okay. Give me Cali's number and—"

"What is wrong with you?" I knew before looking up it was Megan's mother.

What surprised me was Grijalva standing beside her. That's why he hadn't come with me. He was probably talking to Mrs. Thompson.

The woman grabbed my arm and yanked me away from Megan before Grijalva stepped between us and forced her to release me.

She pointed to me. "My husband talked to the Ranger's commander. He said he'd take care of this. He told me he called the sheriff's department, too."

Grijalva blinked in confirmation. "He did."

Mrs. Thompson stomped her foot, something I'd rarely seen a grown woman do. "She's stalking my daughter. Arrest her or issue a restraining order or whatever."

"Let's calm down here." Tall and straight in his uniform, Grijalva carried a smooth assurance. Mrs. Thompson, face red and eyes shooting fire, held back from attacking me.

I addressed Grijalva in my professional voice. "Cali. The girl I told you about, is not here."

Grijalva studied me a second, then addressed the two girls. "Did you talk to an older man, say around thirty, here on Thursday?"

They both wore expressions of exaggerated purity. Megan's eyes flicked to her mother before she spoke. "Like I told my mom, the officer came after us out of the blue."

Mrs. Thompson's shield and sword came out. "I want you to stay away from my daughter. You're some kind of sick pervert."

"It's Cali. I'm worried—"

White teeth, maintained with twice yearly checkups and cosmetic touchups, flashed like a Rottweiler at the junkyard fence. "Megan has nothing to do with Cali Shaw. They used to be friends when they were in junior high, but Cali got wild and my Megan knows she'd get her into trouble. She's not allowed to hang out with Cali."

Megan stared at something in the distance beyond her mother. She'd learned to keep her face blank.

"I saw them here. Leaving together," I said.

Mrs. Thompson's lips pulled back in a snarl. "And you 'saw' a man about thirty years old talking to them. I don't know what your game is, but stop lying about my daughter and leave us alone."

I pointed at Megan. "Tell her."

Megan's mother narrowed her eyes in contempt. "Who are you, even? What's Cali to you? That girl is nothing but bad news and she's not missing, but it's only a matter of time before she is. Or before she turns up pregnant. If you don't make teenagers toe the line, they'll get into trouble. And then what? Tragedy. I'm not going to let that happen to my daughter."

A thousand cuts left me bleeding and enraged. Go ahead and try, Mrs. Thompson. But I saw your daughter, her skirt too short, her smile too big, her juices flowing. If she survives, it's by luck, not from your diligence.

Mrs. Thompson spared a hateful glare at me before turning to Grijalva. "If I have to, I'll sue. Keep her away from us."

Grijalva held a restraining hand up to silence me. Mrs. Thompson threw an arm around Megan's shoulders and pivoted her away. Jen hurried after them, not giving me the same opportunity she gave me yesterday.

I shouted at their backs. "Jen, for God's sake. Call Cali. Now. See if she answers."

Mother and daughter hurried away.

Gralva stepped in front of my line of vision. He lowered his face, forcing me to look at him and spoke in a voice like honey. "What's really going on here?"

"Cali is missing. She—"

He shook his head. "I spoke to the girls. They say they've talked to Cali. There is no mysterious guy flirting with them yesterday. The only one upset is you. Why?"

"How do you know they aren't lying?" If I was really crazy enough I'd make it all up, I'd deal with that. If only I knew the girl was safe. "If Cali's okay, why isn't she here?"

"Megan and Jen say she was upset about being cut from cheerleading and took off."

"Where? When?"

Grijalva held up his hand in a whoa motion. "Apparently, she's got a boyfriend in Phoenix but they don't know his number."

"Did you get her phone number? Have you talked to her?" This wasn't enough.

Grijalva brushed a hand along my shoulder blades, directing me to walk toward the parking lot. "When I called it went to voicemail. The girls say she keeps her mailbox full so she can screen calls and no one can leave a voicemail. They promised to tell her to call me next time they talk to her."

"And you believe them?"

He kept walking.

"Did you call Cali's mother?"

He nodded. "The number on file at the school isn't working. She didn't give them a new number. The emergency contact information lists a person no one knows whose number is also no longer in service."

"This is a girl on her own. No one cares." My voice sounded tight and anxious.

"The school's records show Cali misses frequently. This

doesn't seem to be unusual for her or her mother to go off-grid."

"Until I see Cali, I'm can't trust she's safe."

"You aren't related to her and you aren't a cop anymore. It sounds harsh, but it's not your business. I'm looking into it."

Anger popped and fizzled inside me. "What have you found out?"

He sounded too calm for this situation. "It's not a public matter."

"You're not doing anything, are you?"

We made it to the fence into the parking lot. Grijalva stopped and stared at me, as if trying to see inside me. "Why are you so intent on this?"

The voices whispered and argued, giving me their suggestions on what to say, what to do. At least now I recognized their bad advice. "A girl's life is at stake. We can't afford to take it lightly."

"You're going to have to step back and let the cops do it."

I couldn't tell him that my voices knew things my conscious mind didn't, and they were shouting at me that something was wrong. He wouldn't believe me and he'd probably tell Patricia, who would tell Mitch, and he'd give me the boot.

I needed the Rangers. It gave me the only purpose left in my decimated life.

Patricia caught up to us. "Rafe's gonna hang with me for the rest of this shift. It's only a half hour. We both think you should go home."

I waited while an angry mob erupted in my ears. I'd messed up again. "Yeah, okay." They watched me walk to my Juke and climb in. With a final wave, they turned and headed back to the ball park. They laughed and Patricia punched his arm. Friends.

I remembered friends.

I started my engine, then quickly shut it off. They might want to get me out of their hair, but I couldn't leave, yet.

20

The homeless guy ambled along the sidewalk in the park. I scrambled out of my car and set a course to intersect him.

It didn't take long to catch up to him. He walked like an old man, shuffling, with a slight limp. His tattooed arms stretched out from a plaid shirt with ripped sleeves. He wore grubby gray jeans thin as cheesecloth.

"Hey, hello. Remember me?"

He stopped but didn't turn, as if wondering if my voice really called to him. Only his head turned, maybe so he could run if he needed. When he saw me, he spun all the way around and greeted me with a huge, mangle-toothed grin.

"Hi, Jamie."

Mention of my name stopped me short. The Chorus rose with warnings and orders to attack or run. "Uh, hi." I didn't put a question mark at the end, but I was puzzled. In an attempt to put him at ease, I pointed to his arm. "That's a beautiful tattoo."

Rotten teeth in a slobbery mouth grinned at me. "See the cars in the jungle? I love the cars. They all mean something to me."

Green vines twisted through chassis windows and around

tires of at least a half dozen cars, taking up most of his arm. My stomach twisted at the Jaguar hood ornament peeking through a cluster of red hibiscus flowers. I pointed to one different from the rest. "What is that? It looks new."

His laugh sounded deranged. "It is! All those cars and now I'm in love with airplanes. That is a B52. Really big bomber."

"It looks sore. Do you have antiseptic for it?"

"It's fine. Just new. It'll heal." He touched it gingerly and exposed those awful teeth to me. "You must really like high school baseball."

I glanced behind me and then to the stands. "I'm. Yeah. Baseball is great."

He smelled of sour sweat and clothing gone too long without washing. Dirt streaked his face and collected in the folds on his neck. His skin had the copper glow of desert exposure. None of that seemed to matter to him as he continued the conversation. "Who's your team? I'm guessing Ventana, since you've been to almost all their games."

He stepped too close and my brain twisted. He smelled like ruin and it felt as if the stench had a life of its own and might crawl away from him and slither up my nose, burrow into my sinuses and live with me forever. Just because fine cologne didn't waft from him didn't mean he wasn't owed respect. "Did you find Petunia?"

He tilted his head and paused. It was look I'd seen before and I waited patiently for his head to clear. "You remembered her name. That's wonderful. She's home and well."

He must have a place to live besides the park. It was good for him to have something to love and care for. "I'm glad she wasn't hurt."

"No. She just got a good run, I guess." It felt like he worked at the conversation, like maybe he wasn't used to making small talk.

Me, either. I hoped to put him at ease. "She's lucky to have someone who cares about her so much."

His diseased grin made me cringe, but the compliment clearly pleased him. "I always take care of what I love."

"Thank you for asking after Petunia. You've always been nice to me."

We'd only met that once and I'd blown him off. Why did he seem so friendly to me? A thought jolted me. "How do you know my name?"

His face fell. "Remember? The night Petunia ran away?"

My head erupted in a roar. I'd gone home from the park. Ran on the desert, met Sherilyn and her children. Then I'd locked myself in my house. All night. Took a pill. Woke up stiff. "Sure."

No. I didn't take a pill that night. Did I? The meds ate my life and confused me. I had to stop taking them if I wanted to really live. But sometimes I welcomed the blackness.

He nodded with enthusiasm. "Yeah, I didn't recognize you at first. That's how it is when you meet someone in uniform the first time and then you see them in regular clothes, so it takes a minute. But at the end of the day, you were just as nice both times. So, you remember now? You got my name?"

This made no sense. I was home Thursday night. He looked so eager for my friendship, though, I focused on our conversation. "I've always been bad with names. Sorry."

He waved that off. "Don't worry. I can't remember things like I used to, either. Shax. My name is Shax."

Frank and Maggie argued about Thursday night. Maggie held firm that I'd slept on the chair in the living room. Frank said I'd taken meds and used Shax as proof I couldn't be trusted. A few others gave opinions. I closed my eyes and repeated to myself: "I'm Jamie Butler. I'm Amanda's daughter. I'm a retired Buffalo cop. I live in Tucson. I like hockey."

When the voices returned to a low rumble, I opened my eyes. It couldn't have taken more than three seconds, but Shax wore a suppressed grin.

"You okay, Jamie?"

Something about Shax felt familiar somehow but it must have been from seeing him at the ball park. The way he said my name made my skin crawl. "Fine."

Since he seemed to remember some things, even distorted, I decided to give it a try. "The other day there were three cute girls in yellow and black cheerleading uniforms." I turned and pointed to the fence. "There, by the fence. They were talking to a man, maybe in his thirties. Dressed in a blue golf shirt and jeans. Do you remember them?" My description of the creep sounded generic, one of a thousand men.

Shax squinted where I pointed, as if trying to see it now. He shook his head. "That was the day you got those girls in trouble. I saw that. By the fence. Those snotty girls, they were being nasty and mean and you stopped them. That was good, what you did for me."

He must be confusing me with someone else. "Okay. But that's not what I need you to remember. Before that, they were flirting with that man. Have you seen him around since or before that?"

Shax acted as though he wanted desperately to help me. He squeezed his eyes closed like a five-year-old might. Finally, he balled his fist and banged on his temple.

I grabbed his arm. "Stop it. Don't. It's okay."

He searched my face with eyes almost desperate. "I remember...."

The voices shouted at me to rattle him but I waited. "Take your time."

Tears formed in the corners of his eyes. "The girl."

Grijalva was suddenly next to me. I hadn't heard him approach. "Is everything okay here?"

Maybe he'd had training with the mentally ill. He had a calming vibe to him that worked better than many cops I knew on the force, who liked to come on strong, intimidate and overwhelm. I'd dealt with more than my share of people with a loose grip on the physical world.

With Shax's wrist still firmly in my hand, I answered Grijalva, but stayed looking at Shax. "It's fine. I asked Shax a question and he was trying to remember. But it's okay. It's not important. You don't need to answer me, Shax."

The distress melted off Shax like a candle left in the Tucson sun. His damaged smile returned. "I don't remember any guy with those girls. Just you. Then later, when you came back with that girl."

That didn't make sense, but not much about him did at that point.

He nodded at me and looked delighted. "Is she your daughter?"

I didn't flinch outwardly but inside, I collapsed.

"Cause, she looked like she could 'a been your daughter, you know."

I croaked through a dry throat. "I don't have a daughter."

Unaccountably, Shax threw his head back and howled with laughter.

21

Shax wouldn't quit laughing. Slobber ran from the sides of his mouth and he bent over, slapping his knee.

Grijalva took hold of my arm and directed me away. The residents of the park shrank from us as we trudged across the grass, in and out of the shade from the palms. Our uniforms didn't make us a welcomed sight. Shax's shrieks of hilarity dogged us.

Grijalva's voice cut through most of the racket in my head. "Obviously, the guy's mentally ill. Don't let him get to you."

Frank: *"You'd miss a puddle in a rainstorm."*

Shax was mentally ill. I felt qualified to identify it. But I was still missing something. It hid under the surface like a submerged stone. Waves of distraction rippled above it and I couldn't make it out clearly.

"I thought you were on your way home." Grijalva sounded less irritated than I assumed he'd be.

We stepped from the curb at the edge of the grass into the blazing parking lot. "I saw Shax and I wondered if he'd remember seeing that guy with the girls. He wasn't any help." But he knew something, I felt sure.

We approached my Juke again and I hit unlock on my key. The car blipped and blinked its lights. "Okay, I'm really going home now."

With that same static expression, he said, "Do you have to? Pete's shift is over and I was technically off-duty a couple of hours ago. We're going to change and grab a drink someplace. Why don't you join us?"

You can't mix alcohol with meds. "I don't drink."

His eyebrow barely twitched, and I was beginning to understand it as a sign of big emotion. "So have a seltzer water. Unless it's too hard to be around alcohol and not drink. If that's the case, we can hit a coffee shop."

Avoiding others' drinking didn't faze me. I did have shorts and shirt in the back of my car, since sometimes I liked to run at parks after my shift. The idea of hanging out with other people, especially with cops, made everything inside me quake. Was I ready for this? Maybe after this morning, with all the strain, it would be best to retreat to my pool and the mosaic. But I'd handled this morning and felt strong. And I wanted to be normal, sit with friends. Still, I'd probably make a fool of myself. I wouldn't be able to carry a conversation. I opened my door. "It's not a big deal."

He leaned on the door and his eyes twinkled. "You told me you're new to Tucson and Pete said she didn't think you had many friends. Why not spend an hour with us? What could it hurt?"

Patricia appeared behind Grijalva. "I thought you'd gone home. Hey, why don't you have a drink with us? I called Deon and told him he's still on kid duty."

I eased into my car seat. "Thanks, but I can't."

Grijalva's eyebrows popped up. "Can't?"

Patricia got tough. "That's bullshit. The one time I can get away for a little while and you're going to bug out. No way."

Maggie seemed to be the only one urging me to go. The rest had varying reactions, all negative. But Tara thought I could trust Maggie more than the others. Grijalva and Patricia pushed together, staring at me.

Patricia prodded. "Oh, come on. I'm going to change in the car. We'll meet at a bar close to the cop shop, so Rafe can check out and pop over."

I'd probably be sorry. "Okay."

Patricia's wide grin made me feel better. "Just for a little while. It'll be fun."

Grijalva dipped his chin and gave me a gentle look. "You okay with this? I know I practically begged, but if you're uncomfortable, you don't have to."

"No. It's fine. I mean, it's good. I'd like to." Frank wasn't the only one laughing at my awkwardness. Wings of excitement and fear tapped my gut. I was out of practice being a regular person but I was eager to give it a try.

Grijalva took off while Patricia gave me directions. Then got confused and I ended looking it up on my phone. It was farther away than she'd thought.

She spun around and scooted off, obviously pleased with the impromptu party.

I climbed into the Juke, already second guessing my decision.

It took me a while to find parking and by the time I padded onto the patio in my running shoes and shorts, Patricia was already there. The brewery nestled between tall downtown buildings but managed an open courtyard in back, shaded with palo verde trees. I settled into a metal chair and leaned on the table.

A dark-haired waitress with snapping eyes popped over, probably a student at University of Arizona. Patricia ordered a pitcher of their IPA and two glasses and I ordered a large iced tea with extra lemon. Before the drinks arrived Grijalva joined us.

He looked good in his uniform, but his khaki shorts and black t-shirt didn't hurt his looks at all. He sat and poured a glass of cold beer.

"Have you known each other a long time?" I asked.

Patricia slapped Grijalva's shoulder. "It's been what, six years since we worked together? I was brand new, right? The first two years you have no idea what you're doing, anyway."

We all agreed.

Patricia continued. "I get partnered with John Wayne Franklin. What a numb nuts. He's one of those guys who says, 'women have no place in law enforcement.' So you know what I'm up against."

Yeah, I knew.

A hint of smile surfaced on Grijalva's face. "Numb Nuts retired last year. Moved to Minnesota to be near his daughter."

"Not far enough away, but maybe he'll fall into a snow drift and freeze to death." Patricia placed an arm around his shoulder and squeezed his neck. "Rafe took pity on me. Taught me everything I needed to know. His famous saying...."

They recited it together. "Do what you gotta do so you go home tonight."

Grijalva raised one eyebrow. "Good thing I did. 'Cause that training came in handy when she saved my life."

Patricia grinned and drank her beer.

I waited for the story.

Grijalva took a sip and began. "Twenty-three hundred hours and I'm driving. Matt Johnson's riding shot gun. Sarge put him with me to keep his dumb ass out of trouble. We called him Haz Matt because he was a hazard to himself and everyone he rode with."

We all knew the type.

"We get a burglary alarm call at one of those McMansions in Oro Valley. Most of these calls are false alarms. More like a welfare check. The home owner tripped the alarm by accident and we make sure everyone is okay. No big deal."

He took another sip. "Haz Matt and I are already on Ina Road. Pete and Numb Nuts roll in from La Canada. The dispatcher says the alarm company's monitoring and they hear someone inside the residence. Okay, now we're thinking this might be legit."

Patricia couldn't let him go. "Yeah, and Numb Nuts tells me to stay outside and watch the front door, like I'm a golden retriever or civilian ride along. Meanwhile Rafe and Haz Matt go inside and Numb Nuts follows them."

Grijalva took it from there. "We surprise the burglar, some kid, maybe twenty-two. He's in the living room going through the vestibule. He complies with our commands. Numb Nuts and Haz Matt grab him, cuff him and take him out to one of the cars."

The story-telling felt like coming home.

"So while Frick and Frack are arguing about who gets the collar—who even says that except TV cops, right?" Grijalva paused for a drink. "I'm inside. The house hasn't been cleared. There may be a victim or another suspect. I'm pie-ing the corners, making my way through the other rooms. My gun's drawn, wrists crossed, flashlight on."

Patricia sat up. "And I've had enough of the boys arguing. I see Rafe's flashlight going from room to room. And then I see a pin prick, like a penlight, in what I think is the master bedroom upstairs."

Grijalva tagged her. "So instead of staying outside, like her partner ordered, she runs inside."

Patricia rushed on. "I don't know how I ran up the stairs without making a sound. It was all Mexican tile, but I was a frickin' ninja. I couldn't say anything to Rafe for fear of alerting the second suspect."

Grijalva, talking faster: "I'm grumbling to myself about Numb Nuts and Haz Matt, while clearing rooms. I should have been paying more attention, but man, that first guy convinced us all that he was working alone."

Patricia continued with her eyes bright. "I cleared the master bedroom and all that's left is the bathroom when Rafe barges in. He's not anywhere near as ninja as I am."

They told a good story. A jolt hit my heart and I remembered Cali. Was she okay? I forced the voices into silence and told them what Rafe had said. She wasn't my business. Guilt dropped heavy in my gut. How could we be laughing when Zoey Clark was out there somewhere, her mother suffering in a dark haze?

Maggie sounded insistent, repeating words she said to me often. *"Life goes on. You must go with it."*

Patricia said, "The guy in the bathroom lunges out, gun up. And I'm yelling, 'Gun. Gun. Gun.' And he fires at Rafe."

They both paused and I got the feeling they'd told this story together before.

Grijalva continued. "Pete shoots him center mass, two hits and the asshole goes down." He winks at me. "Exactly like I trained her."

She added the last bit. "His bullet missed Rafe by a pubic hair."

They drained their glasses and split the rest of the pitcher.

"After I finished training I had the best partner." Was I really jumping in? "Kari. We hit it off. Had the same rhythm, you know?"

They nodded, eager to hear more.

"It was that thing where we could almost read each other's thoughts." Kari. Where was she now?

"One night, maybe three o'clock in the morning, we were cruising around Buffalo, and we get this domestic." I couldn't help grinning. "We go inside, get the husband and wife separated. He claims she's been cheating on him. She's denying it and accusing him of drinking too much and imagining things. Finally, Kari asks the guy how he knows she's been unfaithful."

I took a sip of iced tea, not even minding it wasn't beer. "And he says, 'Do it, do it.' Very insistent. The wife is refusing. Finally the guy pleads with her. 'Show 'em. Show 'em the rug burns on your knees.'"

Patricia laughed and patted the table. "Unbelievable. Oh my God, do you remember responding to the fire on Craycroft?"

Grijalva chuckled, probably what passed for cracking up for most people.

Patricia could hardly keep from laughing. "We get there and all these people in this second story apartment are screaming and trying to hand a baby out the window. Rafe dashes upstairs, 'cause he's gonna be a hero."

Again, they passed off and he said, "I force the door open and race inside. But there's no smoke. No flames. Just all these idiots screaming at the window."

Patricia laughed so hard she snorted.

Grijalva kept a straight face. "So I look around and see the toaster oven on the kitchen counter and there's a piece of toast inside with a little flame."

Patricia got a little control. "Funniest thing I ever saw. Rafe opens the door and blows the flame out."

Now we were on a roll I thought of another. "Kari had more street savvy than I did. Even though my mother was a cop, she was overprotective. I knew how to take care of myself, like self-defense and being aware of my surroundings, but down and dirty went past me. So another domestic, we arrive and the guy is sitting on his porch, his head bleeding. When we asked him what happened, he said, 'I was tryin' to get me some stank on my hang down and she hit me upside the head with a smoothie.'"

Grijalva's mouth ticked up.

Patricia grinned but she was working it out. "I get 'the stank on his hang down,' but you lost me with the rest."

I nodded. "Me, too. I looked at Kari and she was barely keeping it together. She motioned like this." I held my hand up and pantomimed ironing. "An iron. It smooths out wrinkles."

The stories went back and forth and then turned more personal.

They made an effort to include me while they caught up with each other. I knew some about Patricia from our shifts together. But I learned she'd miscarried her second child and spent several months in therapy before feeling good enough to have another. Grijalva shared how his divorce stretched on for years while they wrangled custody of his son and daughter and the rights to his pension.

When they took a breath, I butted in. "Rafe is an unusual name."

He sipped his beer. "Not really. It's short for Raphael. I didn't want to be known as a Teenage Mutant Ninja Turtle."

"Plus," Patricia said, "We've already established you're no ninja."

Rafe seemed genuinely interested. "Jamie. Is that a family name?"

My walls crumbled a little more. "No. Not that she'd ever say, but I think my mother wanted a boy. At least, she never tolerated any girly stuff from me. No pink dresses, no frilly bedspreads or fairy princess Halloween costumes."

Patricia waggled her perfect almond-shaped nails in a delicate peach color. "The last expense to go if we're broke is my weekly manicure."

Rafe rolled his eyes at her, then focused back on me. "What about your father? Didn't he want you to be his princess?"

The Chorus surged into a noisy wave. "I don't think Dad cared. My whole childhood was kind of me and Mom. He didn't pay much attention to me."

The beer made Patricia a little louder than usual. "That sucks. My husband doesn't do puke at night or those stupid school plays, but he's all over tea parties and homework help."

Rafe frowned at me. "I'm sorry."

I shrugged. "To tell the truth, I didn't miss it. Mom did a great job raising me so I've got no complaints."

Patricia slapped the table. "Recess is over. It's movie night at our house and if I don't get home to monitor the pizza order they'll get pineapple and chicken or some hideous thing. It's my job to teach my kids pepperoni is the only pizza worth eating."

We crossed the parking lot together. The sun must have kicked into double time because it hung much lower than I'd have thought. Or maybe, for the first time in a century, I'd had fun and lost track.

Patricia banged on the roof of her minivan two cars away. "Now we've popped your cherry, you can start calling me Pete like every other soul on Earth."

Nobody bothered me on my drive home. The peace prompted me to add a few extra minutes to take Gates Pass from downtown over the Tucson Mountains. I parked in a pullout near the top and watched the sun slip over the Baboquivari range.

Rafe said they were looking into Cali. That should end it. Except Frank kept growling at me and even the Chorus pitched and muttered. The voices didn't always speak truth. Rafe was right, though. It wasn't my case. I could barely handle my own life.

"You're too stupid to save some kid," Frank repeated.

Dusk sent long shadows and relief from the heat when I puttered down my street and pushed the button to open my garage. Two blonde heads bobbed in the driveway across from me. They scribbled with chalk on hands and knees.

I started for the door into the house and made a U-turn. What harm could it do to say hello to my neighbors?

Before I made it to the street, the gray sedan rolled past. Keeping that slow pace. A chill cascaded down my spine and the noises in my head rose. "I'm Jamie Butler." And I've had a good day, I continued to myself. You all be quiet and go away.

Each step across the street required conscious effort. The voices rumbled, but at a low level. No one shouted warning and Frank hadn't uttered a word since the get-together at the brewery.

Sherilyn scurried around the garage, pulling items from the dozens of boxes and stacking them on shelves. She didn't hear me walk up the driveway toward the girls. It would be so easy for anyone to harm her children.

Kaycee glanced up. She dropped her pink stick of chalk and bounded up, a happy grin revealing her perfect pearls of teeth.

Her movement caught Cheyenne's attention and she shouted. "Jamie!" As if I were some long lost relative. She beat Kaycee to me and before I could protect myself, she threw her arms around my hips.

Kaycee circled hers around my knees and I was trapped. "Those are beautiful drawings."

Cheyenne stepped back and surveyed their work. Kaycee held on a few more seconds, then, with eyes on Cheyenne, took the same critical pose.

Sherilyn brushed her hands together and hurried from the garage. "How's it going?"

"I stopped over to see what these budding da Vinci's were up to." It seemed almost effortless to start a conversation.

Sherilyn opened her mouth but Cheyenne hollered first. Overcome with excitement, it seemed she'd lost her inside voice. "We could decorate your driveway. We'll do a really great job. Kaycee makes perfect suns and I am the best at flowers."

"How can I say no to such an offer?" The two girls scooped up their chubby chunks of chalk.

Sherilyn wiped her hands on her cutoffs. "It doesn't rain here enough to wash that off. You're likely to have scribbles until the monsoon."

"It'll add to the charm."

The memory came at me without warning.

Grime is ground-in on the knees of her jeans and it's going to take some work to get it out. Her hands, elbows, and t-shirt are covered in a kaleidoscope of dusty chalk. A proud grin shows off braces. On the driveway, written in balloon letters from one side to the other, blue outlined with pink, it says, "Welcome Home!"

I can't wait to park and get her in a squeeze. I'd been gone for three days at a law enforcement conference.

Larry steps from the side of the garage, all smiles and waves. I'm confused because he's supposed to be at a software seminar and Mom was scheduled to babysit.

My stomach churns at the idea of him being home alone with her for three days and I'm only half aware of her squeals and hugs.

Larry is tickled with his surprise and says he'd decided to cancel out on the training so he could have some daddy/daughter time.

He hadn't told me and I immediately blow up. I don't know why it enrages me, so I can't explain it to him.

I apologized. But it wasn't enough to stop the pit growing between us.

Now they had their supplies, their little legs sent them flying toward my house. "Wait!" I caught them by their t-shirts and reined them in. "I'll walk with you across the street."

They allowed me to keep hold of them until one foot hit my driveway, then they pulled away.

Sherilyn shouted, "Mind if I keep at this while Jackson sleeps?"

I waved her off. "Go ahead."

I knew the girls were safe with me, but what assurances did Sherilyn have? She'd seen me all freaked out, talking to people only I could hear. She needed to pay more attention. Protect the precious gifts she seemed to take for granted.

I eased myself to the pavement and picked up a piece of chalk. My crude drawing of a dog delighted them, so I drew an equally bad cat. They looked the same to me, but the girls named them Ruff and Mewy. I complimented their artwork.

We checked on the baby birds. How they'd survived this long seemed a miracle, and I didn't believe in those. Some wily coyote was probably letting them get big enough so they'd make a meal instead of a snack.

By the time Jackson woke up and Sherilyn had to quit, I'd turned on the driveway lights. I walked the girls safely across the street, we said our good nights, I survived more hugs, then traipsed through my garage and into my house.

I had an urge to call Tara. She'd been pushing me to "make connections," as she called it. She'd be proud of me. But it was nearly eight o'clock; she had a right to her private time. Besides, this was the opposite of a crisis.

What a turn-around from this morning. A surge of confidence buoyed my steps. I'd get through Mother's Day and maybe even reclaim something of my life. Yes, I could do it.

The glow of my kitchen light shimmered on the pool, inviting me for a swim. On the patio, I stripped off my shorts and shirt and jumped in, loving the splash, cool relief, and freedom. I floated and swam until I felt all the tension wash away.

Wet footprints puddled on the Saltillo tile as I made my way to the bedroom for dry clothes.

I stopped, listened. The air conditioner kicked on. Whispers, far away chatter, like the soft tinkled of wind chimes. No Frank. No soft sobs from Peanut. Even Maggie seemed to be taking the night off.

Hunger punched my stomach. I munched while I chopped veggies and ham for my salad. Before I dug in, it occurred to me I'd left my clothes in a heap on the patio. I collected them and dumped them in the laundry room, retrieving my phone from the shorts pocket.

That's when I saw the missed call from Mom. I carried my food outside and sat poolside. My feet cooled in the water as I perched on the edge with my plate on my lap. A black and white roadrunner engaged in a stare-off with me, clearly wanting his evening drink, not appreciating my interference. I forked a crispy, cold bite into my mouth while waiting for the call to connect.

Without greeting, she rushed on. "Where were you?"

"I went for a short swim. I just saw you'd called. You said you weren't going to call so I didn't expect it." I swallowed and before she answered, I rushed on, like Cheyenne might. "I had a really good day. After my shift at the tournament I went out for drinks with another Ranger and a friend. Then when I got home, the two little girls from across the street came over and drew all over my driveway with chalk."

Mom didn't share my enthusiasm. "Honey, you're not supposed to be drinking with your medication. You didn't drive afterward, did you?"

"I had iced tea. But the point is, maybe I'm making friends."

"You sound almost manic. Stop a minute and think about this. What do you know about these people? The Ranger? Have you worked with him much? And what kind of friend is this?"

"This time the bitch is right. Someone talks nice to you and you're all Sally Field. 'They like me!' Moron."

A horrifying memory battered me, one I wished would stay hidden.

In the dark, outside the picture window in their dining room, the light from the chandelier over the table casts shadowy glow over the yard, making the grass look like a bed of nails. The trees struggle in the wind, black splashes with flashes of light from the window. The battle rages outside, and inside and I can't distinguish the coming storm from the war in my head.

"She's going to put you away. He's already hurt you. You must stop them." Frank hisses, then yells. Then he screams so loud I can't resist.

The wooden knife handle pulses with life in my hand. They keep eating, both reading, no conversation. The door is locked but I have a key.

Beethoven drowns out my stealthy entry. So quiet on the thick carpet, they don't see me. I want to stop. Run away. But Frank is urging me on, giving me no choice.

I raise my arm, knife aimed at the spot where his sweaty gray hair tapers to pale skin.

Mom's chair dumps over. Her body slams into me, knocking me to the floor, making Frank finally shut up.

She easily wrests the knife from my weak grasp.

Sorry. So sorry. Pills. Sleep. Hospital.

I unclenched my fist and flattened my palms on the pool deck. "The Ranger is a woman. She's got a couple of kids."

Mom probably nodded with that knowing expression. "That makes sense. Mother's Day makes you want to connect with children. Like the kids across the street. That's understandable. But, for your own sake, you need to take it slowly. Find out about people before you rush in."

I stabbed some ham and cheese and lifted it, set it back

down. The image of Cali's shy expression, her beautiful blonde hair. Was she really okay? Did the creep who took her make her answer her phone? "How do I get to know people if I don't spend time with them?"

A long sigh. "Just be careful. I don't have to tell you; your closet is pretty deep. And what if people start wondering why you retired so young? What happens if they check out your past?"

The Chorus woke up, with the volume of a busy restaurant at dinnertime.

Frank: *"Did you forget who you are? If Pete or Rafe knew about you, they'd set speed records for running away. And Sherilyn—obviously she's a twit."*

Mom softened. "Don't listen to me. I've had a lousy day."

Glad to change the subject, I asked, "Election?"

A glass clinked on the counter. Wine, no doubt. Deep red. "No. This damned investigation. She's all over me."

"Sorry you have to deal with that."

"She's digging into your case. So keep a low profile. "

Guilt washed down the back of my throat like thick sludge. "I'm not exactly making waves down here." Except with Mrs. Thompson and Megan.

"What are you going to do about Cali Shaw? What about Zoey Clark?"

"I know. I'm out of sorts today. Don't mean to take it out on you."

I spoke my truest emotion. "I'm sorry."

"Okay." Brisk again. "Enough about me. How's the mosaic coming along?"

This was safer ground. "Great. Going to look nice on your deck."

"Oh, honey, you should keep it. That kind of thing isn't really appropriate for snow and cold."

"How is the election planning going?"

She charged like a dog let off a leash. "I've hired Toby Benson, one of the best strategists around. I hate to sound cold-hearted, but your father's pension is making this campaign much easier to afford." She rushed on. "Not that I wouldn't rather have him with me."

The Chorus rose in a confusion of anger. Maggie's voice felt soft and satiny. *"Your father is gone."*

I hoped my answer sounded normal. "Dad would be glad he's helping out."

"I suppose. Toby has some great ideas, and with the increase in convictions over the last two years, we've got the law and order vote on our side. These days, that's the trend, so I'm feeling confident."

With little input from me, Mom let her enthusiasm for Toby and the campaign carry the conversation. The roadrunner and I continued to stand off, and the Chorus carried on their chatter without me.

She sucked in a breath. "Damn. Look at the time. I've got to get to bed. We're shooting a commercial tomorrow and makeup only goes so far."

I hung up, the buoyant feeling of earlier now a burning memory. Today's emotional rodeo showed the status of my health. Not as good as I'd thought.

The bite of salad I shoved into my mouth tasted old and wilted. It stuck in my throat as my attention focused on a clump of something near the filter outlet. I swallowed and nearly choked on dread. My knees stung as I crawled across the pavement to lean over the edge and pull the sprig from the pool. Drops of water, like blood, dripped onto the concrete from the drooping blossoms of the lilac.

Impossible. The voices rose, keeping time with my racing heart. Putting depth and power into my words, I said, "I'm

Jamie Butler. I'm Amanda's daughter. I'm a retired Buffalo cop."

Barely able to keep from running, I dumped the flower in my kitchen garbage. With shaking hands I poured ice water, sliced lemon and squeezed it in. Obviously, someone had a lilac bush in their backyard. I'd smelled it and now the flower in my pool. Nothing to be panicked about. A spring flower. No problem.

The salad sat on the breakfast bar. I needed to eat. I'd promised Tara and Mom that I'd take care of the basics.

My phone rang.

Caller I.D. said Mitch Harris, my AZ Ranger commander. Maybe someone couldn't make it to the horse races tomorrow and he wanted me to take an extra shift. The distraction would be good.

But that wasn't the case.

After a quick greeting he said, "You agreed to back off from the Thompson girl. But I got a call from Jim and he's fit to be tied."

The weight of dread pushed me to lean on the granite counter. I'd gone out, had some laughs. Spent time playing with those little girls. I should have been following up on Cali. "Maybe you can get the Pima County Sheriff to look into this girl, Cali Shaw. I think she might have been kidnapped or gone off with this predator at the ball park."

"Yeah. You said that. And they assigned an officer. He checked it out. It's fine. But you're still causing problems."

"I know, but—"

He interrupted. "I hate to do this. But I'm going to suspend you."

"Wait—"

"Not permanently and not officially. But until you've had a chance to calm down."

The Rangers was all I had. Without that purpose, the chance to do some good, I'd lose my tether. "Please don't do this."

He left no room for negotiation. "I've done it. Sorry, Jamie." He hung up.

"Someone's finally seeing the real you, huh, moron." Frank sounded gleeful.

I picked up my salad and dumped it in the trash, plate, fork, and all.

22

He ran the tattered bandana through his fingers, then held it to his nose. It smelled like her. He knew because he'd been in her house, her bedroom. He'd touched her things. The red hoodie that no longer smelled like its original owner, but instead now smelled like Jamie.

She was coming apart. He saw in the way she questioned herself. She had to wonder if she was the last one to see the little girl, the confusion at the possibility she'd been at the ball park the night the girl disappeared, the shock when she found the bit of bandana at the doorway. He congratulated himself on that detail.

He hadn't expected her to weather Mother's Day. She was stronger than he thought. But that only made her ultimate downfall sweeter.

The girls were weak but they were holding on. He needed to make sure he didn't take them too close to the edge. As long as one of them survived to the end, it would be okay.

Not long now. He was pulling the rope tighter, drawing her closer. Soon, he'd make her pay.

23

The sun stayed tucked behind the Tucson Mountains and wouldn't strike me for another hour. It couldn't be more than seventy-five degrees just after 6 a.m. Surprisingly, I'd slept some last night. Frank and the Chorus raged for an hour or so after Mom's and Mitch's calls. Eventually, Maggie soothed them all.

With Tara, and a few others before her, I'd worked on addressing most of the voices that visited me. Obviously, Frank demanded his share of attention. I made sure he never felt too neglected because it was Frank who got me in the worst trouble. He'd been the one to demand I jump from her bedroom window on the second floor. He was also responsible for me showing up at my parents' door wielding a butcher knife.

Maggie had been with me as long as I could remember. Tara called her the Mother and suggested she got her name from the loving television mother on a sitcom popular when I was a child. She wondered if I needed Maggie to comfort me because Mom could be cold.

I understood Mom's love for me came packaged differently than most mothers. But Tara had lots of ideas about the voices. I didn't agree with all of her theories.

Aside from Frank and Maggie, there were others. A group I called the Three liked to ambush me. I couldn't discern how many spoke, but they always spouted three statements of doom and destruction. Tara and I concocted an antidote for them. I chose three declarations as a balance. "I'm Jamie Butler. I'm Amanda's daughter. I'm a retired Buffalo cop."

If those didn't soothe me, I'd add other statements about myself. I had so few that I'd recycle them, repeating my rosary.

Then there was Peanut. So sad. So alone. Even Tara agreed I wasn't ready to talk to her, yet. I wasn't sure I ever would be.

Mom thought I'd conquered the voices. She didn't know it was more like taming them. Tara thought I'd always hear them. I knew I would. They were part of me and I'd miss them if they left completely.

This morning they were all active. It sounded like a convention in a grand ballroom. I needed activity and my mesquite tree out front needed trimming. Before I picked up my saw, I checked in with Frank. Aside from his usual obscene commentary, he didn't seem inclined to violence.

Tara and I had discussed how to deal with this day. I'd planned to take the assignment at the horse races and had barricaded myself against letting Frank or anyone else take over. Since Mitch had scrapped that plan, I was at odds. Maybe I ought to get a Petunia of my own. When I thought about Shax, it led to Cali, and I had to stop thinking about her.

I set the ladder under my tree, but the Dempsey's mesquite branches hung so low over their front walk I repositioned myself under their tree instead. Mrs. Dempsey had complained to me about hiring someone to take care of trimming. Mr. Dempsey might putter around a golf course a couple of times a week, but climbing a ladder with his forty-pound belly begged disaster. Mrs. Dempsey couldn't lift the saw for more than thirty seconds.

I lopped away, letting the conversations swirl. It reminded me of spinning the knob on an old radio with the sounds moving and melding, nothing sticking with any meaning.

A slammed door and slap of feet interrupted the static. Within seconds Cheyenne's voice rounded the corner from the oleander. "Good morning Frank. Hi, Maggie."

I started down the ladder, thankful that I looked before I stepped. Kaycee's pink hand rested on the second lowest rung and she stared up at me with her clear, blue eyes.

"You're out early, little miss." I tried to sound cheerful but I took in her bare feet, her baby doll pajamas, her sleep ruffled hair. No mother.

I maneuvered around her hand, dropped the saw and gently reached for her, wondering if she'd let me pick her up. She raised her arms when I bent.

Oh, the feel of her little body, soft and squishy, smelling of sleep, sun screen, and baby sweat. It burned through me to hold her like that, the sweetness more than I could bear.

Still no Sherilyn. I had no choice but to keep hold of Kaycee and make my way to Cheyenne, who squatted outside the birds' enclosure. "What are you doing up so early?"

I'd forgotten about the birds and was surprised to see them in the shade of the oleander, huddled close and backed under the branches. Their parents were obviously keeping them fed, whether I watched over them or not. They didn't move and their shiny black eyes watched us.

She squinted up at me. "We had to say good morning to Frank and Maggie. Mom said it's okay."

I glanced at the house across the street and noticed the gray sedan parked down the way. With as often as it appeared, obviously it belonged to someone who lived on our street. I needed to isolate the voice that kept pointing it out to me and assure whoever it was that the car wasn't a threat. "She knows you're here?"

Cheyenne turned back to the birds and poked her finger through the wire. "She said as long as you're out here we can visit the birds." Cheyenne sang in a high-pitched voice. "ABCDEFG, HIJK, elomento pee."

Kaycee squiggled to get down and I set her next to Cheyenne, where she imitated her sister's squat and stuck her tiny finger through the wire.

The front door across the street opened and Sherilyn appeared in a long t-shirt with Jackson on her hip. "I hope you don't mind the girls coming over. They wanted to see the birdies and Jackson had a dirty diaper."

"Find your own damned daycare," Frank fumed.

I made myself wave and smile. "They're fine." She'd let them run outside without shoes. Across a street by themselves.

"I'll just be a minute." Sherilyn slipped inside and shut the door.

I stood with the two girls. Cheyenne stopped singing. "Kaycee says you like little girls but I think maybe you're like the witch in Hansel and Gretel and you only pretend to like us and then you'll eat us when we let our guard down."

Maybe they were both right. "I don't eat much red meat."

Cheyenne stood up and folded her arms across her chest. "Mom, she told Daddy that you are sad."

"I am sad sometimes."

Cheyenne tilted her head. "Because of your little girl?"

My heart stopped. The Chorus crescendoed. "What... what little girl?"

Cheyenne toed Kaycee. "The one that talks to her."

The door across the street opened again and Sherilyn popped out in shorts and tank top. "Breakfast!"

Kaycee jumped up and pumped her fat little legs straight for the street. I lunged for her arm and caught her as her bare foot slapped the sidewalk. Cheyenne placed her hand in my free one and tugged at me to cross the street.

"Like Daddy says, safety first."

Sherilyn collected the girls and thanked me.

I went back to my ladder and finished trimming the Dempsey's tree. The sweet smell of mesquite and Texas sage rose on warm wings. If I concentrated on the moment, the sunshine, the pebbles that made up my front yard, the warming day, the spring smells, then I wouldn't have to think about Mitch's call. I could let myself believe Rafe's assessment that Cali Shaw was safe. If I focused on the beauty of the desert I could convince myself today was simply another date on the calendar.

Next door Mr. and Mrs. Dempsey wandered onto their front porch. Mr. Dempsey, thick white hair that looked silky enough to stroke, waved. "Well, would you look at this, Mother."

Mrs. Dempsey, heavy purse draped over her forearm and tucked into her belly, crunched along the gravel of their yard into mine. Her polyester pants singing with each step. "Bless your heart! What a Mother's Day gift. Those ol' branches were getting to be such a bother."

Mr. Dempsey hollered from his walk at the volume of someone hard of hearing. "You sure saved me a lot of work, young lady."

Embarrassed by the effusive thanks, I mumbled, "No problem. I was trimming my tree so my tools were already out."

Mrs. Dempsey patted my arm. "That's just the sweetest thing. Ted is taking me for brunch. It's a Mother's Day tradition. Would you like to join us?"

Mr. Dempsey pointed his garage opener. "Don't know why I'm taking her out today. She's not my mother. But you're not my mother either, so you're welcome to come."

"Thank you for asking but I've got a lot to do around here."

Mrs. Dempsey cackled in a carefree way I envied, and yelled at Mr. Dempsey. "I'm the mother of your children. That deserves a nice brunch once a year." To me, she said, "Honestly, that doesn't begin to pay for the price of motherhood."

I knew the price of motherhood. Before she could ask about my plans, I started in. "Did your son and daughter call this morning?"

Again, that laugh, so free of burden. "Heavens it's two hours later in Omaha and neither of them have called yet. Ted and I, we never slept that late. Too much to do and church on Sunday."

Mr. Dempsey backed their Lincoln into the driveway and tapped the horn. "Oops. Gotta go. Ted gets peckish if he doesn't get his Grand Slam." She turned and picked her way across the yard in her sandals. "Sometimes I think Mother's Day brunch is all about him."

After trimming the trees and dragging the branches to haul off later, I still had a long day ahead. My pool gave cooling relief and the mosaic table filled the rest of the morning. I fixed a lunch I had to force myself to eat.

The temperature hovered in the eighties, a perfect day to run and maybe wear myself out. In my running shorts and shoes, I ventured out from my garage, ducking under the door before it closed. The baby birds hunkered close in the cover of the oleander, the sun creeping across their pen.

Standing in the shade of my house, I fiddled with the settings on my athletic tracker. A long run seemed the best option for managing my stress, unless I wanted to obliterate myself with meds.

The memory of the maracas rattle sent a chill cascading down my spine. The rattlesnake in the wash called to me and I decided on a different route for today. Frank didn't need an opportunity to tempt me.

An old Charger eased down the street. Tangerine orange, with a white stripe along the side. Someone had taken care of this old guy. A truly classic car in mint condition.

It pulled over in front of my driveway and all my alarms sounded. The window rolled down and from the driver's side, a friendly voice called out. "Hi. Jamie. I was hoping you'd be home."

The steel melted in my body. With legs that didn't want to run the other way, I walked to the car. "Officer Grijalva. What are you doing here?"

He shut the mighty engine down and stepped out of his car. "I don't get many Sundays off and I wanted to take Geraldine here for a spin. I was heading out toward Three Points and when I got close to your turn off, just pulled in on a whim."

Frank growled.

A normal person would say something. Make a friendly comment, smile. "Nice car."

His wide grin held no darkness, no secrets. "How 'bout it? You up for a ride?"

At least I had an excuse. I looked down at my clothes. "Just going for a run."

He raised his eyebrows in a "so what" way. "I'll buy you a shake at this great spot up the road."

Drinks yesterday. A ride and shakes today. Did I need this much contact? Did I want it? "A shake isn't compensation for a missed run."

He grinned. "Fair enough. What would happen if you took the day off? It's Sunday. Come for a ride with me."

Frank said, *"You know what happens when you make friends. They leave you. Like Larry. Like Sue. Like Kari."*

Tara harped about making friends. Mom advised caution. Wasn't it time I decided something this simple for myself?

The sun warmed the back of my head and I looked at the side of the house, the route I planned to run. "Maybe some other time."

Rafe's face, so still and neutral, seemed to convey disappointment. "Seriously? You'd take a run over my dazzling company?"

Even for me I had a mix of emotions. Tara's line of reasoning echoed. What could be so risky about riding in a car with this guy?

"He could find out more about you, and he'd be gone in a puff of dust."

"You wouldn't be any worse off than you are now."

Or, he might stick around long enough for me to get attached, then he'd rip out my guts when he left. Better to stick to my run.

He waited for me to change my mind but I had nothing to say. He gazed down the street, then into my eyes. "Okay...truth. It's my Sunday with my kids, but I let them go with their mother because it's Mother's Day. So I'm lonely and feeling abandoned. Thought if you went for a ride with me, it'd take my mind off it."

Frank burst through my paralysis. *"Bullshit!"*

Here's what a few years of therapy taught me about Frank. For all his vitriol and foul language—the demands of violence I should visit on others—his main concern was my safety. If we were alone, I'd let him know I appreciated his concerns but that Rafe could be trusted. We didn't need to fear every person.

I wasn't alone, though. Being firm with Frank worked best if I actually spoke to him. When I didn't have that luxury, I did my best to convey the message internally. Since I mostly kept to myself, when this need arose, I would pull out my phone and talk, like half the American population speaking into their devices.

"I shouldn't have just come over. Bad habit of mine."

He'd put himself out by coming here and I handed him defeat and rejection. A ride. That's all. Soon enough he'd figure out any one of the million reasons for not wanting to spend more time with me and never show up again. Rejection wasn't something new to me. Obviously, it stung him. "Okay. A shake sounds good."

A subtle change in his face but his eyes sparked with pleasure. "You won't be sorry."

The black leather interior warmed the backs of my legs, but not scorching, as it would in another month. The snap of the belt buckle vibrated through me, like the clang of a jail cell. No turning back. My brain raced, trying out and abandoning conversation starters.

"This is a great car. What year?"

Rafe backed into my driveway and then headed out of the neighborhood. "It's an '87. I had one like it back in the day. This baby is my project for Sundays when I don't get my kids."

Maybe he wanted me to ask about his children. He'd mentioned them twice. "This is a Shelby, right?"

He glanced at me, clearly surprised. "You know about Shelby Chargers?"

How could I forget the freedom of opening it up on a straight road, the thrill of control around tight corners in the mountains. "It was the only sunroof I ever owned. Not practical in upstate New York most of the year."

"You had one, too? Oh man, I loved that baby more than anything." He turned onto Ajo Highway, heading west. "Well, obviously not more than my ex. Since I sold the car to pay for her wedding ring."

"I sold mine because...." I started to speak but he accelerated and the rush of air in the windows drowned me out. Thank God, since the next words, "the car seat wouldn't fit in back," would have launched into questions I avoided like hidden mines.

He shouted above the wind. "Should have kept the car. She was way more reliable and faithful than my wife."

He saved me from conversation by reaching for the tape player. "Hope you like heavy metal."

He pushed a cassette into what was probably a state-of-the-art stereo system in 1987. Def Leppard's *Pour Some Sugar on Me* screamed louder than the wind, and thirty years pitched off my shoulders.

The song took me back to a year into my tour of duty, based in Ft. Huachuca, sixty miles east of Tucson. It was my first brush with Arizona and my early crush on the desert.

We were drinking beer and I was waxing my Shelby Charger under the shade of the mesquite. One more good time laughing with the other enlisted men and women. The radio cranked up. No worries except that I didn't drink so much I'd be hungover when I drove the commander around the next day. Loving life untethered with personal expectations. Mom thousands of miles away. No boyfriend. Just me being me. Before I met Larry, got married, added responsibilities on top of responsibilities, and wore myself down with the burden of love. Before it was all taken away. Before I lost myself.

Rafe drove fast, well over the speed limit. Some law enforcement officer. Every now and then he'd glance my way and that teen-boy elation lit his still face. After twenty minutes he slowed and a smattering of dusty, sun-faded buildings littered either side of the road. A flag fluttered above a tiny brick Post Office but nobody moved in the afternoon heat. Rafe slapped his turn signal on and took a right into the ghost town. Behind a stand of scrub brush and creosote, a building little more than a singlewide trailer squatted in a gravel parking lot amid several cars and dirty pickups. It declared itself The Sugar Shack in all its faded and tacky glory.

The Charger's rumbling power broke abruptly and Def Leppard cut off in mid-scream. It seemed way too quiet.

Rafe extended his arm, palm up, toward the Sugar Shack. "As promised. The world's best milk shake."

The nostalgia trip continued. A baby in a carrier sat on top of the splintered wood picnic table out front. The mother, a tattooed woman in cut offs, flip flops, and T-shirt with sleeves torn out, fed ice cream to the baby dressed only in a diaper. The father sipped from a straw inserted into a paper cup big enough to serve as a swimming pool. He stood over a dark-haired girl of about six who wore a tattered princess dress and fairy wings. An ice cream cone melted down her hand and arm, quickly gathering sticky mud.

An older couple perched on the end of the same table. A thin woman with hair like dandelion fluff smiled with such delight at the baby and little girl. She and the young parents carried on a friendly conversation while her husband ate his sundae with a vague expression, maybe not hearing it all clearly.

A teenaged Latina leaned on her elbows inside the wooden-framed window. Rafe pulled up a fist pistol and cocked his thumb, pointing at her. "A chocolate shake for me, and...?" He tilted his head at me.

With the voices of the people at the table and others crowding my head, I didn't spare the brain power to make a decision on flavors. "The same."

The girl shot back at Rafe. "You got it." She spun around and shouted the order, then turned back to Rafe. "About time you got that hunk of junk out of the garage."

Rafe admired his car. "Geraldine is feeling her oats." Rafe

pointed to me then to the girl. "Jamie, this is my bratty niece, Heidi. Bratty niece, this is my friend, Jamie."

A dark beauty, Heidi resembled Rafe, except for her toothy grin. Easy and freely given. "I don't know why you'd want to spend your time with this old straight-faced man."

Rafe spoke while I tried to dig down to find some bantering. How long had it been since I'd shared teasing. "She felt sorry for me."

That wasn't so far from the truth. "He asked me for a ride and a shake. I couldn't say no."

Heidi laughed. "He's such a loser." She reached behind her and shoved the shakes our way, taking Rafe's money. "Aunt Sophie was here with Myah and Rico earlier. She was wearing these giant sparkly earrings. Did you let the kids pick those out for her?"

He raised his eyebrows and mischief poured from his eyes. "Looked good, huh? I told the kids she'd love them."

"They are the ugliest things and I'm pretty sure she hates them." She raised her hand and high-fived him.

I was saved from much conversation when we carried our shakes to the table and Rafe settled himself between the two couples. I climbed in opposite him and stayed quiet while he teased and asked the others questions. The chocolate ice cream melted on my tongue, unleashing more memories both welcome and painful.

She is six and I let her order a shake too big for her tummy. I'd been craving strawberry, but delight to let her order the chocolate she so wants. I finish it, of course, waiting while she lets most of it melt. The creamy cool of that summer evening, watching her run after fireflies on the grass, while I suck the last drops, growling in the straw.

She chats about the shake and bugs while I bathe her before bed, wash tiny feet, green with fresh cut grass, soothe the mosquito bites with dots of anti-itch cream. I tuck her in, smelling of baby shampoo

and read her the book with the lush illustrations of pink and purple
fairies. I stay with her long after she falls asleep, listening to her
breath get deeper as she flies off with gossamer wings into her own
fairy dreams.

I pushed the shake away, only half finished. Rafe noticed, but he didn't say anything. He kept up a friendly give and take with the no-longer strangers at the table.

Rafe pointed at me. "Jamie is new to Tucson. What do you think she needs to do or see?"

The young mother said, "When people come see me, they always want to see Biosphere II. I think that's boring."

Her partner puffed air. "It's cool. I like the Air Museum and the Boneyard."

I sucked in a breath at the name.

The younger woman waved him off. "That's even worse. It's just miles and miles of old military planes."

The older woman piped up. "I've always enjoyed the Sonoran Desert Museum."

The discussion took off without me and I only needed to smile and nod.

Frank had his usual awful comments about everyone. A few voices thought I ought to empty my shake on Rafe's head. But that was all the usual chatter and nothing I couldn't contain.

Rafe finished and said good bye to his niece and his new friends at the picnic table. He didn't say much as he fired up the Charger, exchanged Def Leppard for AC/DC, and we raced back to my house. He pulled into the driveway and shut down the rolling circus.

We both climbed out and he met me in front of the car. "Better than a run, huh?"

I couldn't be sure I smiled. I'd hit my social limit.

"How about a real date? Friday? I'll take you downtown." He looked hopeful.

I rubbed my forehead to bring down the noise. "Thank you. I had fun today. But." A nice person, a normal person, would be tactful. "No. I don't think it's a good idea."

Maybe I surprised him by refusing. "Not a good idea? Because I'm Mexican?"

Now it was my turn to be surprised. "No. Of course not."

"Then why?" I realized his tactic. He was doing that thing salesmen do. Trying to get me to give him a reason for rejection, then shoot it down so I'd be forced to say yes.

"I'm not dating. It's me."

His lips barely turned up but he looked amused. "That's the worst excuse I've ever heard."

I shrugged my resignation.

He grew serious. "Here's the truth. I liked you right away when I met you the other day. I got the vibe you thought I was okay, too. I asked Pete about you and she said you're a great partner, smart and easy to get along with. She doesn't know much more."

"I'm a private person."

"Yeah. I get that. Sometimes, you work the job and you see stuff and people don't understand. Can't relate. You can't tell them and you hold it inside. So I think maybe something bad happened and now you're down here trying to forget it."

He stepped to the pit inside me. I didn't want him to fall in. I took a few steps back toward my house. "I've got to go. Thanks for the shake."

He leaped to block my way. "It's not just you."

I hesitated.

"Ever since my divorce, I don't get out. My friends are all her friends. Our families have been tight for two generations. I need to make some new friends. Thought maybe we could do it together."

He'd ventured too close for me and I didn't know how to

respond. So I turned it away from myself. "Have you found Cali Shaw?"

He seemed startled at the abrupt shift. "Is that why you agreed to go with me today? To get information about her?"

I shook my head. "You haven't tried to find her, have you?"

Disappointment dropped his shoulders. "I thought we had fun today."

We did have fun. And I'd blown it. As usual. "I have a terrible feeling about her. What are you doing about her?"

An icy edge crept into his voice. "Look, time is critical for Zoey Clark and the department has funneled resources to her. Cali has the reputation for taking off. We can't justify pulling someone from Zoey's case."

"But..."

He shook his head. "I'm sorry. That's just the way it is."

I closed my eyes and waited for the fire inside me to die down. "Thanks again for the shake."

I kept them closed until the Charger fired up and drove away. Frank kept screaming the whole time.

When I opened my eyes and reached to punch in my code on the door lock, I joined him.

24

It couldn't be here. Pain ripped across my chest, my muscles contracted and my head exploded with agonized cries.

How long did I stand there? I hoped I hadn't screamed but with the roaring in my ears I couldn't be sure. I tried to swallow and heard the clicking of dry throat.

Sherilyn's chirpy voice traveled across the street, though the chaos. "Hi, there."

My hand shook when I raised it in a weak wave. The noise swirling in my head threatened to overwhelm me. I clamped down on my teeth and stared at my front door latch, hoping I was hallucinating.

But the black and yellow hair bow stuffed in the handle was real. The other bow, abandoned in the mud under the lilac bush had been red, and this one yellow. But it was so much the same. It was happening again.

The rough feel of polyester on my fingers proved it was no illusion. My hands shook as I pulled the bow closer. Two long, blonde hairs stuck in the clip on the underside of the bow.

It felt like a rattler in my hand. My brain buzzed with opinions. How had the bow ended up on my door?

"Your fault. The girl is dead. Because of you." Frank's accusations hit me clear as a lion's roar.

My mind raced with other explanations. Did a voice speak or was it me saying, *"The girls are playing a trick on you. Probably watching you and laughing at your reaction."*

Sherilyn sauntered up my walk. "Howdy."

I couldn't answer.

She held out a green glass bottle, condensation dripping. She grasped one of her own. "Thought we could have a beer and maybe get to know each other a little."

The last thing I needed was to disintegrate in front of a witness. "I don't drink." I blurted it out more bluntly than intended.

She reacted as if I'd slapped her. "Oh. I'm sorry. I'll—"

I worked up what I hoped passed for a neighborly face. "Anymore."

While Frank wanted me to shove Sherilyn, someone else rooted for me. *"Hold it together."*

With a little more control I said, "I mean, I take medication and it doesn't mix with alcohol. I'm not an alcoholic or anything."

Frank snickered. *"'Cause being an alkie is worse than being crazy."*

A cute twinkle lit her eyes. "I've got apple juice, if you'd rather. It's mostly the conversation I'm after."

I clenched and unclenched my fingers to stop the tingling. The bow's clasp bit into my palm. "Where are the kids?"

"Donnie got home in the middle of the night. They're all cuddled up on the couch watching *Minions* for the billionth time. It may not be quality time, but they all love it and they're together."

"Donnie's alone with the girls?" Through all the noise in my brain, this news upped the volume.

She tipped a beer to her lips and drank deeply. "Phshaw. He's their daddy. He can get their drink of water and change a diaper. I deserve a little break from someone being hungry or dirty or laundry needing folding or dishes washed. After all, it is Mother's Day." She laughed in an easy way I might have done once. Please, don't let anything happen to make her lose that joy.

"So, if you don't want juice and you can't have the beer, which I'll be happy to take care of for you, do you have anything you want to bring to the party so we can visit?"

The three took her up on the invitation.

Stay away from her.

What does she want?

Grab the bottle and slam her on the head.

Time with Rafe had tapped me out, and now the bow. Normal people accepted simple invitations. "I'll get some ice water."

Frank wasn't happy.

Sherilyn followed me up the walk and acted as though she'd keep going inside my house. I blocked her. "I'll get it. You can wait here."

Frank laughed. *"She's figuring out you're a weirdo."*

I tried to make light of it. "Thought you'd like to keep an eye on your house. With your kids there."

Frank's voice held threat. *"Because you know what daddies do, don't you, cupcake?"*

I shut my mind to the scenes, the arrests, the terrible things people did to the weak and helpless.

The bow. What to do about the bow? I used Sherilyn as a buffer so I could let the issue steep without having to think about it. I stepped inside and set the bow on the dining room table and tried not to look at it while I poured my lemon water.

I joined Sherilyn on the bench out front.

As one therapist told me early on, it was good to establish habits. For me, the ice water with a thick lemon slice acted as a reminder to stay cool and calm. A person could create triggers to channel positive emotions, not only be victim to triggers for negative reactions.

An empty bottle sat at Sherilyn's feet, the other nestled in her grip. She grinned, looking like a mischievous elf. "Okay, Jamie Butler. Tell me all about you."

I swallowed a gulp. "Not much to tell. Why don't you start. You came from Oklahoma?"

Her relaxed smile looked a little loose. One guzzled beer on her tiny frame probably buzzed through quickly. "Me and Donnie went to the same high school. He dated my best friend. But she cheated on him and ran off and got married, had a couple of kids, and got divorced again. She doesn't come from good stock. We got together to heal his broken heart. He hired out on Union Pacific, I shelled out kids, and here we are, in Tucson, Arizona. And frankly, glad to be away from that small town."

She stopped, took a pull on her beer and tipped it my way. "You. Go."

"Retired cop from Buffalo, New York."

She let out a high-pitched giggle. "That's it? Come on. Husbands? Kids? Lesbian lovers?"

Frank urged me. *"Tell her all about it. Watch her run, throw her junk back in the boxes, and move away."*

"Nope," I said. "Just me."

She tucked away her boozy grin. "And the voices."

The volume rose, the wave of confusion making me freeze and struggle to hold it in.

After a few seconds, I drank deeply and forced myself to look Sherilyn in the eye. "Yes. The voices."

Her matter-of-fact attitude was not something I'd seen

before. "I figured. I know that look you get. And that day, you were talking away and I didn't see anybody."

What could I say?

She patted the fist in my lap. "It's okay. My old Grandma Curran heard voices. She talked to them all the time. Weirdest thing ever. But that's just the way it was. She said it wasn't a handicap. It was a bonus. You know, she had names for 'em. One, she said, kept track of her schedule. She had twelve kids, so that was a big deal. And one of them knew all the recipes by heart and would tell Grandma so she never had to look 'em up."

Maybe like the voice I called Digit, the one who remembered numbers. The crowd inside my head jostled and murmured. All I could do was clutch my water glass and stare at Sherilyn.

"People made fun of her, especially when she was growing up, so she learned to keep her mouth shut when people other than family were around. In that small town it kind of scared folks. But we all grew up with it and it was natural to us." Sherilyn paused to drink her beer. "You look scared to death. I'm telling you, it's okay with us. In fact, I think Kaycee hears voices, too."

That little girl deserved to be happy, not tortured being so very different from everyone else. At least she had a mother who understood.

"Grandma said sometimes the voices told her things that hadn't happened, yet. And then it came true. If Kaycee hears them, too, then I'm wondering if she didn't know something about you right away. And that's why she's so taken with you."

The words struggled from me. "I don't know about that."

"That, and I saw you in your cop uniform the day we looked at the house and I figured you're a good neighbor to have."

Uniform or not, I doubted I'd do much good for her family.

She downed her beer and I did my best to keep up with her

conversation. She seemed to accept I had little to contribute and carried most of it.

Doing my best to stay focused on her kept thoughts of the hair ribbon at bay, but after she returned to her family, I was left alone with the bow.

Just me and the crowd inside. I couldn't call Rafe. After I'd brushed him off earlier, he wouldn't want anything to do with me. Pete had two kids, and Mother's Day meant she'd be busy.

I circled my table, staring at the ribbon. Black and yellow, a polyester jumble. Did it belong to Cali? I finally punched Pete's number on my phone and waited for her to answer.

She sounded curious when she picked up. While we greeted each other, her kids kept a racket going in the background. With a voice steadier than I felt, I told her about the bow stuffed into my door handle.

She listened. "What do you think it means?"

I rubbed my throbbing temple. "I'm afraid that creep has Cali and he's taunting us."

She sighed. "That's a big jump. My guess is that the girls are pissed you got them in trouble and they're toying with you."

The long blonde hairs clung to the clasp. "What if you're wrong?"

The kids' noise became a screaming fight. "I gotta go. Trust me. This is nothing and those little caviar-crunchers are baiting you. If you respond, you're going to get kicked out of the Rangers and maybe be up on charges for harassing minors."

I lapped the table a few more times. Pete was right. There was no other reasonable explanation. Only my paranoid imagination. I'd taken a small incident, three girls flirting harmlessly with some guy, and turned it into a personal crisis.

I wandered into the kitchen and opened the refrigerator. A scant serving of romaine, a quarter tomato, and a smattering of other veggies made my entire food inventory. Tomorrow I needed to grocery shop. Tara, groceries. A normal day.

The yellow and black drew me in.

My phone only contained a handful of numbers in its contacts. The old phone, like my old life, had vanished. Somewhere I'd stashed an address book. I'd been teased about it, but countered that in the Apocalypse, at least I'd be able to send letters and make phone calls.

It took an hour to rifle through boxes until I held the red leather notebook. Flipping through pages, the names and faces fell from my memory, each dragging regret of how I'd lost them all. People I used to know. Friends I thought cared. All gone now. I couldn't blame them.

I found her number and took a chance it would still reach her. I was met with the standard voicemail greeting, but the number still worked. With a hesitant voice, I identified myself and asked her to call me back.

I waited. It took some time to pour my ice water and lemon, then I entered the darkness outside my French doors. A flick of a switch illuminated my pool, the reflection of ripples dancing along the cinderblock fence.

She wouldn't call me. Why should she? We hadn't talked in years. Even before it happened. My bare feet slapped the patio and I stopped to stare at my half-finished mosaic table. A therapy project I was too agitated to work on.

I jumped when my phone rang. A deep inhale. "Be quiet," I told them. "Let me have this moment."

They settled a little and I pressed the button on my phone. "Kari. Thank you for calling me back."

Her voice, so familiar, brought a painful lump to my throat. But her tone didn't welcome me. "It's been a long time. What do you want?"

Despite her harsh answer, I ached to reach out to her. "How are you?"

"Do you care?"

"I know it's been a long time, but of course I care. You're my friend. You always will be."

Her laugh picked an old scab. "Is that right? Friends don't get their mother to transfer them if they get a little more recognition. Friends don't abandon you when it's out of sight out of mind."

Her bitterness burned. I took a moment to follow her back in time and remember. "I was proud of your commendation. I admit it hurt my feelings when you applied to transfer. Mom said you'd requested a different partner, that you'd complained I wasn't carrying my weight."

She didn't reply.

The strain in my voice came through. "I wanted to call you so many times, but I didn't know what to say. I hoped you'd call me but you never did."

She sounded like a block of cement. "I loved being your partner. I'd never have asked for anyone else. But I was transferred and it killed my career. I'm riding it out now, only two more years to my pension."

Close to twelve years ago. Could we have both been so mistaken? I couldn't remember all the details, only the hole in my life when she was gone. Misunderstandings destroyed something good. I rubbed my temple and tried to focus.

A moment passed before a softer voice continued. "I'm so sorry...about...what happened. So sorry."

They were all pushing and shoving, wanting to be heard. I held them back as much as possible. "That's kind of why I'm calling."

She didn't answer.

"I need to ask you for a favor." I held my breath.

Skepticism crept into her voice. "What kind of favor?"

I rushed on. "Can you get me the files? Her case. I've never seen it."

"Whoa." She inhaled. "That's not a favor. That's asking me to risk my career on the eve of retirement."

My head throbbed and hands tingled. "I know. I wouldn't ask if it wasn't important."

There was no sympathy now. "Ask the Sheriff. She can do it for you."

"She thinks the less I know the less it will hurt. But my therapist and I agree it's time to face it. All of it."

A long pause. "What do you know?"

"Only what Mom told me. A career criminal confessed and was convicted. She never said who and wouldn't give me the details. I accepted that for years. But I need to know all of it now."

She sighed. "I can tell you the guy who confessed was Grainger King. He was picked up for a rape about a week after...." She stuttered.

The crickets and cicadas wound up in solidarity to The Chorus, The Three, Frank, and all the rest.

"He'd been linked to at least three other incidences and he confessed to them all. He died not long after his conviction. Cancer or something like that."

All Mom said was that they'd found the killer, got him locked away, and I needed to move on.

Blindsided by the horror of a memory so fresh I held my breath.

The room is so cold. My arms and legs are strapped to the bed and all I can do is flail my head. I can see Mom by the bed rail. But Frank won't let me talk. He's screaming at her. He's saying unbearable things to the only person in the world who loves me. I can't make him stop. He doesn't believe her when she says it's finished, that the murderer is caught. He's going to kill her and then go after the other one. He tells her about the blood that will flow. She shakes her head, doesn't know Frank is not me. She is walking away and she doesn't hear me call to her. She only hears Frank threaten to murder her in her sleep.

"Jamie? Are you still there?"

"Yeah. Here. I need you to…. Can you find the evidence box? Take pictures of what's there and send them to me?"

She grunted. "No way. It could cost me my retirement and it won't change anything."

I played my last card. "What if it was you?"

There was no catching up. No asking about family or coworkers. Only a terse goodbye and it was over.

Light from the pool waltzed around my backyard. Night noises buzzed alongside the constant chatter. No one had good things to say and they kept at me. In that mass of voices someone whispered what I needed to know. I listened but couldn't find the one.

I could take a pill and probably sleep. But if I did, I'd never hear the key information.

I clamped my hands over my ears. "I'm Jamie Butler. I'm Amanda's daughter. I'm a retired Buffalo cop. I'm 46 years old."

My only chance to break something loose lay at the other end of the phone connection. With my ice water refilled, I sat at my mosaic table and worked, hoping to distract myself so I wouldn't make the phone call.

Before I could stop myself, my fingers dialed his number.

My insides jittered and I wanted to clutch the phone with breathless excitement, at the same time I wanted to throw it into the cinderblock fence. Not many people had loved me in my life. But once, Larry had loved me.

I expected his voice and was struck dumb when Sue

answered. The caller I.D. on this phone wouldn't warn her. I gripped a tile. "Hi, Sue."

I pictured her, short dark hair, eyes bright and waiting for the next laugh, body a whirr of movement. So different from me. She'd frown, placing my voice immediately. "Jamie. Wow. This is a surprise. And on Mother's Day."

There was another Mother's Day so long ago.

We are sixteen and Sue and I are on our own in her mother's kitchen. So many meals I'd eaten at that table. We follow her mother's pot roast recipe exactly. This Mother's Day her mother can take it easy. The lemon pie fails, but we bought ice cream just in case. Outside, we pick lilacs for the table from the bush between our two houses. Chris McMann and Darrell Hodges drive by in Darrell's beat up Nova and we stop to flirt. They invite us for a ride and we tell ourselves we'll be back before the roast is done, and hop in. We don't account for running out of gas.

Sue's mother covers for us, as usual. We returned to a juicy roast, removed in time, and a perfect lemon pie. Mom, who surprisingly makes it in time for her invitation, is impressed, and never knows Sue's mother saved us. But Mom manages to sneak in a comment about women needing more skills than keeping house.

Sue's mother didn't work and she always had cookies and an extra place at the table for me. She'd kept my refrigerator stocked after the news hit. She was probably the one who threw out the food when it went uneaten.

I thought of what to say. I miss you. You are better for Larry than I was. I'm glad you had more children. I don't hate you anymore. "Can I talk to Larry?"

She didn't say anything but a moment later Larry said, "Jamie?"

"Hi."

He sounded flat. "We haven't heard from you in over four years and all you say is 'hi'?"

I set down one tile and picked up another. I tried harder. "Okay. How are you? The kids? Sue?"

The words and tone were guarded. "Kids are doing well. My business is stable enough. Sue quit her job last year and loves being home full time. What are you doing?"

The smile slid onto my face so I'd sound convincing. "The desert is great. I'm settling in, have friends, lots to do. I volunteer for the Arizona Rangers."

An uncomfortable pause built between us.

We'd shared the same bed for fifteen years. Carried the same scars, wore the same masks of forgetfulness. How could we have so little to say to each other?

"I'm really surprised they let you join."

I tightened my stomach against the one-two.

He sighed. "I don't want to sound mean, but don't you carry a gun? How did you manage that?"

A bead of blood oozed between my fingers and I dropped the tile. "Mom did her magic with my files. It's all clean and sweet. Retired at age 45 after twenty years on the force."

"But you're only 46. You retired two years ago."

"See? Magic."

Larry only used sarcasm at his most bitter. "Yeah, Amanda always knows best."

Enough. Like a surgical procedure I needed to cut quick, minimize the bleeding, and stitch it up before it festered.

"After the... when I was...." I took a deep breath and started again. "Was the investigation conducted right?"

He hesitated. "I'm not sure what you're asking."

"Mom has this thing about the slightest appearance of nepotism. I was wondering, did she put enough resources on the investigation."

Edgy or just annoyed, he said, "Why is this coming up now?"

I gripped the table. My voice bordered on hysteria. "Just tell me, damn it. I'm asking now and I want to know."

"Sure. Yeah. Let's see." He wavered in a very un-Larry-like way. "You're the cop and I'm the computer geek, so you know, I don't... I didn't." He exhaled, and when he started again, his voice cracked. "I couldn't deal with the details. I'm sorry. She was gone and you were just as gone. Your mother wouldn't let me in to see you. She took charge of the investigation and wouldn't tell me anything. I should have fought. But I didn't. I couldn't."

His tears unnerved me, scraping bone on bone. Without any warning, my eyes watered and overflowed. "It's how Mom deals with pain. She takes charge. She works."

He drew in a quivering breath. "With your mother so determined, I assume everything that could be done was done. They couldn't find him for a long time. But he got arrested for another crime and confessed. Short trial and I didn't go. I couldn't."

"You sound fine with that. As if it doesn't eat at you every day."

"I have a family. A busy life. You need to let it go. It won't help you get better."

"I don't need to get better. I need to find her killer."

Dead silence. He couldn't have been more shocked than I was. Someone inside me put those words in my head, in my mouth. The someone who knew.

"They found him, Jamie."

"Did they?" I shot back. "Are you sure?"

"You sound like her. Your mother."

Frank hissed and snarled. Suddenly, he spoke out loud with my voice. "At least she cares. Why don't you?"

"Right. Let's step back ten years where you tell me I should be a better father."

"You should have been. You left us both." These weren't my words, but sometimes Frank's voice won out.

"Left you? You have no idea how hard I tried to be with you. Both of you. But as soon as she was born she was all you needed. Every time I tried to step up, spend any time alone with her, you swooped in like a jealous bird and snatched her away from me. You say you wanted me to be a better father, but you did everything you could to stop me."

"I—" Too much brain clatter to think this through. Did I try to keep him from her? Like how Mom put up barriers between me and Dad? It's possible I did the same, not meaning to but always emulating her. I realized we'd been silent for some time. Larry had always given me space to respond.

"If I did, I'm truly sorry. Neither of you deserved that."

Again, silence. Then the sound of a sob. "I loved her. And I love you." He sniffed and his voice strengthened. "But I've got a wonderful life now. Sue and I have made a family. I can't go through this with you. Please, don't call me again."

When I hung up, the only voice left in my head was Peanut. She cried alone.

I wiped blood from the tiles and reached for my phone. I needed to make the call I'd been avoiding.

25

I tried my voice in pretend conversation until no sound of stress strummed when it came out. Then I dialed Mom.

She sounded tired. "I was having a glass of wine before bed. How are you? Why are you calling so late?"

Damn. I hadn't wanted to appear anything but normal. "I guess I forgot about the time change. Sorry."

"That's okay. It's been another tough day, that's all."

"The election?"

She sipped. "That investigator is a pain in the ass."

"There's nothing to find, so she's going deep. She'll move on to someone else soon."

Mom's voice tightened. "No one is completely clean. This isn't an easy job and you have to make deals to get things done. But you're right, there's really nothing out of the ordinary. Nothing no other sheriff hasn't done."

Sheriff was a job I'd never wanted. Compromise could cross the line to corruption. I suffered guilt in the case of my early retirement. By law, I wasn't eligible for full bennies for another eight months. I didn't know where Mom stole the time, in manufactured unused personal leave, changing my hire date, giving me credit for working when I was locked inside the walls of a mental ward? Mom never explained and I never asked. Just cashed my checks each month.

She always stressed about elections and they'd never been close. "John Overton is a tough opponent, huh?"

"He's a punk. Let's talk about you. What's going on in Tucson? Are you working out, eating well?"

I paced and braced myself. "I've been thinking about tha-tha.... That night. The evidence that was recovered. You know, the ponytail elastic and the necklace."

"You shouldn't dwell on that. The details will only upset you."

"Tara thinks it's good to face it."

Her voice sweetened like warm caramel. "Well, I'm not sure I agree with that. Even so, if you want to remember it, please be under Tara's supervision. You shouldn't allow yourself to get upset when you're alone."

"I'm not upset, I—"

She interrupted, still keeping a soothing voice. "You're upset right now. I can tell. Why don't you take a sleeping pill and get a good night's rest."

Frank was thrashing around in my head.

"It's time for me to come to terms with this. I think it was my fault and I'll never get over it if I don't find out why."

A hint of frustration sliced her words. "We've been over this. You had a date. That's normal and natural. It isn't your fault. It hurts me as much as it does you. But the responsibility lies with the piece of shit who did it. And he's dead. End of story."

Frank growled *"Goddamn liar. It doesn't hurt her as much as it does you."*

My feet ached from pounding on the patio as I paced. "That's just it. I need to see the evidence, read the case file. I have to know for sure he was the one."

"It won't bring you closure. It will only be another obsession, like those voices. Accept it, or you'll never get better."

"I'm not obsessing. I have a right to know."

She stopped at that and when she spoke again, she sounded stern, the same as when she'd caught me with a joint my junior year. "You're talking like you did back then, when you went to Forest Hills. You're making no sense, being irrational. Take your Seroquel."

Two years ago, even six months ago, I would have agreed with her. I might have believed that I was going crazy. But not now. I clung to the quiet voice inside of me, even if I couldn't hear the whole message.

Arguing with her would only make her worry more. I sounded tired and defeated. "Okay. You're right. I'll see Tara tomorrow. You've got enough to do without taking care of me. I'll take a pill and sleep."

"That's for the best. Tomorrow will be better."

I agreed with her and hung up.

Maybe tomorrow would be better, but I wasn't done with today, yet.

26

I resisted the oblivion of the pill. I needed to unravel the connection. Common knowledge dictated the simplest explanation was usually the best. Maybe I was only complicating the problem, creating pathways in my imagination.

I circled the table with the hair bow. The blonde hairs seemed like ropes strangling me. Escape took me though the French doors to the sparkling pool, glowing in the desert's dark night.

The girls hated me. They knew I suspected Cali had gone with the creep. I hadn't backed off when they TPed my house, so they upped their antics. Now they watched to see if I'd overreact and get myself into trouble with Jim Thompson, the puller of strings.

Or Cali was missing. In the hands of a killer who taunted me. He'd hurt her to get at me.

Except the man who stole my life was supposed to be dead.

Around the pool I trudged. Each time, I passed a cinderblock shoved behind a fan palm. A thick nylon tow rope looped it several times, the knots tight. The length of the remaining rope was measured carefully, allowing for the share that would be knotted round my ankle.

Frank instructed me on the device not long after I moved here. He mentioned it from time to time, though I didn't need the reminder.

Tonight, he nudged me closer every loop around the pool. The Three joined in.

"*It's quiet under there.*"

"*Peaceful.*"

"*Silent.*"

I don't want to remember this, but I do.

She's eighteen months old and needs me, but my flu is so debilitating I can barely stand. Larry insists on giving her a bath and I can't argue. I keep the doors open so I can hear. She's giggling and splashing. He's singing silly made-up songs. I start to doze and wake to her shouting about not wanting her hair washed. She hates it. I struggle to stand on shaky legs. For one night, she can live without washing her hair.

I call to him. He says it's fine. She's crying. I'm angry. I tell him to forget the hair. I'm nearly in the hallway and he's standing in the doorway, his back to the tub. She suddenly stops bawling.

No longer weak, I'm there before him, shoving him out of the way. She's on her back, eyes wide, mouth open, water covering her face.

I yank her out. She's sputtering and coughing. I glare at Larry as I carry her to my bed. I'm still shaking when I cuddle my little Peanut close to my side.

I passed the cinder block again. "*What are you sticking around for?*" Frank asked.

"*No one cares.*"

"*They hate you.*"

"*It's peaceful down there.*"

Rafe might have wanted to be friends, but I'd shoved him away. Patricia obviously had a complete life without me.

Larry said, "Don't call me again."

Kari wished I'd stayed silent.

Only Mom cared about me.

The rope looked like a friend. The water, welcome relief.

"Do it."

"Now!"

The splash drowned out all of the voices. The cool wave buried me. I closed my eyes to the glow of the pool light.

It's all right.

Finally.

27

Boom, boom, boom.

I didn't open my eyes but clutched the hoodie closer to my chest.

The doorbell dinged. Then again. And a third time.

I squinted, locating my shorts and t-shirt in a heap on the tile next to the wicker saucer chair I'd curled into right after taking a pill.

The banging resumed as I unfurled from the chair. The clothes and my hair were still damp from my midnight swim. The plunge had given me enough respite to realize I'd let the voices take too much control and they'd led me down the path of paranoia and self-pity. The road that steered me away from myself. The pill felt like defeat, but it kept me from destruction.

I limped to the window, limbering up from my cramped sleep with each step. My fingers slipped through the blind slats and eased them open so I could peek out. At first I didn't see anyone, then a quick scan revealed two little figures, fists raised to bang again. If I didn't move, maybe they'd go away.

They rang again, then pounded. Cheyenne put her hands around her mouth and sucked in full lungs. "JAMIE!"

If I didn't do something she'd have Mrs. Dempsey over here. My soggy clothes sent a shiver over me when I threw them on. The lock clicked and I swung the door open. The sun shone almost overhead, late morning already. "Does your mother know you crossed the street?" I sounded less severe than I'd expected.

Kaycee's round face beamed. Her fuzz of blonde hair contained bright splotches of red and blue paint clumps.

Both little girls clutched wrinkled newsprint pages. Cheyenne might be miffed if she knew a grass green streak ran from behind her ear to her collarbone.

Kaycee thrust her paper toward me, her chin up. Still damp with drying paint, the page swirled in royal blue and brush strokes of red. It nearly burned my hand with the memory.

Tiny fist with a bulky wooden brush handle flicking blue paint onto the paper, over the edges, swiping the plywood we'd set up in the garage for an easel. Her singing reverberating off the walls. Painting after painting hanging from clothes pins attached to the metal shelving units.

We surveyed them all while sipping Kool-Aid and nibbling Vanilla Wafers, as if patrons at an art gallery. Finally choose our favorites to take inside and tack on the refrigerator.

Cheyenne flipped her paper around and held it front of her like a shield. "We made you pictures." She held it out to me. "Mine is our grass and trees from Oklahoma."

I held both paintings and struggled to remember what to say to children. "It is very green."

"Thank you." She took it as a great, and highly deserved, compliment. "Kaycee says hers is the lake. But you can't really tell. She's not old enough to do anything but make a big mess."

"I think it's lovely." I did. But it was too beautiful for me.

Cheyenne waited with an expectant tilt of her head. Kaycee grinned at me and said nothing. I stepped farther onto my front porch and checked across the street. Sherilyn stood on her porch, the door open behind her.

She waved. "Baby's sleeping."

I waved back. The two girls kept staring at me. "Well. Thank you."

"Aren't you going to put them on your 'frigerator?" Cheyenne zipped past me. "We can help you take the old stuff off. 'Cause if you don't change out the pictures they get rusty."

Kaycee hadn't moved so I reached to her and she placed her soft hand in mine. I dragged her into the house, leaving my door open.

Cheyenne didn't have any trouble finding my kitchen and stood in front of the refrigerator with her hands fisted on her hips. "Where's all your stuff?"

"What stuff?" I set the pictures on the counter and bent to take her hand. She resisted when I tried to pull her toward the door.

"The mag-a-nets and pictures and notes and stuff. The stuff people gots on their 'fridgerators."

She pulled her hand away. "If you don't have mag-a-nets, how're going to put our pictures up there?"

Now I had to hang them up? "I'll use tape."

"Okay. That's a good idea. I'll watch Kaycee while you go get some."

The junk drawer in the kitchen held only a few items, not like the overflowing mess of that other drawer, full of Happy Meal toys, rubber bands so old they cracked and broke, bits of change, nuts and nails, and myriad household detritus. In this drawer, the tape didn't even touch the scissors.

Cheyenne pulled her study in green from the counter and held it up against the refrigerator. "Put the tape right there." She leaned her face toward the right top corner.

I slapped a piece on and we did it for the other three corners and then for Kaycee's lake. Cheyenne took Kaycee's hand and they stepped back, glowing with pride. I had the crazy urge to offer them Kool-Aid and Vanilla Wafers.

"Okay. Thank you. Now you need to go home," I said.

They seemed okay with that and followed me to the door. Together, I ushered them out my door and down the walkway, where we met Sherilyn. Her front door stood open and she held the baby monitor.

Sherilyn rested a hand on Kaycee's head. "You're so good to these munchkins. They just love you to bits."

"I'm new, that's all." Wait until they get to know me.

"Nope. There's something about you. Kaycee fell in love and Cheyenne is not about be left out. So, you're stuck with two new friends."

Uncomfortable but not unhappy, I shifted my gaze down the street in time to catch a flash of what looks like someone wearing a red hoodie. Voices surged in my ears and I'm bombarded by a thudding heart, electricity thrumming through my veins. "Uh." I held up a hand to Sherilyn. "Wait a minute."

Flip flops slapping on my heels, I sprinted down the sidewalk and up the driveway of the house. Whatever I planned to say or do when I encountered whatever flagged my attention, I didn't know. The voices urged me on and I didn't resist.

Nothing but a barrel cactus blooming with yellow flowers and a cinderblock wall greeted me when I rounded the garage. If someone had been there, they'd scaled the wall and were gone. I trudged back to Sherilyn.

She eyed me with curiosity. "What was it?"

I shook my head. "Nothing. I thought maybe someone was there. Have you noticed a gray car with tinted windows cruising around?" I pointed up the street. "It's parked there sometimes."

Sherilyn squinted in the sunshine to where I pointed. "Nope. Why?"

Again, I dismissed it. "Nothing. I'm jumpy, I guess." Over protective of children that weren't mine. "Thanks again for the pictures, girls." I started toward my porch.

"Three," Sherilyn said, out of the blue.

I turned around. "Pardon?"

"Friends. You have three new ones, if you count me."

An unexpected lump clogged my throat. She knew about the voices and still, she wasn't running away.

Cheyenne piped up with her bossy attitude. "Give me that. It's not yours."

Kaycee whisked her hands behind her back and set her mouth in determination.

Cheyenne took her case to Sherilyn. "Mom. She picked something up from the ground and I don't think she should have it."

Sherilyn bent down to Kaycee. "Show me what you've got."

Kaycee drew herself in and gave her mother an untrusting glare.

"Come on, let me see," Sherilyn coaxed.

I pushed my hair from my face, realizing I'd slept on it wet. It surely had crimped in weird angles. I hadn't brushed my teeth, either. Why didn't I scare the little girls?

Kaycee slowly pulled her hands from behind her back and held them out, fisted tight.

Sherilyn fought a smile. "Okay, now open up."

Kaycee glared at Cheyenne, who hovered over her. She unclenched her hand one plump finger at a time.

Cheyenne lost patience and wrenched the prize from Kaycee. The younger sister wailed at the injustice.

Cheyenne held up the silver chain, a charm dancing at the end. "Is this yours?" she demanded from me.

No. Oh please, God. No.

28

A dark blanket lifted from my eyes.

"Jamie?" Sherilyn stood in front of me, concern clouding her expression.

"Yeah." I swallowed. "Sorry."

With shaking hands I plucked the necklace from Cheyenne's fingers. Her mouth opened in offended protest. "I wasn't going to keep it."

I tried to answer and managed to croak. "I know. It's okay. I didn't know I'd lost it."

The thin silver chain. A runner's charm dangled, catching the glint of sun. It looked so much like hers. But this wasn't the same.

I choked as the memory pushed at me. She'd made varsity her freshman year. They'd put her as anchor on the 4X4 relay team and she'd brought home the district championship. So proud.

We'd gone to her favorite restaurant to celebrate. Sitting around the table with only crusts of pineapple and ham pizza, Mom pulled the jewelers box from her bag. Mom beamed when she received the excited hug. I cried at so much happiness.

The same necklace, scratched, mud ground into the tiny creases. Rusty brown on the chain. Probably in an evidence box, hidden in the cool dark. Like a grave.

Sherilyn made a hasty retreat with her young ones in tow and I all but ran to my house, slammed the front door, and clicked the lock. I deposited the necklace on the table next to the hair ribbon.

Frank's vitriol erupted. "Shut up!" The words echoed against the Saltillo tile floor. Megan and Jen couldn't know what the necklace would mean to me. If they'd placed it there as a prank, it was an unbelievable coincidence. That left an equally unbelievable scenario. Someone who supposedly was dead was taunting me. Car keys in hand, fist on the door handle, it occurred to me I must look and smell similar to Shax. I took time to shower, eat the rest of the food in my refrigerator, and drink two glasses of ice water and lemon.

While I sipped, Frank and I talked. An hour spent letting him spew, reassuring him I wouldn't let anyone hurt me, and giving him a chance to wear himself out. It relieved the pressure in my head and calmed the tingling in my fingers. Feeling stronger and more grounded than I had in a while, I backed the Juke out of my garage and drove across town to Ventana High School.

For the illusion of authority, I'd donned my Arizona Rangers uniform, complete with shiny badge. A poster on the door of the high school directed all visitors to sign in at the office and that's where I headed. The school smelled of books, floor wax, thousands of cafeteria lunches, and the buzzing of young bodies.

The necklace rested in a plastic sandwich bag, the best I could do for an evidence bag. It was tucked into my breast pocket. With a relaxed and easy smile, I stepped into the front office and waited for the secretary to look up from the stack of papers in front of her.

Middle-aged, she resembled every school secretary I'd ever known. Stalwart, reliable, kind-hearted, stern, all wrapped up in a Mom package. She addressed me with a pleasant face. "How can I help you?"

Here goes. "I'm Officer Butler, from the Arizona Rangers. I'm investigating an incident and would like to interview a witness who is a student here."

She sat back and eyed me. "This is new. I've been here fifteen years and no Ranger has ever wanted to interview a student. Who is it?"

"Megan Thompson."

Her eyebrows arched up. "Huh. Our policy is to call the parents before allowing any contact from people outside the school district."

Did that policy originate at that moment? "Sure." I'd get further by staying friendly. "I can see that. I'll contact her parents and speak to her at her home, under their supervision."

She nodded. "That would be best."

I stared to leave, then, as if I just remembered, I added, "There is another student in question. I understand I can't speak to her now, but can you tell me if she's here today? Cali Shaw?"

The secretary thought about that. "I'm sorry. Unless you're a parent, that's private information."

My frustration grew. "I only want to know if she's been in school the last couple of days. I don't need to contact her."

She studied me and reached for the headset of her phone. "Let me see if the principal is available. He might be able to help you."

The principal, who would want specifics, and when I could

only give him my private fairy tale, would call Mitch and he'd have my badge for good. "That's not necessary. I appreciate your protecting your students. I'll get in touch with them through their parents."

Frank tried to butt in, but I kept him quiet. I remained firmly in charge as I made my way to my Juke and cruised the parking lot until I found Megan's CRV. I passed the next hour writing in a journal and keeping all of us on an even keel.

I needn't have bothered. When I met Megan at her car door, her mouth dropped open momentarily. She snapped it closed and up came the hip, her head tilted and her lips formed a sneer. "Officer Butthead. You're not supposed to be here."

"Where is Cali?"

Head tilt to the other side. "Staying after for math tutoring. She's not all that bright, you know."

Was it me or Frank who wanted to slap her? I pulled the envelope from my pocket and held it out for her to see inside. "Is this Cali's?"

She peered at it and her expression slipped for a fraction of a second, then reappeared. "How should I know? Half the kids on the track team have one."

"Does Cali?"

She shrugged. "Maybe."

Hot tar bubbled inside me and I paused to cool it. "Cut the shit. If this is Cali's, then her life is in danger."

Megan spewed a mean laugh. "Her life is in danger. Hysterical, much?"

I shouldn't have, but I grabbed her arm. "This isn't a joke."

That got her attention. Fear filled her eyes and she pulled away, reaching for her car door.

I threw my hands in the air. "Sorry. I'm sorry. This is important."

She wrenched open the door and pounced inside. "You're going to be so sorry, cunt."

My biggest fear was that I wouldn't be the only one.

29

Not remembering the details, I'd managed to get myself through downtown. The phone rang and when I glanced at the ID, my stomach contracted.

Let it go.

Don't talk to her.

She's the devil.

I punched it on and held it to my head, since Mom hated the connection over the car audio.

"Oh thank goodness. I've been so worried about you."

Smile, so she can hear it. "No need to worry. I'm fine."

Someone spoke to her and she probably held up her finger and scowled as I'd seen her do a million times. "What is going on out there?" Said with the same inflection as when Darrell Hodges and I were studying Civics behind the closed door of my bedroom.

I ignored the demanding tone, attributing it to all her stress. "The usual. It's gorgeous today, not supposed to get above 85. I'm making real progress on the table. I'm scheduled to work at the courthouse for the Rangers tomorrow."

"Honey. Listen to yourself. You're wound too tight. I can hear it in your voice. What is wrong?"

Now Frank had something to say. *"Tell the bitch to stick her tongue in a light socket."*

"It's this time of year. I'm not as bad as last year, but even Tara says it's bound to cause a little anxiety, especially after last year."

Throw the phone away.

Tell her to go to Hell.

Run your car into that pole.

Even though they didn't speak often, today The Three acted up.

Her heels clacked on the old tile of the station in Buffalo. I'd been part of that scene and knew the cold blast of fear Mom spread in her wake. Admin probably ducked their heads to their computers, uniforms snatched paper or grabbed a phone and pretended to talk, anything to look busy. "Whatever it is, Honey, you need to get it under control."

"I'm fine."

Frank piped up. *"That's all you've got? You moron."*

A car door slammed and a few dings sounded before the engine started. She said, "I thought you trusted me."

"I do, Mom. You've always been there. My best friend."

Frank shouted. *"She's your worst nightmare."*

Tension strung in her voice. "If you trusted me, I wouldn't have had to hear from Tara that you've missed some appointments lately."

"Are you checking up on me?"

"We all agreed when you moved down there and started with Tara, that if there were any problems, I would get involved. You do remember signing the DPOA, right?"

Mom only wanted what was best for me, but Frank was cursing her. Tara's theory about Frank and Mom was that both of them fought for control of me. Until I took control of myself, they'd continue in this stomach-churning tug-o-war.

"I'm much better now than when I moved down here and I've been thinking it's time to rescind the power of attorney. Having you as that safety net might be holding me back from total independence."

I expected a blowup but I got a sad response. "Oh, Honey. I know you are becoming healthier, more like the Jamie you used to be. But there's still a long way to go. This stage you're in could be a false sense of growth. I know you don't remember, but you've had these before."

"Remember? Holy shit, we were there." Frank.

A horn honked behind me and I realized I'd been sitting at a green light.

"As soon as we weaned you off the heavy meds, you'd be okay for a few days and I had such high hopes. Then you'd start talking to yourself again, get frantic, and lose it. It didn't take long before we had to medicate you again."

I pulled into the parking lot of a Waffle House and left the car running for the air conditioning. "I got upset because while I was on the drugs, I forgot about it all. Every time you'd take me off, I remembered and had to suffer the shock. Instead of letting me process it, you sent me back to oblivion." I quit talking but the Three didn't.

Because of her we suffered over and over.

She doesn't want you to get well.

Hang up.

Mom sounded surprised. "Where did you come up with that? Is it what Tara is telling you?"

"No. It's what I'm telling me."

"You're not talking to yourself again, are you?"

"No. I'm not talking to myself." To Frank and Maggie. Technically not talking to the Three, the Chorus, and definitely not Peanut. But most of them talked to me.

Rustling over the phone and a slight grunt told me Mom probably made it to her destination and was climbing from her car. The slam of the door confirmed it. "It's important you make it to your appointments with Tara. It's the only thing you have to do. I can't afford to leave Buffalo right now, with the campaign and this damned investigation. But if you need me, you know I'll come out there. You're more important to me than this election."

Liar.

She loves her power more than you.

She's never loved you.

"I know how much being reelected means to you. And the county. I'll see Tara later today."

Her heels clacked on cement. "Maybe take some time off from the Rangers at least. You don't want to relapse."

Wherever she was heading, she'd arrived and now needed to end our call. I pictured her pinched face as she tried to give me attention. "You're right. I'll relax, maybe read a couple of those novels you sent."

"Good girl. I'll talk to you soon." She hung up.

I was stressed, yes. But I didn't feel close to the edge. Was I lying to myself?

I eased onto the busy road heading toward home.

The mid afternoon sun highlighted the saguaro cactus that lined the stretch of road leading through Sonoran National Park. The white blooms crowned the majestic old timers and I could imagine *her* eyes lighting up when I told her the surprising fact that saguaros only grow in the Sonoran Desert. And that they grow so slowly a cactus measuring less than two inches could easily be ten years old.

So many fascinating things she'd never get the chance to

know. A lifetime of experiences and memories I imagined for her. I looked up from a stop sign where I'd been idling. No traffic at this empty piece of desert.

How had I ended up on this road? I didn't remember driving here. I checked the clock on the dash. I didn't remember the last two hours. Where else had I been in that time? And who had been at the wheel?

I turned my car toward home. That's twice in a matter of days I'd lost track of time. Maybe Mom was right and I was more upset than I'd thought. Mother's Day, this thing with Megan. And Cali. If I could only see her.

Maybe it was time to admit I needed help.

Whether he hated me or not, I had to call Rafe. Somehow, I would convince him to find Cali.

I parked the Juke in my garage and stepped out, practicing what to say to Rafe.

A scream shattered my thoughts. "Jamie!"

Sherilyn raced across the street. One flip flop flew behind her but she didn't slow. "Help me!"

I reacted by reaching for my gun, snug in the holster of my utility belt.

She grabbed my arm and tugged, panic driving her. "Kaycee. She's gone!"

30

"Stop!" I said it to Sherilyn but I meant it for everyone who broiled and churned. "Slow. Tell me."

Tears surged from her eyes and she panted, but she was able to speak. "I was in the kitchen making cupcakes. Jackson was in his walker and the girls were taking a nap." She caught her breath. "Supposed to be. But Cheyenne came in after a long time and asked where Kaycee was."

She sobbed. "I swear. I didn't hear her. I don't know how long. The front door was closed but not locked. I didn't think she could open it by herself. She's alone. Somewhere. Oh God, we have to find her."

They all yelled and screamed and threatened to overwhelm me. Someone reminded me of the gray sedan. It had to be related.

I concentrated on Sherilyn. "You need to stay here with Jackson and Cheyenne. Call 9-1-1, and get the Dempseys to send neighbors to search the subdivision."

I whirled around.

"Where are you going?" Sherilyn sounded slightly calmer.

"The desert." I ran by the bird playpen. One baby flapped

his wings on the rocks out of the shelter of the oleander leaves. The other was gone.

Your fault.

He's going to make you pay.

He's going to kill her.

"Kaycee!" I shouted into emptiness. The cicadas whizzed their strange music, letting it swell and ebb.

How would a toddler view this expanse and choose a path? I ran, following my route to the dirt road and down the drainage.

"Kaycee!"

Cholla cactus choked the road. Hostile vegetation that could snag soft baby skin and stick burning needles into sensitive flesh. Cat's claws sprang from bushes, where unsuspecting little legs could be shredded.

"Kaycee!"

How far could she make it, plump legs, pillowy feet in strapped-on flipflops, puffing dirt along the narrow path?

"Kaycee!"

The drainage ended and I raced along the trail too narrow for a car. Lizards skirted from the creosote to the Mormon tea, under dead branches. The small holes I never paid attention to now loomed underfoot. Snake? Tarantula? Gila monsters?

"Kaycee!" I shouted into the heat, my throat begging for moisture.

Thickets tangled with brush and trees, maybe hiding javelina. Coyotes might be lurking in packs of two or three, delighting in something with no defenses, with a gait so slow. Bobcats eager to pounce.

"Kaycee!"

A voice whispered, *"Remember."* Remember what?

"Kaycee!"

I'd gone a mile from the house. Was it even possible for her to get this far? Why would she take off? Where was she going? I dropped down to the wash.

Caught sight of a flash of pink. "Kaycee!"

In the shade of mesquite, laying still in the sandy wash, Kaycee looked like a giant doll with glassy blue eyes.

"No! Oh please, no." My lips moved but everyone pleaded and begged, cried and swore.

I lunged for her, knowing I was too late. Another girl gone. I'd failed. We'd all failed.

Her eyes focused on me.

"Thank God!" I knelt to her, afraid because of her stillness. "Kaycee, are you okay?"

She didn't answer but I wasn't really talking to her. I scanned her body, stretched out in the shade and noticed the two blue streaks about an inch long in her rolly thigh. Her leg twitched and she closed her eyes.

I couldn't tell if she'd started to swell but it seemed likely that the thigh with the puncture marks was puffier than the other.

Rattlesnake. Most likely the one I'd seen here the last few days. He'd been big and old, and maybe that would work in her favor since the babies' venom is much stronger.

Frank cursed me for not thinking to bring my phone.

"Kaycee," I touched her cheek gently, wanting to reassure her.

She didn't open her eyes. Her breathing grew labored.

She's dead.

Zoey is dead.

Cali is dead.

Not dead. Not yet. But if I didn't act quickly....

They carried on, cursing, yelling, fighting. Somehow I kept my focus and slid my hand under Kaycee's matted blonde hair. I lifted her and cradled her head in the crook of my neck. With my other arm under her behind, I let her legs hang down, keeping the snake bite below her heart.

Running would jiggle her, maybe cause the venom to circulate faster. Keeping her stable would take longer, giving the venom more time to work through her. One didn't seem any better than the other. I could kill her either way.

Tucking her as close to my body as possible and trying to run as though my feet were clouds, I retraced our steps. Frank accompanied every movement by telling me how worthless I was. Others weighed in with accusations of how I was letting her die. They repeated how I wasn't fast enough to save her, how the same thing would happen to Cali. Looping over and over while all I could do was focus on getting Kaycee to safety.

We made it out of the brush and into the drainage. Kaycee hadn't moved or uttered a peep and her breathing was barely there, but she was alive. I couldn't see her leg from how I held her and I wasn't about to take the time to look. Up the drainage to the trail road.

"She's alive." I shouted it. "She's not going to die."

The voices accusing me of Kaycee's death drowned out the sound of my feet in the sand. They wanted me to believe otherwise.

It felt as though I ran through quicksand. My mind conjured a vision and I felt I could not only see down the trail, but around the curve to the lot next to my house. I saw the road and the walk to Sherilyn's front door. Impossible for me to see a half mile away, through the desert and twists and turns of the trail, but I saw Sherilyn pacing the concrete stoop outside her front door.

When I actually rounded the curve toward my house, a crowd of neighbors stirred in the street between Sherilyn's and my house—the Dempseys from next door, a retired couple who lived next to them, an older Latina woman who I'd assumed babysat her grandchildren. A few others I didn't know. The middle-aged and younger adults were all at work and the kids at school. I ran from the desert. "Call an ambulance! Rattlesnake bite."

Mr. Dempsey said, "They're on the way."

Mrs. Dempsey focused on the bundle in my arms. "Poor little thing."

The grandmother babysitter held a phone to her ear, and it sounded like she relayed information to the emergency dispatcher. Sherilyn ran from her house. Her scream pulled a cord strung from my head to my soul and it vibrated like an electric eel, shooting through me. "Kaycee!"

In a moment Sherilyn snatched her from my arms and knelt on the hot pavement, surrounded by neighbors. She rocked the child, sobbing and sputtering nonsense words.

Kaycee's arm flopped with each sway forward and back. She didn't respond.

The toddler's face, normally pink-cheeked with a shy smile sneaking out, look so still, a blue tint began coloring bags forming under her eyes. I couldn't bear to see that arm, wobbling back and forth, back and forth.

As Sherilyn's teary jumble of words poured over Kaycee's still body, the soft plunk of stone hitting the pavement caught Frank's attention. *"Well, look at that."* Below Sherilyn, where it had popped out of Kaycee's pocket, a one inch square tile lay on the street. The cobalt blue looked like neon.

I bent over and snatched it, slipping the piece from my backyard project into my pocket. Why did Kaycee have it? Did she pick it up from my house when she and Cheyenne brought their paintings?

Lilacs. I'd lost time this afternoon. Now this. Frank laughed. *"You're too stupid to put it together."*

The ambulance shrieked at the entrance to the neighborhood. From far away something like my voice sounded strong and firm. "Mrs. Dempsey. Will you stay with the other children while Sherilyn goes to the hospital with Kaycee?"

I sprinted to Sherilyn's house.

Cheyenne stood on the couch that was set in front of the wide living room window. Her face looked the color of snow, her eyes round and frightened. "Is Kaycee dead?"

I wanted to scream along with the voices in my head. "The ambulance people are going to take care of everything. Can you find your mother's phone for me?"

As if glad to have something useful to do, Cheyenne hopped off the couch and ran into the kitchen. "She was talking when I got up. She talks to my grandma all the time."

I followed Cheyenne into a kitchen in mid-baking chaos. Cheyenne found the phone next to the stove and handed it to me.

Mrs. Dempsey filled the doorway behind me. "Hello. You must be Cheyenne. I'll bet you're a great big sister."

"Mrs. Dempsey is going to stay with you. She's a really nice lady."

Cheyenne's eyes shimmered with tears. "I want to go with Mommy."

I squatted down. "She's got to take care of Kaycee right now. So you need to take look after things at home until she gets back."

Cheyenne sniffed. "Can you stay with me and Jackson?"

"I am going to help your mom until your dad can get here." I pulled her into my arms and kissed the top of her head. "Mrs. Dempsey will need help with Jackson."

Cheyenne's bottom lip trembled but she nodded.

When I raced back to the ambulance, they were strapping Kaycee onto the stretcher.

Mr. Dempsey had the neighbors on the sidewalk, giving the EMTs room to work.

Sherilyn stood above the two EMTs, a young man and woman who could have been twins. She held her hand to her mouth, her eyes shiny with tears. She slowly focused on me. "She stopped breathing." Sherilyn's own chest heaved and she panted. "Dear God, she stopped breathing. I don't. It's. I..." Sherilyn broke into sobs.

I drew her into a hug. "She's going to be okay." Though I doubted the truth of this. "Hang on. She needs you." Nearly the same thing I'd said to Cheyenne and it worked as well with Sherilyn.

She sucked in a sob and turned back to Kaycee. They loaded the little body into the bay of the ambulance. The blood had drained from Sherilyn's face but she'd stopped crying. She leaned toward her baby. I knew. Oh God, I knew how much she longed to cradle her precious child.

"I'll meet you at the hospital. Here's your phone." I folded her fingers around it.

She didn't pay any attention to me as she crawled into the ambulance after Kaycee.

The ambulance blipped the siren and pulled a U-turn, then headed out of the neighborhood. I hurried toward my car in the garage.

Someone else should be going. A friend or family. But she'd only moved here three days ago. She was alone and terrified. There was only me.

I opened my car and slipped behind the wheel. "I'm okay."

Frank laughed. *"You're nowhere near okay, cupcake."*

31

I found Sherilyn pacing and frantic in the emergency room lobby. She ran to me as soon as I stepped through automatic glass doors into the chilled air. "She was blue. And her leg. Oh my God. It started to swell. I tried to call Donnie. He's on a train. All I could do was get a hold of one of his buddies to get the dispatcher."

I hugged her and the Chorus let loose in a symphony of discord.

You can't help her.

It's your fault.

Kaycee is dead.

"What did the docs tell you?"

She wiped her eyes. "They said they're giving her the antivenom, but she's so small and they can't predict anything." Her voice squeezed to a squeak. "She wasn't breathing."

"But they resuscitated her. They'll do everything they can and they can do a lot. Don't give up hope."

Frank: *"You know she's a goner."*

"She's not going to die!" I said it with enough force to shut Frank down, but it must have helped Sherilyn.

She straightened her shoulders and sucked in a breath. "She's not."

We waited. I assured Sherilyn that Mrs. Dempsey would take good care of Cheyenne and Jackson. I brought her soda and water she didn't drink, snacks she didn't eat. Mainly I managed Frank and the others and sat in silence while Sherilyn paced and talked to her mother on the phone.

I thought about calling Tara and cancelling our appointment but I couldn't risk worrying Mom. Maybe Kaycee would recover and everything would be fine.

After a while, a woman in scrubs came into the waiting room. Sherilyn gasped and rushed to her. The woman introduced herself as Dr. Taylor, a pediatrician. She had Sherilyn sit.

"Kaycee is holding her own. I wish I had better news for you, but right now, it's touch and go. We have her on a ventilator because the venom has paralyzed some of her functions. It's a good thing you found her when you did because she had no time to spare."

Sherilyn shook her head. "She's going to get better, though."

Dr. Taylor hesitated. "We're hoping for the best."

It's your fault.

They're all dead.

Murderer.

Dr. Taylor stood. "She's in ICU now. I'll take you to see her."

Sherilyn jumped up. She stuck her hand out to me. "Come with me."

"NO!" Frank ordered.

I clamped down on my back teeth "They usually only allow immediate family."

She squeezed my hand. "I need you. I can't do this alone."

She could, but I wouldn't tell her no.

The hospital's smell of antiseptic and cleaning supplies set me on edge. The cold air on my skin felt like walking in a morgue.

Bile rose, burning my throat and I braced for the memory.

Leather straps loop my forearms, cinched to the metal frame, covered with the loosely woven white hospital blanket as if they can conceal my imprisonment from me. Have I been here days? Months? The catheter irritates me inside and out, humiliating and insufferable. I beg and scream, call for Mom to save me. The horror inside my head is inescapable. Accusing, threatening. Hating.

I want to die. Always the smell and cold air. And the white.

I mumbled under my breath. "I'm Jamie Butler. I'm Amanda's daughter. I'm a retired Buffalo cop."

Dr. Taylor held open a swinging door. "This way." She led us into the unit. "I'm only allowing you five minutes right now. But soon I'll let one of you stay as long as you want."

A circular desk filled the space with rooms radiating like spokes. A handful of women and a few men seemed busy, each doing their own task, at monitors, with clipboards, trays of vials, stethoscopes slung around the necks of older staff, younger people with iPads.

Suddenly Sherilyn's grip tightened and she yanked me toward a room. She let out a cry when she saw the little form in the bed. Too many machines, a tube down her tiny throat, her face bloated and pale.

Sherilyn let go of my hand and raced to the bed. She leaned over and spoke with strength, like the fierce mother she was. "Hi little Kaycee, girl. Mommy's here. You need to try real hard to get better. Okay? 'Cause me and Daddy need you to come home and play with Cheyenne and Jackson. We need you to make our family perfect."

There wasn't a note of fear or anguish in her tone. She talked for the five minutes we were allotted. Dr. Taylor returned and coaxed Sherilyn out of the room.

When she turned to me, she looked shocked. "Are you okay?"

"That's the question of the day. No, she's not okay." Frank's derisive laugh helped motivate me.

"Sh-sure."

Dr. Taylor eyed me and I rallied further. "Hospitals. You know."

Frank said, *"It's not hospitals, it's dying children."*

Sherilyn took my hand again. "You haven't moved from the doorway and you're so pale. Are you going to be sick?"

A surge of energy bolted from our connected hands. "I'm here for you. Not the other way around."

It's the least I could do for now. Kaycee hadn't wandered away from the house on her own and ended up in a wash with the rattler I knew lived there. Someone inside me knew what happened.

They weren't talking to me. My fingers stroked the smooth tile in my pocket. I didn't need them or anyone else to tell me this was my fault. It was all connected and I was the only one who could figure it out.

Donnie burst through the emergency room doors. Amid Sherilyn's sobs, she let him know what had happened. He was allowed to take a turn with Kaycee.

With Dr. Taylor shepherding us out of the unit, Sherilyn slipped her arm around my waist, making me drape mine over her shoulder. She tucked into me. "Because of you I could be strong for Kaycee. You saved us both."

Or killed you.

32

I had a short time to walk the river path before my appointment with Tara. I held my phone to my ear and let Frank have his say. It relieved pressure from my head and the tingling in my hands subsided.

Settled on Tara's sofa, I unclenched my fists and spread my hands on my thighs. I told her about Kaycee.

"Why do you think Kaycee's accident is your fault? You weren't babysitting her. You didn't entice her into the desert. And you certainly didn't put her in the way of the rattlesnake."

You know.

You saw.

Your fault.

The voices hadn't spoken in a session for months. I didn't welcome their presence now. "It's more a feeling. Like I should have noticed something I didn't. Is it possible I've gone from hearing voices to having a personality that takes over? Someone doing things I don't know about?"

She considered this. "I suppose if you suffer another trauma it's possible. Not likely."

"What about Mother's Day. What if I think I've done okay

and really, I suppressed my emotions and it's coming out in another personality?"

Tara frowned at me. "Do you feel on the edge? I'm not getting that from you."

We talked about Kaycee and my worry over taking on a new psychosis, and by the way Tara circled, I knew she wanted to convince me of my paranoia regarding the accident. I held back telling her about Cali.

"Do you think with Mother's Day you might be stirred up and somehow reliving the guilt you feel from four years ago?"

"No." Except, maybe that was true. "This is new." Again, I avoided telling her about the necklace and hair bow, the Hot Tamales. It sounded like a crazy person attaching meaning to random incidences.

I fidgeted. "Can we do the memory work now?"

Tara considered me in silence. "I advise against it. Let's put it on hold for a week or so, give you time to rest."

Time was running out and if my memories could somehow help find Cali, I needed to push on. I folded my arms and met Tara's kind eyes. "You can walk me through it here in your office, or I can get there alone, by my pool. But I'm going to finish this today."

That drew a concerned reaction. She knew the temptation of the pool. "That's not a good idea."

We stared at each other for thirty seconds before she must have sensed my resolve. "Okay. But I will stop you if I think you've gone further than I think you can handle today."

I closed my eyes and listened to her calm voice walk me back to the gate of the Boneyard.

"Remember the concept of then and now. You can come back whenever you need." She let me go with her invitation. "Tell me where you are."

"Lilacs clog the bushes all though the junkyard. I'm almost

gagging on their sweetness. I used to love them but now they make me want to throw up. Mud puddles pock the ground and the dirt smells like death. It's cold deep in my bones. Clouds hang so low and heavy I hunch against the weight. Mom marches off in one direction and I follow two officers another way. Everyone is calling *her* name. I can't open my mouth. I'm so afraid."

I swallowed, my mouth too dry. Tara said I didn't need to do this today. I could stop. But one voice hammered at me. *"Remember."* I kept walking.

"Junkers heap on either side of the muddy path. Deep green grass and saplings sprout from between rusted heaps of metal. Everything is damp. The light is dim even though it's probably the middle of the day."

Every muscle tensed and I reminded myself I sat on Tara's couch in Tucson. The sun blazed outside. Now is not then.

"Someone yells. 'Here!' It's a subdued tone. I can't breathe because I know what it means. Still, I race after the two officers in front of me."

I didn't want to see this. Voices begged me to stop. But we all had to face it. Cali needed us.

"Scrubby trees and purple laden lilacs keep the ground shaded so more mud than grass covers the ground. I probably scream, I don't know. I want to look away but I can't. I should go to her, but I'm paralyzed. Her pink skin, so perfect three days ago is scraped and bloodied, mud smeared, purple bruises staining skin I'd slathered in sun screen all her short life. Blonde hair, always so beautiful, is dull with mud and blood, patches ripped from her scalp. But her face. Oh God, her face. Nothing like an angel in sleep. Her bulging, glassy eyes, settled in swollen flesh, mouth open as if in a scream. Purple bruises ringing her neck. Her toenails, the paint neat and unmarred from the pedicure we'd done together not even a week ago."

I paused to control my sobs, and worried Tara would stop me. She didn't, so I returned to the junk yard.

"He'd strangled her, obviously. A murder of rage and violence at the end of three days of Hell. The mist is turning to light rain, falling on her, but not washing her clean. Drops hitting her eyes and she doesn't blink."

Again, I had to stop. But the pause was brief.

"I suppose the other searchers are gathering. I don't know because everyone is screaming inside me. I haven't met Frank before but he's suddenly there, yelling at me to reach my hand to the car beside me. It's the only thing that makes sense and my fingers close around the steel jaguar leaping from the hood. I wrench it loose to the deafening roar in my head. It must have been there decades to make it possible for me to break off."

I panted and hesitated. *Now is not then.*

"It's cold in my palm but burns at the same time. The pain as it rips open my chest isn't enough to ease the agony. It will never be enough. But I try again and again. The blood flows until my hand is too sticky and Mom's arms hold me like steel bands"

All that's left was for me to scream my rage.

My child.

My life.

Only slivers of ice remained, condensation dripping on the coaster, the lemon slice wedged at the bottom of the glass. The yellow and black hair ribbon and the silver necklace seemed to jeer at me from the pine surface as I lapped the table.

I'd been at this through the predawn when I'd awakened after only a few hours. Unable to sleep, I spoke to the voices, trying to find the one who knew. The message like a bee sting, *remember, remember, remember.*

When I'd called, the hospital had given me the vague information there was no change in Kaycee's condition. I wanted to know more but was reluctant to call Sherilyn and disturb her.

The snake bite and Cali missing. They had to be connected. Somewhere, someone inside me knew. Until I could sift to that voice, I needed to work another way.

I waited until the business day started and I could call Rafe without seeming like a hysterical lunatic.

Frank kept up a steady tirade, biting, snarling, keeping me on the defensive. *"You know what's going on here."*

The others weighed in from time to time and the Chorus

chimed in at about half volume. But mostly, I talked with Frank. "There's got to be an explanation."

"The explanation is that he's killing girls and it's your fault. Just like the last time."

Around the table again. The ribbon. The necklace. I couldn't stop the memory, like a rerun of the worst horror film.

Gray drizzle. Sickening lilacs. Pink skin, scraped raw with mud.

The doorbell jerked me from the scene. Heart beating at twice normal and with a roar in my head, I slipped toward the window along the porch and peered through the slats of the blinds.

"What does he want? Don't let him in?" Whispers and shouts.

I blinked to silence the whole lot. Or at least lower their noise to the background.

I opened the door to Rafe in his uniform. He wasn't happy.

"Damn it, Jamie. What are you thinking?" He pushed inside before I had a chance to step onto the porch.

I didn't back up enough to let him past the entryway. I could pretend I didn't know what he meant but there didn't seem to be much point to that. "Cali's missing. And you don't seem interested in finding her. I had to do something."

He set his jaw as stared at me. "We got another call from Jim Thompson. I can't cover your butt if you keep this up."

There was one more play to make. The gray sedan. "I need you to look up a license plate number." I closed my eyes and called Digit from among the voices. I dictated the number to Rafe.

He didn't write it down, but looked over my shoulder and his gaze found my dining room table with the two objects there like a macabre centerpiece. He shook his head. "It's like you're obsessed with proving your instincts are right."

"It's not my instincts. It's experience."

"What experience?"

Frank shouted at me to hurt Rafe. Maggie's soft voice floated to me. *"Tell him, Dear. He can help."*

I shut my mouth and stomped into the living room.

Rafe followed. "It's hotter than hell in here. Why don't you have the a/c on?"

I'd opened the French door in back and the kitchen window in the cool of the night and hadn't thought about it since. Now I noticed the sweat soaking my T-shirt. "I like it hot."

"You're obsessing. That's not good."

"You don't know what's good for me."

He wiped at his moist forehead. "You're right. I'm sorry."

An earlier version of me would have shut the door and turned on the air, would offer him a cool drink. "You slapped my hand for contacting Megan Thompson. I apologize and promise not to do it again. You can write that in your report. Now will you check on that plate?"

He raised his eyebrows. "That's it?"

If wishes came true. "What do you want from me?"

Without invitation, he sauntered past me and dropped onto the couch. "I want to know you. Tell me what you're hiding. Why you can't let the cops deal with Cali?"

He sat inches away from the hoodie. The Chorus sounded like a New York traffic jam. It took me a moment to decide to tell him more. "The details of this case are similar to one I worked a few years ago."

He rested his arm on top of the hoodie and I nearly cried out as if he'd slapped me. If he thought I acted strangely standing in the middle of my living room staring at him, he didn't show it. "Tell me how this is like that case."

He must have noticed the lumpiness underneath his arm. Without seeming too interested in the sweatshirt, he picked it up.

It was as if he seared me with a white-hot iron. I leaped forward and jerked the hoodie from his grasp. He flinched and the chuckle I tried for stuck in my throat like a gag. I took a couple of mincing steps toward the dining room. "Sorry. I shouldn't leave my stuff laying around like that. If I'd known you were coming over, I'd have cleaned up a bit."

He stood and followed me, making a show of inspecting my house. "Cleaned up? This is like a museum. No dust, everything in place." He nodded at the table. "Except these, of course."

I held the hoodie close and didn't try to talk.

Rafe approached me in that quiet, powerful way of his. Without touching me, he made me feel warm in a protective embrace. "Tell me."

Frank exploded. *"Don't trust him."*

Rafe's serene aura worked on me. Not even Tara made me feel this safe. I met his gaze and held it for several beats, searching, probing, looking for the lie.

With a sigh of surrender, I began. "A missing girl in Buffalo. She was gone for three days before they found a clue. A ponytail elastic with hair. Blonde."

"The missing girl was a blonde, like Cali?"

He couldn't know that each word, each memory, every single thought, sliced like a butcher knife through my flesh. I nodded. "It was in an abandoned car by a junk yard. So we searched."

Rafe shook his head. "Criminals can be so stupid. Leaving such obvious clues."

Cement blocks pressed on my chest, more pain. "Oh, he left it on purpose. He wanted us to find it."

Rafe caught the starkness of my tone. He didn't say anything.

"We found the girl's necklace on a path toward the middle of the yard." That's what I said, but my body felt and saw the mud.

Rafe's eyes shifted to the necklace on the table, then back to me.

"We discovered the body after that."

After the one last clue, of course. I hugged the sweatshirt. Finding a body sounded antiseptic, neat and tidy. Not like what I saw every night and prayed to forget.

Frank had taken over then, not only my head, but my body. Not soon enough.

Rafe whispered and I almost didn't hear because of the others. "I'm sorry."

It was the right thing to say to an officer who'd failed. It would never be enough, but it was all he had to give.

I blinked dry eyes and cleared my throat. "Someone confessed. He was convicted and died in jail."

He studied me and then the objects on the table. "Where did these come from?"

I watched him to judge his reaction. "They're Cali's. The killer left them for me to find."

That impassive face. But he was working on everything I'd said and putting it together. "You're telling me the confession was false?"

I nodded.

"And you think he tracked you here and is targeting you with Cali's disappearance?"

Suddenly weak, I plopped into a dining chair. "That's exactly what I think."

He studied me for several seconds. "After Jim Thompson called me this morning, I made a call of my own."

My stomach contracted.

"I called your old station in Buffalo."

I quit breathing and waited for the sky to fall.

34

Someone told him all about me. They'd probably coughed up the gory details. Why had he bothered listening to my story?

Rafe gave me that indiscernible face. Probably assessing the level of my sanity. "You must have been a pretty big deal there. Everyone seemed to know you."

He toyed with me like a cat with a cockroach. "I was there a long time."

That face of his, so carefully stripped of emotion. "I got shunted uphill pretty quickly and landed on the sheriff's desk."

Even in my over-heated house a chill spiked my skin. "Must have been a slow day."

His eyes zeroed in on me. "Maybe, but she didn't waste much time. Told me you were an exemplary officer, retired with honors and full benefits, no smirch on your record. And she hung up."

That sounded like Mom, down to the term "exemplary." Guess no one had mentioned that Sheriff Amanda Carmichael was my mother. I had my father's last name, so Rafe probably hadn't made the connection. That's one in our favor. High-five,

Mom. I changed the subject. "That's all interesting, but we need to find Cali Shaw."

The kindness and heart-stopping masculine strength in Rafe's face showed no reaction as he studied me. His dark eyes snapped with intelligence. It wouldn't be long before he figured out he should put distance between us. Rafe probably heard the low hum of the refrigerator, maybe a bird in the back yard. For me, Frank grumbled about weak-assed pansies in uniform, the Chorus chattered about how long it was taking him to flee, Maggie soothed. Peanut kept her silence, waiting for me to ask her.

"Okay." Rafe dipped his head toward the front door.

"Okay?"

He looked at the ribbon and the necklace, then started for the door. "Let's go talk to Megan. See if we can find out where Cali is."

He intended to help me? "She'll be at school."

He let a smidgeon of disgust into his voice. "Jim Thompson said until you apologize or are in custody, he's keeping Megan at home." When I didn't jump up, he glanced over his shoulder. "You know where she lives, right?"

Stopping long enough to scoop the necklace and bow into a drawer, and to place the hoodie back on the couch, I hurried after Rafe and lock the front door.

I called the hospital again and got the same bland non-information of no change. While he drove, I told Rafe about Kaycee. I gave him the license plate number again. "I have no reason to think it, but I think someone in that car might be responsible for Kaycee's accident."

He kept his eyes on the road and after a minute, he pulled his notebook and pen from his pocket and handed it to me. "Write the number down and I'll run it later."

We got caught in morning traffic. Even though Rafe knew

the backroads through Tucson, as cops always do, it seemed we cruised past twenty grade schools, with their hovering parents dropping their kids off in regulated lines, snarling the commute. Do what you can, parents, have your child escorted from your car to the school doors. That isn't where danger lurks.

We crossed under I-10, leaving the older, seedier parts of town and entered into the realm of landscaped neighborhoods and upscale shopping centers. Towering palm trees, wide sidewalks, a spit and shine my side of town didn't try to accomplish. I directed Rafe to the golf course and into the eucalyptus-shaded subdivision. Though the temperature climbed to the eighties, here, the well-toned seemed to wrestle it into feeling ten degrees cooler.

We pulled up in front of the door with the pink-potted entryway. My stomach soured at the sight of Megan's shiny Toyota parked in front of the closed garage door. So much handed to her and she grabbed more, scorching everything in her path.

I checked my phone for messages. Would Sherilyn think to call me if Kaycee's condition changed?

Rafe looked at me with concern. "You're going to play nice here, right? Let me do the talking."

Whispering and jeering continued in the background.

I climbed out, not committing to anything.

Rafe hurried around the hood to join me, walking a half-step ahead. He rang the doorbell. For all the fancy flourishes of old-growth plantings and well-kept common space, this house had the flimsy desert construction of my neighborhood. A TV vibrated with the overly cheerful strains of a commercial and feet thudded down the stairs. In a short time, the door whisked open and Megan stood in front of us in a pink sundress so short walking quickly would expose her Victoria's Secret. She'd learned nothing about throwing open her door without checking. I wanted to grab her shoulders and shake her, make her understand how her stupid and careless habits could get her killed.

Her head jerked to the left, as if checking to see if someone else witnessed her. She thrust her hip out and set her shoulders with deliberate attitude. "I can't believe you came here again."

The overpowering scent of rose potpourri or the giant Yankee Candles sold in every mall across the country, came rushing out on cooled air.

Rafe merely twitched his shoulder to warn me against answering. He tucked away his charm and was all stony cop. "We need to talk to your friend, Cali. She's not answering her phone. Where is she?"

As if against her will, she side-eyed to the left again. "I'm not Google."

Rafe nodded. "And I'm not fooling around. I can cite you for destruction of property, or you can cooperate."

She folded her arms. "Go ahead. Daddy might have something to say about that."

"I'm sure he will. He'll also be interested to hear about your latest antics. My guess is our story isn't the same as yours."

A door opened and closed inside the house to our left. "Megan?"

The girl straightened and her arms dropped to her sides. The sneer quickly morphed into a wide-eyed look of concern.

Mrs. Thompson rounded the corner to see me and Rafe outside the door. Mama Bear snarled and advanced without hesitation. "Unless this cop is here to witness your apology to my daughter, you'd better march yourself off my property."

I tensed against the temptation to tell Mrs. Thompson about her despicable darling daughter.

Rafe bristled but held himself with his usual dignity. "Hello, Mrs. Thompson. We're here because we need to do a wellness check on Cali Shaw. There's no answer at the address the school has on file and the cell number for Cali's mother, a Kandy Shaw, says it's an invalid number. We thought Megan might have some information."

Rafe had been investigating. He believed me.

Mrs. Thompson, stuffed into her paisley capris, sweat ringing her underarms, pulled off one gardening glove. "I'm not surprised you can't get in touch with Kandy. That woman is so irresponsible she probably quit making payments and had to get a new number."

"Do you happen to have a new number for her?"

Mrs. Thompson scowled in annoyance. "I have a number. Who knows if it's valid. And let me tell you, I had to do battle royal to get it from her. She wasn't about to cough it up until I told her Cali simply could not stay over a long weekend until I had a working number. You know, Kandy wouldn't give up a chance to go away with some man. Always a different one, mind you. But she seems to find them and get them to take her on vacations. She leaves that poor girl with anybody who will have her."

I couldn't look at her because her sanctimonious expression would make it impossible to ignore the calls for violence raging inside me.

Rafe didn't shout at her to get the damned phone number, as we all wanted to do. She peeled off a glove. "Wait a minute. I'll have to get my phone."

With Mrs. Thompson as witness, Rafe asked Megan, "When was the last time you saw Cali?"

Mrs. Thompson turned that irritated face on Megan.

Megan's voice rose an octave to sound more like a little girl. She gave her mother a worried look. "I'm not supposed to hang out with Cali so I only see her at practice. And since we're suspended, I haven't been."

Mrs. Thompson snapped at her. "Oh for heaven's sake." She stomped off to get her phone.

Megan followed her mother's retreat with a look of contempt she then turned on us. She stuck out her hip again and she did a little wag with her neck, like a stiff version of an inner-city tough. "I talked to Cali this morning. She's got, like, better things to do than hang around school. She got cut from the squad because she missed practice after we were suspended, and it's not like her mother makes her go to class. So, you're wasting your time. She's fine."

Rafe nodded. "You're probably right."

She rolled her eyes at his patronizing tone.

Mrs. Thompson returned with her phone. With slightly more civility than Megan, she gave Rafe the number. "Cali's got no discipline and no role model for a mother. I tried to help her out when she was younger. I really did. But why would she listen to me? I'm a drudge, with rules and curfews." She paused to let her wisdom soak in. "Is that it? Because I don't want to see you around here anymore. Is that understood?"

Rafe's wide, white grin told her how ridiculous it sounded to give ultimatums to a cop.

She managed to look cowed and angry at the same time and added more muscle than she needed to shut the front door before we'd said good bye.

I was already in the car with my door closed before Rafe eased behind the wheel. "Call her now," I said.

He frowned. "Let's go back to the station and do it."

I tapped the dash with my open palm. "Now. Or give me the number and I'll call."

He fished his phone from his pocket. "I'll do it."

Rafe ran his finger down his notes to highlight the number and dialed with his thumb. That time it rang three times before a laughing woman blasted on with, "Speak to me!"

"Ms. Shaw?" Rafe held the phone slightly from his face so I could hear her response.

The laughter died. This woman knew authority when she heard it. She had the low, scorched voice of a life-long smoker. "Kandy. Yes."

"This is Officer Grijalva of the Tucson Police Department. I'm calling in regard to your daughter, Cali."

Her first response was irritation. "What's she done now?"

The corner of Rafe's mouth twitched, maybe with the same disgust I felt. "She and some friends vandalized a residence and we're trying to locate her."

Kandy's scratchy voice sounded bitter. "Vandalized. You mean like egging or keying a car or something?"

"Something like that."

"Christ. Is that all? You don't have real criminals to worry about you gotta convict kids for harmless pranks?"

Rafe hardened his tone. "The issue, Ms. Shaw, is that we can't locate your daughter."

She laughed and it turned into a cough. "Good for her."

"Where are you, Ms. Shaw?"

A lighter flicked and she inhaled. "Right now I'm sitting on a balcony in Cancun drinking a mai tai. And if I wasn't talking to you, I'd be having the time of my life."

"That bitch should burn in Hell," Frank said.

Rafe's mouth twitched again, the only sign of his impatience. "We checked out your residence and no one was there, nor was her car anywhere around the neighborhood. Can you tell me where Cali is staying while you're having the time of your life?"

She inhaled again, taking her time answering. "I don't know who told you she's home, but I wouldn't leave a sixteen-year-old alone for a week. What kind of mother do you think I am?"

"The kind who should be fed to hungry dogs," Frank said.

"We tried to reach her by phone and didn't get an answer. You can see why we're concerned."

An inhale. "Don't worry yourself on her account. She's plenty capable, believe me. I spoke to her this morning. She lets her messages sit in her inbox and it fills up, that way, she can screen her calls and decide who to answer and you can't leave a message. It's an old trick. She's fine."

Rafe stared out the windshield. "I'd like to verify that myself. Can you tell me where she's staying?"

"Jesus. You can't mind your own business? She's with my mother. In Mesa. I'll give you her number." Kandy rattled off a number and I scrambled to write it in Rafe's notebook. "She goes there when I travel."

"Thank you, Ms. Shaw. I assume if you see my number on an incoming call, you'll take it,"

Her long exhale made me imagine her blowing cigarette smoke in Rafe's face. "Of course, Officer."

He disconnected and started dialing the number I'd written.

I stated the obvious. "She's lying."

He nodded. "Probably."

"I've never understood parents who cover for their kids. Especially when they could be in danger."

Rafe held the phone to his ear. "Sometimes, like with Mrs. Thompson, they think they're protecting their kid. Other times, like Cali's mother, they want to be the cool mom. The best friend."

A memory scorched me.

The scream of the blow dryer drowns out the hideous indie band that is her current favorite. My roots beg for mercy as she pulls and smooths my shoulder-length hair. She snaps off the dryer and steps back, eyeing me in the mirror. "You should wear your hair like this all the time. You look so hot."

I frown at her, my nerves stretched tight and my stomach swirling. "Hot is not a word for a woman my age.

She shoves my shoulder. "Stop that. You're not that old. Most of my friends tell me how cool you are and Troy called you a MILF, an image I'll never get out of my head."

"Thanks for sharing, now I'll feel slimy when he's around."

She bends over and hugs me, framing us together in the mirror. Her silky blonde hair falls over my shoulders, her blue eyes bright and as excited as mine. "I'm kind of glad I got Dad's hair and eyes, but thanks for the good bone structure."

I can't help laughing. "You sound like your grandmother."

She jumps up and bounds for my closet. "Thanks. I was going for that Queen Amanda thing. I love that she's set the standard for us strong, kick-ass women."

I am grateful that I'm not the kind of mother I'd had. Mom never needed my advice on anything, certainly not hair and makeup. She didn't raise me to have the girlfriends who giggled over boys and experimented with the latest fashion trends at slumber parties. For Mom and me, life was a series of goals set, met, and moving on.

But never for *us*. We would have been friends.

The phone connected and Rafe spoke. "Mrs. Shaw?"

An angry woman responded, "No. That's my daughter. If she owes you money you'll have to get it from her. I'm not responsible for her debts."

"Nothing like that." He introduced himself and explained he was performing a wellness check on Cali, who was supposedly staying with her.

She paused, then in the same harsh tone said, "If Kandy said Cali is here, why don't you believe her? Cali is here. She's been here for a week."

They exchanged a few more words but Rafe couldn't get anything else from her and hung up.

I slapped the seat between us. "That's an obvious lie. Cali was at the ball field four days ago."

He nodded and didn't say anything for a minute. "Is that the last place anyone saw her?"

She'd slipped into the gray sedan, a memory that jolted me. The voices wouldn't connect those dots. "As far as I know. "He started the engine.

35

We pulled out of the fancy neighborhood and Rafe pointed us south.

"Where are we going?"

He concentrated on the late afternoon congestion. "Maybe someone at the park saw the girls and can help us find the man they were talking to."

"The guy is holed up somewhere with the little blonde, banging —" Frank said.

I muttered for him to shut up, then winced, afraid Rafe heard. The constant crackle and static of the radio might have masked my utterance because Rafe showed no reaction.

"You can't hide your crazy from him forever."

I called the hospital again. The same young male voice answered as the previous two times and he was clearly annoyed to have to tell me no change, again. There had to be some change by now, but I wasn't sure if I could handle what that might be.

We didn't talk for the next twenty minutes in the stop and go of the street lights. Since retirement, I didn't miss the frustration of having to get someplace and a rush of humanity clogging my way. These days, my only destinations were wherever the Rangers sent me and my time with Tara. I easily managed that by leaving extra early to avoid the stress of being late. Trying to get to the park now felt like wading through tar.

We finally battled our way through downtown and east to the park. If the population had changed or shifted from yesterday, an outsider like me wouldn't notice. It seemed the same collection of weather-worn men and a few women, lounged around in their colorless clothes. Their grime and defeated air made them look nearly indistinguishable from each other.. Rafe parked in the lot and we climbed out.

Technically, the hottest part of the day was mid-afternoon, but it always felt to me the real burn arrived an hour or two before sunset. The rays seemed to laser into my skin and the air felt too still to breathe. In another month, we'd be in the worst of it, where the wise stayed indoors from nine or ten in the morning until four or five in the afternoon. By Buffalo standards, today felt like dead of summer, Popsicle in the shade, long afternoon nap weather. For Tucson, it was spring.

I scanned the nearest clump of homeless. Four men, ranging in age from young adult to seasoned graybeard. One lay with his head on a backpack, one stood and fidgeted from foot to foot, talking in rapid fire to a drowsy man with a blank face. Another guy, hair like sun-bleached steel wool squatted next to a grocery cart filled with dusty belongings. No Shax or the perv who'd talked to the cheerleaders.

Rafe hadn't joined me so I turned to see what held him up. He backed from the trunk of his car with a case of bottled water. "Want to help me here?"

I rushed to him and took his load so he could grab another case. He slammed the trunk closed. "Come on."

With the peace offering, we approached four different gatherings of people. At least one person in each group knew Rafe by name. He passed out water and asked them if they knew Shax. Most of them did. Had they noticed a man about thirty, six feet tall, with dark hair, talking to girls at the fence between the ball field and the park? None of them had anything useful to pass along.

The sun slipped behind the Tucson Mountains that stood between the heart of town and where I lived, on the western edge. Long shadows spread from the palm trees scattered around the park.

"There," I said and pointed toward the slight figure of Shax ambling toward the group at one of the picnic tables. I hurried to intercept him and Rafe kept up with me.

When he saw me, Shax pulled up short. He didn't haul around a pack or push a cart. He wore different, if not equally shabby, clothes than he'd had on the other day. More proof he had a place to live off the street.

He met me with a sickening smile of diseased teeth. "Jamie, Jamie, sweet desert flower."

Rafe narrowed his eyes at Shax.

The Chorus hummed and groaned.

Knows your name.

Knows your name.

Dangerous.

"You remember me from a few days ago?" I asked gently. Setting him off again wouldn't be good.

He scratched at his tattooed arms. The tendrils of vines snaked up and down through the cars, tails, eyes, claws, vehicles lost in the green leaves. The plane tattoo looked raw. "Jamie Butler. Good cop. Doing your job."

"That's right."

Rafe and I approached him slowly and he waited, like a skittish stray dog who might bolt if we spooked him.

The light of the day faded and we stood in growing gloom. "Do you remember the afternoon we met?"

That damaged grin brightened. "I do. You wore your uniform. Like it was your skin. Your skin. Yes. And you got mad. Very mad. Wanting to take care of kids. At the end of the day, always protecting children."

"Yes. Those three girls. The tall blonde one and the others with darker hair. Remember them?"

He closed his mouth and nodded, eyes round like marbles. Was he high? Or had his brain mangled reality, making it hard for him to navigate society? "The pretty girls in the bumble bee dresses."

"Good." I leaned toward him a little, getting a whiff of stale garbage. "Do you remember who they were talking to?"

He grinned again, like a little kid winning a prize. "Me!" His face clouded. "They were mean. Said awful things to me. They got all the money and the pretty, pretty faces and all that sweet honey. They smelled like you want to eat them, but they taste like spoiled cabbage."

I tried to bring him back. "But there was someone else there, too. Do you remember who that was?"

He looked confused. "They were too good to have a conversation with me. Not like you. You helped me."

That gave me another opening. "How is Petunia?"

Rafe hadn't said anything but he watched our exchange with intensity.

Shax's forehead furrowed. "Petunia?"

"Your dog. You lost your dog that day and wanted me to help you look for her."

He shook his head. "I don't have a dog. I don't have a yard to keep her in. Once I had a lot of things but someone took them from me. " His wistful expression deepened. "I even had a

Jaguar. I loved driving it fast. Loved that powerful cat springing ahead."

The image of the jaguar launching from the car hood made me gasp at the pain. Hot and burning my chest. I forced myself to see the park. Then and now.

Shax's loss sank into me. I didn't have anything to offer to make it feel better. Except knowing how it hurt. "I'm sorry."

He tilted his head and eyed me with an expression I couldn't identify, sort of a curious anger. "Do you know how it feels?"

Voices I had no names for whispered to me. *"Look at him. Remember. Remember."*

"I helped you that day. After those girls were talking to the dark-haired man by the fence. Think, can you remember that guy?"

He focused on the grass, now a dull gray in the twilight. His head popped up. "Not that day. You didn't help me in the day. It was at night. You came back. With the girl."

He was confused, so I tried to help him focus. "I was here the next day, at the baseball tournament."

He shook his head like a whirlwind. "No. No. No. Not when you wore your uniform. Not then. At night. You came here at night. You and the girl."

I gave Rafe a defeated look. This was going nowhere.

Rafe took over. "Tell me about that. Jamie helped you that night? How?"

Shax addressed me. "You saw me at the fence. Like in the day. At the fence watching the girls. I like to watch the girls. I don't touch them. I just watch."

Rafe prompted him. "And Jamie helped you?"

Now he looked at Rafe. "Yes. She did. I followed them across the park. They walked fast and I kept up with them. Just watching."

In the park that night? It must have been someone else. He was confused.

Now Shax smiled at me. "You gave me twenty dollars."

I leaned toward him, into his decaying stench. "That wasn't me. I wasn't at the ball park that night."

His eyes got that glassy gleam again. "Oh no. It was you. I remember the twenty dollars. I bought us all something. You were our angel. Twenty dollars. Food and...." He slapped his hand over his mouth and gave me a horrified look.

Rafe used that soft, commanding manner of his. "And what? What next?"

Shax shook his head and backed away. "I'm sorry," he said to me.

Rafe followed him one step. "Sorry for what?"

Shax spun away and ran.

I caught him within a couple of steps and grabbed his arm.

He screamed and tried to break free but Rafe took hold of him. They wrestled for several minutes, Shax crying and flailing, clearly terrified.

Finally, Rafe was able to calm him enough that he could let go.

Shax panted, his head down, not looking at either of us.

As gently as possible, I tried to reach him. "Shax? What are you sorry for?"

He didn't answer.

Rafe used a more commanding tone, though still kind. "We're not going to hurt you."

Shax raised his head toward Rafe and his eyes flicked to me, then quickly away. "I remembered why she gave me the money." He ducked his head as if I might take a swing. "She said I wasn't supposed to tell anyone about seeing her with the pretty girl."

36

Rafe didn't say anything as he maneuvered through the lighter traffic of early evening. The sun had disappeared but sent slashes of oranges and pinks to blend with the deepening purple of night falling over the desert.

My head was stuffed with voices. Concentrating on what to say to Rafe felt like rowing into the wind. "I wasn't at the park. I didn't see Cali after the afternoon at the game."

He didn't indicate he'd heard me and I wondered if I'd said it out loud or only in my mind.

We skirted Sentinel Peak, the mountain that looked over all of Tucson with an A of white rock, I assumed to celebrate the University of Arizona. Headlights wound up to the overlook, people enjoying the cool of the evening, while I wound tighter and tighter, trying to calm the raging in my head.

I couldn't stand the silence in the car. "Shax is not reliable. He's confused me with someone else."

Staring at the road, he said, "What's going on?"

Frank told me to grab the wheel and steer us off the road.

Rafe frowned at me, then turned his attention back to the road. "There. Right then. Where is it you go?"

Despite the scream of warning from the Chorus and Frank's violent urgings, I snapped back, "I don't know what you're talking about."

His face pinched in annoyance. "You're sure making it hard for me."

"I'm not asking anything from you."

"No, you don't ask anything from anyone, do you? You've got Pete, who wants to be friends and you shut her down. She says you aren't buddies with anyone else in the Rangers and no one there seems to know anything about you. Why is that?"

"Why make friends when they'll disappear as soon as they find out about you?"

Annoyance seeped into the fine lines around his eyes. "I ask you a question and it's like you have to filter your answer. You don't have to be so careful. Just talk to me."

Frank shouted at me. *"Don't tell him!"*

He's bad.

Don't trust him.

He wants to kill you.

Silently I told The Three: I'm Jamie Butler. I'm Amanda's daughter. I'm a retired Buffalo cop. I live in Tucson.

His frown told me I'd taken too long to answer. I spat my words at him out of embarrassment. "Why should I talk to you when you don't believe me?"

His sigh carried his frustration. "About what?"

My head pounded. "Cali. She's been kidnapped and maybe Shax—"

He put his hand up. "Stop it. You and I both know Cali isn't missing. She's been in touch with her mother and Megan. She's not staying with her grandmother, that's obvious. She's probably shacked up with her boyfriend."

"I'm not making this up."

"Tell me why you're doing this? Is it because you're lonely and want attention?"

"You can't believe what Shax said."

He shook his head. "I don't believe you went back to the park and ran off with Cali, no. But what is going on with you?"

The war raged inside my head.

I closed my eyes and silently told the voices to shut up. They lowered the volume enough I could speak calmly. "Tomorrow we should go to the school early and talk to more of Cali's friends. Megan is too good at lying and others won't be that skilled."

Rafe's jaw hardened. "No. This is it."

"But—"

Those dark eyes dripped sadness. "I thought we could be friends."

"Why? What about me says I need or want friends?"

"My God. First of all, even if it's sexist, you are an attractive woman. But after that, you're caring and kind and even with all your caution when you talk, it's obvious you're smart. I'll bet somewhere inside of you, if you'd quit trying so hard to hide it, you have a sense of humor."

"BULLSHIT," Frank yelled.

There was a woman like that once. She never had a lot of friends because she was different. But she had a best friend who didn't mind her occasional distance because it didn't happen often. She fell in love and even if he didn't know about the crowd inside her, he accepted her and they laughed, had adventures, made a life and a child together. The wonder of that baby and the joy as she grew, brought laughter and vitality, a race into each new day to discover what abundance it had in store.

That woman lost everything bit by bit. The last blow stripped the fire from her and left her like snow-covered silt.

I sounded like still water. "You're not going to look for Cali?"

"No, Jamie. I'm done."

Rafe remained silent as we left the congestion of restaurants and stores and sailed past the neighborhoods, finally to the last street on the edge of the desert. The blinker sounded like thunder as he made a left. No streetlights disrupted the darkness and only scant house-lights pocked the night. A vote of the HOA kept our neighborhood designated as a Dark Sky area, the better for star gazers. The deep cover of night usually comforted me. Free of the glare of prying eyes or a reality too harsh to bare.

I couldn't wait to flee into the darkness and away from Rafe and his judgement. But my fingers on the handle squeezed and wouldn't open the door. Was it better to stay with Rafe or face this new unknown?

A sparkling silver Nissan Altima took up my driveway. Who?

The Chorus ratcheted up, whispering and questioning. I pushed on Rafe's door and struggled to stand, eyes riveted to the Nissan.

Rafe sped away as soon as the door clicked shut and I wallowed in a growing sense of doom. I didn't have long to wait before the mystery was solved.

My front door opened and Mom stepped out on the porch.

37

"What a surprise!" Did I play delight correctly? Would it convince her?

She strode down the walk, face set in a stiff smile. "I can't get a straight answer from you. If I have to fly all the way out here, then that's what I'll do."

When she was close enough, I threw my arms around her. "It's great to see you." And it was. Two years since we'd been face to face. She'd brought me here, into the healing sunshine, away from the pain and searing memories, and then she'd climbed on a plane and flown out of my physical world.

Now she was standing here and her embrace felt somehow weak. I pulled back. "Are you okay?"

Dark bags hung under her eyes and her skin had a pasty look. "It's this whole election. I'm putting out fires right and left, trying to keep the morale up when we've got the special investigator shoveling crap and sticking her nose into everything. And I've been worrying about you."

It's all your fault.

You only cause her problems.

Stab your eyes with the car key.

"I'm sorry. I didn't mean to make you worry. But you'll see, I'm fine." I wouldn't tell her about Cali. She didn't need more to worry her.

"We'll see how fine you are. I know you like the sunshine and warmth down here, but it might not be what's best for you. If you aren't doing well, I'll have to move you back." Mom gave me a tired smile. "Don't look so upset. It would be nice to have you closer."

Forest Hill.

Cold. White.

Shackles under the bed.

I couldn't say anything but she didn't seem to notice.

Mom strode to the front door. "Why don't you come inside? I've been here all afternoon so I started dinner."

I glanced across the street to see lights but no vehicles in the driveway. Was Kaycee okay? Where were Mrs. Dempsey and the kids?

I hurried inside the house. The nauseating smell of hamburger frying met me. Mom stood at the breakfast bar chopping onions. She glanced at me and back to her knife. "I had to run to the grocery store. You didn't have anything except the dregs from a farmer's market. I'm making goulash."

I wanted to say something about goulash being her specialty. But Frank tried to force me to say that, of course, she would make her lousy goulash because it was the only meal she could manage.

I clamped my hands over my ears and pulled them away quickly before Mom noticed.

"I don't know why you insisted on this place at the edge of the known universe. The store is so far away."

"The knife is within reach." Frank said.

I answered him. "She's here to help."

Mom's head popped up. "What?"

"Nothing." Walking took all my concentration with Mom watching me. "I think I'll go sit out back and relax a minute. I had a long day."

She didn't say anything while I filled a glass with ice water and a lemon slice. The crowd in my head kept at me. If I could make it to sit by the side of the pool and speak with Frank, the others might fade. Then he could tell me where Cali was.

"...call Tara."

The last words spiked through the noise. I whirled around. "I'm sorry. What did you say?"

"You're pale and talking to yourself. Honey, you're not well. I'm going to call Tara and see if I can take you in immediately."

"No!" I hadn't meant to shout.

She whipped her head back as if I'd struck her. "I really think it's best."

"Please. I'm sorry I yelled. But I'm trying to cope on my own. Can you let me work it out?" My grip on the cold water glass felt like a lifeline.

She studied me. "Clearly, you're upset. Maybe if you take a pill."

I wrenched the door and walked outside. "I know how to take care of myself."

She followed me. "By yourself? What about the cop who dropped you off? Is he the one you went for drinks with the other day?"

I understood her concern for me. In a weird way, it paralleled Frank. But both could be destructive if I let them.

Mom usually kept her temper better, but this election cycle must be taking its toll because she bristled. "I didn't spend thousands of dollars on doctors and hospitals and countless hours supporting and comforting you to see you throw it all away because a good-looking man charms you."

"Rafe is a nice person." Though after tonight, he wouldn't be a friend.

"Honey, you don't need cop friends. Their lifestyle, the hours, the drinking, the stories. It will draw you in. It's not good for you. It's why you shouldn't be an Arizona Ranger."

The low rumble of the Chorus distracted me and I concentrated on Mom's lips. "I like the Rangers. Makes me feel useful."

"There are other ways to be useful."

"But I'm trained for this kind of work."

"Of course. But it's obviously a strain. You look terrible. I'll bet you're not sleeping. And what about the voices? Are they back?"

"Lie," Frank told me, though he needn't have bothered.

"No voices," I said.

She folded her arms, clearly unconvinced. "You don't need to cover up to me. I'm here to help you."

"Okay, yes. I hear the voices. But it's not 'again.' It's still. I've heard voices my whole life, Mom."

She waved that off. "You haven't. Imaginary friends aren't the same as a psychotic break. Every child has made-up friends."

A spark of anger forced words. "Do they have made up mothers named Maggie?"

Her face dropped. "There's no need to be cruel. I was a working mother. I felt, and still do, that having a successful career was the best role model I could give you."

"I'm not complaining. You've showed me love, loyalty, and support my whole life. If I'd felt neglected or unloved, do you think I would have chosen the same path?"

Mom looked away, one of the few times I'd ever seen her doubt her choices. "Maybe I shouldn't have been so hard on you. I thought it was my job to help you succeed. But you never had the temperament to be a cop."

"I loved being a cop. And a mother." Oh God, I'd loved being a mother. "It wasn't my career that broke me. And being a cop didn't cause the voices. I've always heard them. I just lost the ability to manage them, and any reason to care."

Maggie's soft voice pushed through. *"That's not true, dear. I haven't always been with you."*

Peanut unexpectedly began to cry. Her plaintive sobs cut through me. I knew she wanted me to ask her why she cried. *I'm sorry. I can't.*

Mom shifted from foot to foot. "I know you don't want to hear this, but the voices are in your head. You indulge yourself when you treat them like separate entities."

I'd rarely discussed this with her and wasn't sure I wanted to now. "I know they are all part of me. But trying to ignore them or pretend I can make them go away doesn't work. The issue isn't hearing them, it's learning to live with them."

Mom took my hand and led me inside to the dining table. She pulled out a chair and motioned for me to sit.

"Before you get upset, just listen."

My heart thudded; I braced for whatever was coming.

"I was afraid you'd taken a bad turn. The fact that you've missed some appointments with Tara, and finding out from your company commander that you're temporarily suspended makes it clear you need to distance yourself from stress."

"You called Mitch? You had no right!"

Mom covered my hand with hers. "You're coming apart."

"I'm—"

"I've arranged for you to go to a spa in Palm Springs."

"NO!" Frank, the Chorus, and every voice screamed.

"Mom, I—"

"Just listen. It's not a sanitarium or hospital. It's a spa. There are some people who can help you if you need, but only if you require them. Other than that, you can relax and not worry about anything. Maybe read some novels, watch movies, eat great food, get massages. It'll be just what you need. If you don't improve, then we'll have to move you back up to Forest Hill."

I rubbed my temples and did my best to quiet Frank. "Okay. I'll take time off from the Rangers. But please, I'm not going to Palm Springs. I'm fine, honestly. Just trying to transition from meds to dealing with life on my own."

She sat at the table scrutinizing me. "If you're fine, as you say, why would a Raphael Grijalva be calling my office to check up on you?"

I fought to stay neutral. "It's nothing. I'm helping out with an investigation because of something I saw while on duty."

Her eyes narrowed. "What kind of investigation?"

"A missing girl."

She shifted into her sheriff mode. The one she'd perfected long before she rose through the ranks. The tone she used to keep me and Dad in line. "This is what is going to happen. You're going to resign from the Rangers. You don't need it. They obviously don't need you. I can't believe Tara allowed it in the first place. It is not healing."

If she heard the cursing in my mind, even as a veteran cop, she might be shocked. "The Rangers haven't—"

Her iron voice drowned me out. "Listen to me, if people start digging, they might discover why you retired early with full benefits."

Guilt.

"Is being a Ranger worth ruining your life? Worth me losing everything I've worked my whole life for?"

I couldn't answer for the screaming in my head.

"Think long and hard about this, Jamie. I only want what's best for you."

38

The doorbell burst like church bells, echoing in our silent standoff. After a second, I strode to the door and without looking out the blind, threw it open.

Sherilyn, in her cutoffs and tank top, eyes puffy and dark, hair like a dove's nest, launched herself into my arms and burst into tears.

Kaycee's dead.

Zoey's dead.

Cali's dead.

I wrapped my arms around Sherilyn and hardened myself. Someone needed to hold her up. I hadn't been able to go on when it had happened to me, but Sherilyn had two other children. They needed her. I would be a sponge, pull the pain into me, hold it for her. It didn't matter if I broke doing it. Cheyenne and Jackson needed a mother. No one depended on me.

Sherilyn sobbed and her knees buckled, causing her to lean on me to keep from falling. I didn't say anything and erected walls of brick and concrete to hold back my emotions. I wouldn't allow my mind to picture Kaycee. I concentrated on keeping my arms around Sherilyn, soaking up her tears.

Mom only suffered that scene for so long. She bustled to the front door and took hold of Sherilyn's bicep, pulling us apart with a soft touch. She used the same gentleness with me, as if either of us might dissolve in the harsh world. "What's going on?"

Sherilyn didn't acknowledge Mom. Her attention focused on me. She wiped at her eyes and shook her head. "I told Mrs. Dempsey I'd only be a second. I need to get back to my kids."

I placed a hand on Sherilyn's back. "I'm sure she'll understand. You need to take care of yourself."

Mom scowled at me and cast an irritated glance at Sherilyn.

Sherilyn's eyes filled again. "The best thing for me is to have my family all around."

I patted Sherilyn's back. "Is your mother on her way? Will family be gathering? What can we do to help?"

Sherilyn's tears spilled over and she gave me a watery smile. "You've already helped us more than we could ever repay."

Maybe I breathed, but all I felt was cold stone where my body should be.

"If you hadn't found her when you did, she'd have never made it." Sherilyn broke down in violent sobs again. Between the blubbering, she managed to say, "She is so pale and her little leg is as big as a rhinoceros, but she's home."

What was she saying? I repeated her words to myself. Pale. Swollen. She's home. She made it.

Like someone took a sledgehammer to me, I shattered into a million pieces. Without warning, tears spouted and my muscles turned from ice shards to living flesh. In a flash, I grabbed Sherilyn and whisked her from her feet in a hug like I'd only ever inflicted on one other person. "Thank God!"

I set Sherilyn down and we stepped apart, laughing and crying. Both of us babbling. I understood they'd struggled all night and into the day. It was touch and go, but around noon,

Kaycee finally started breathing regularly and her blood pressure returned to normal. The antivenom did its job. As soon as she was out of the woods, Donnie had to go back to work.

Fighting happy tears, I introduced Mom and Sherilyn and briefly explained about the snake bite.

Mom watched us with a strained smile and said, "That's wonderful she's recovering. I imagine you're anxious to get back to your children. Please don't hesitate to call if we can do anything for you."

Sherilyn nodded absently at Mom and turned back to me. "It's all because of you. I wouldn't have known what to do. You saved her."

Zoey's dead.

Cali's dead.

Your fault.

"She's going to be okay. Let's focus on that." I said it to the voices as much as to Sherilyn. They knew where the blame lay for Kaycee's brush with death. One voice repeated, *"Remember, remember."*

Sherilyn grabbed my hand. "I told you Kaycee knows stuff. She knew you were going to save her. You're meant to be part of our lives. I don't think we're done needing you." She hugged me quickly and bounced away, tears gone, her impish smile back. She winked at Mom. "I don't think she's done needing us, either."

Her flip flops smacked against the pavement as she darted across the street.

Mom closed the door and frowned. "She's one of those neighbors who wriggle into your life and eventually get so demanding you can't walk outside without being bombarded. If you don't put an end to it, she'll take advantage of you."

I headed back to the patio and the peace of the pool. "I don't mind helping out."

"Of course not. But you're hardly in the frame of mind to take care of someone so helpless. You need to concentrate on yourself. You can't save the world. And your failure is what breaks you."

I stood still, my back to her. "I know you flew out here at the last minute and it's a huge sacrifice with all you've got going on. I appreciate your care. Honestly. But you know how I need consistency. Surprises throw me."

This wasn't entirely correct. Not at the same level of a year ago. But it was true enough.

She put an arm around me. "You should probably take Seroquel and get some rest. You'll feel better in the morning."

I sighed with the weariness of having to explain again. "I'm trying to wean myself from the crutch of meds. If you could give me a little time alone."

She looked shocked. "You want me to go away?"

"Maybe go get dinner? We can save the goulash for tomorrow."

She drew me closer. "Why don't I let you relax here and I'll go unpack and finish making dinner. Then we can have a nice chat."

I stepped away from her arm. "Mom." The word came out hard. "Can you just once do as I ask?"

She lasered me with her eyes, searching for the cracks. Conflict over doing what she wanted, and indulging me pinched her lips. "Let's sit down and eat. We'll catch up and I'll go to my room to read. You can have all the solitude you want."

I didn't say a word as I gathered my ice water and brushed past her on the way to my room.

The door slammed to the echo of The Three:

Forest Hill.

Cold and white.

Leather straps.

39

I stayed in bed long past when I wanted to rise. It wasn't as if my bedroom was my usual sanctuary. Serviceable at best, this morning it felt like a bunker away from Mom. After an interval of kitchen cabinets opening and banging closed, I heard the front door open and shut. It slammed and the combination lock beeped as it rammed home.

I dressed in khaki shorts and t-shirt and ventured out. The note on the counter explained she needed to make another trip to the grocery store for eggs and bread and fruit. She'd scribbled a few other items, probably to let me know how short I'd fallen on self-care.

Water splashed into the ice of my glass, glancing off the fresh lemon slice. I carried it out to the patio, where the morning sunshine danced along the pool. The last few days pushed down on me. Cali's disappearance, Mitch suspending me, inching toward friendship only to see it crumble, the horror of Kaycee's snake bite, and now Mom's unexpected appearance.

And yet, despite the increase in the voices' volume and number, I hadn't folded. The challenge exhausted me, but I was holding on. The static of voices—especially the sobbing Peanut and the quiet one I couldn't place who kept admonishing me to remember—hadn't silenced my own voice. And I sounded stronger and surer than I had since before my world had stopped turning.

Mom would be home soon. My stomach churned, but I could handle it. The shrill of my phone cut through the morning.

My first instinct was to ignore it. But what if it had to do with Cali? I pushed myself to stand and hurried in to answer. Kari's number greeted me in the I.D.

Hope flared. "Kari, hi."

It wasn't the friendly tone I'd so wanted to hear. "Okay, so you just can't call me up after so long and not tell me anything about your life. You didn't ask anything about me. I know...knew you so well. I can't believe you've changed so much you don't care."

A lump climbed my throat. "I care."

She sniffed. "I miss you. Yeah, I'm pissed that your mom wrecked my career and that you seemed to discard me. But, damn, Jamie. We were friends and that means something to me."

"Tell me. Please."

She talked for a few minutes about her husband, and how they'd gone through therapy and it seemed to take. How her three-year old son kept her busy, and questioning what she was thinking having a kid in her forties.

I tried to sound upbeat and chipper and told her about Tucson and the Rangers.

It was clear that life had moved on without me, as it should. My old partner now had a family. My ex-husband and his new wife. I'd taken myself out of Buffalo. Other than that, I strove to maintain some kind of regular existence. Changing and growing seemed insurmountable. I couldn't alter what I cared most about, but I was determined to do some good in the world.

When I felt we'd made an effort to catch up, I brought it back around. "Did you get the file and the evidence?"

"After you called Sunday I got curious. Back then, I'd wanted the case solved, mostly for you, so I didn't question it much when Grainger King confessed and was convicted. But I decided to look it up, even though I told you I wouldn't."

"Thank you. I owe you."

"You don't owe me."

"Can you send me a digital copy of the file and pictures of the evidence?"

Kari hesitated and a dragonfly flitted over the pool and dipped low for a drink. "This is the strangest thing. I expected a thick file because so many people care about you, and because of your mom's position. I knew Granger King had been picked up at the scene of a rape/murder about a week after...." She didn't seem to be able to bring herself to say the name. "There were lots of witnesses and a solid case against him."

I pushed through the French doors and opened the drawer with the ribbon and necklace. My fingers ran over the rough polyester of the ribbon. "Mom told me he'd been linked to at least three murders. He confessed to all of them. I need to know what he said about this case."

We fell into our old rhythm with no barriers between us. "I remember he died not long after he confessed to all the other murders."

"So there's no way anyone can question him." The silver of the runner charm glimmered from the bottom of the drawer.

"It seems strange now, but I didn't think about it then. I was relieved you wouldn't have to go through a drawn-out process."

"And now?"

She paused. "Now I think about it, it's wonky. Because his

other attacks were random in a park. But this one was in a home."

"Did you have a chance to read the file? What's it say?"

"That's the weird thing."

I fingered the ribbon, a chill shooting up my spine. "What's the weird thing?"

"There's no record of the evidence being logged."

That couldn't be. "But there was a hair elastic and necklace, her clothes...I don't know what all. It will mention that in the file."

"No evidence box. And the really bizarre thing is that there is no file on her... the incident. And Grainger King's file is missing."

40

So anxious for Mom to leave, and now I couldn't wait for her to return. How could every trace of the investigation be missing? She must have them somewhere. Maybe she had doubts, too. She could have the files and evidence box in her office to study them. But then, she'd have checked them out and there would be a paper trail.

I paced my front walk. Come home. Come home. The sun, so pleasant in the shade of the backyard, blistered my face.

When the sound of a car started down the street heading my way, I stopped at the top of the driveway and waited.

A cop cruiser appeared and pulled into the driveway. Rafe climbed out of the car and with slow steps made his way toward me. His face had a closed look, sharp as a hatchet.

Rafe stopped in front of me and locked his eyes on mine. I'd seen those same eyes smile from inside him, welcome me. There was none of that warmth now. A steely gaze, cold, despite their deep brown. "You need to tell me what happened Thursday night. After you saw Cali with the guy at the park."

The grumblings escalated.

My skin itched. "I left the ball park after my shift, came home. Was home all night. Alone."

His calm cracked. "I want to help you. But if you keep lying, I can't do anything."

Zoey's dead.

Cali's dead.

You killed them.

Why didn't he believe me? "Lying about what?"

He retreated to his cool attitude. "What do you know about Cali Shaw and her whereabouts?"

Whereabouts. No one talks like that in real life. Ice ran through the crevices between my bones. My breath burned. "Did you find her?"

Rafe's eyes narrowed as if he struggled to keep from shouting. Rage rolled off him with such force I could almost smell sulphur. "Quit messing with me."

The cacophony inside me made it impossible to answer for several seconds. "Please, tell me what's going on."

"Damn it. Why won't you let me help you?"

The scene flashed in front of me.

Dead. Her blonde hair streaked with mud and blood. Purple bruises ringing her neck. Her fingernails broken, face swollen. Legs splayed, clothes ripped and missing.

Peanut wailed, but she was only one of so many voices.

"Rafe." I heard myself whisper. "Did you find her?"

"Her car."

There was hope. "But not her? She's still out there. We've got time. Where was it? Did you find any clues in it? You believe me now, don't you? She's missing."

"Oh, I believe she's missing."

Good. "I called my old partner in Buffalo. We haven't put it together yet but I know there's a connection. My mother is here and she's the county sheriff. She might remember something helpful. We'll find Cali."

"This definitely has something to do with you."

"That's what I've been saying. Did you find some evidence in the car?"

"Yes, we found evidence."

If I knew what the other evidence box contained, I could probably tell him what they'd find, but it didn't matter. Whatever the killer left, we could use it to find him. "What is it?"

He flattened his lips and skewered me with his eyes. "Your Rangers badge."

41

I sank to the bench on my porch. Heat from the metal burned through my shorts and the sun drilled into my forehead. The voices took over, so many wanting me to stab my eyes, bash my head against the house, take a swing at Rafe. Others shouting and cursing. Frank saying over and over, *"You moron. You moron."*

Rafe watched me. I don't know how long I sat there. Long enough my thighs felt numb on the hard metal. He came into focus.

I batted at the confusion and focused on my badge in the car. "How could that happen?"

"You tell me."

A fuzzy thought started at the base of my spine and grew clearer. I'd been upset after the baseball game and took a pill to get through the afternoon and night. I awoke in my chair. The hours in between were a blank, like so many in the last few years.

No. I didn't take a pill that night. I took one the next day. Or did I?

I might have been the last person to see Zoey Clark before she went missing. Driving home from the high school the day

I'd grabbed Megan, right before Kaycee went missing. I'd lost over an hour. Now my badge missing.

Frank laughed so hard a shooting pain slashed through my brain.

I jumped up from the bench and jetted into the house. To my bedroom and jerked open the closet door. My uniform blouse hung where it usually did. I whipped it out. No badge. I spun around and scanned my room.

Rafe stood in the doorway. "What are you doing?"

The killer was here.

Zoey's dead.

Cali's dead.

"Someone must have been here. In my house." The smell of lilacs wasn't an illusion. Someone had dropped the blossom in my pool. They'd been here.

Rafe didn't say anything but I knew he didn't believe me.

I didn't have much in my bedroom, but what I did have looked exactly the same as always.

Rafe took in the room, his eyebrows dropping in concern. White walls, no rug on the floor. The bed with no headboard. The dresser with only the malachite sphere. Nothing on the walls, no pictures on the bedside table. If there had been so much as a crucifix over the bed, it would have seemed an upgrade to a nun's cell.

I spun away and rushed into the open space of the living, dining room, and kitchen. Frantic with my need to know. The painting above the mantle didn't give me peace. The other touches Mom added all maintained their natural places. That's when I saw it.

"It's gone." I think I shouted it, but it might have been someone inside my head. I ran to the table under the window that looked onto the porch. This is where I allowed three pictures of her. Her baby face smiled at me from where she stood in the bath-tub, her fingers clutching a blue plastic block, her toothless grin full of mischief. The photo with of all of us on Mother's Day when she wore her favorite red polka dot dress. And the photo with her arms thrust in victory seconds after winning the 4X400 relay.

The track picture was missing. In her team uniform. Like Cali's cheerleader uniform. "He stole a picture."

Rafe came closer and bent to see the two remaining. He picked up the Mother's Day photo. "My God. She looks just like Cali Shaw and Zoey Clark. Who is it?"

I opened my mouth but nothing came out. I closed my eyes and tried again. "Bethany." The word sounded like the granite of a gravestone. "My daughter."

Rafe studied the photo a second and realization dawned. "The case that mirrors Cali's. It's your daughter."

I couldn't even nod.

"You're saying someone knows the details of your daughter's murder. They kidnapped Cali because she looks like your daughter. They planted evidence similar to what was discovered in that case. Then they broke into your house and stole your badge, left it in Cali's abandoned car. And all of this set-up for what purpose?"

"REVENGE!" Frank's shout made me flinch.

Rafe caught my reaction because he frowned at me, as if listening for the voice only I heard.

I plodded to the living room and sank to the couch. "I don't know."

Rafe stood by the table, with Bethany's photo still in his hand. "I want to believe you, but you're not helping me."

Without thought, I planted my hand on the arm of the sofa, wanting to draw comfort from the red hoodie always draped there. My hand landed on the soft cushion of the couch. "No.

Oh, no. He took it! He took it!" The hysteria crept higher and higher into my brain.

Rafe looked alarmed. "What did he take?"

I jumped up and scurried to the entryway. Did I have it in my hand when the little girls barged in? Did they take it? No, I'd walked them across the street and we'd held hands. Would Mom have put it somewhere? No, if she'd seen it, she would have climbed all over me about hanging on to painful memories.

It took no time to speed around the rooms, checking every surface, every place I might have draped or dropped it. My heart raced, as in those seconds, minutes when I'd discovered her missing.

I relived calling hello as I enter the front door. No answer. Her geometry book open on the table. Pages scattered. Hot Tamales all over the floor. Running to her bedroom, to the living room. Not in bed. Not watching TV. To my room. To the guest room. Kitchen. Garage. Back yard. Finally screaming, running down the sidewalk.

A hand clasped onto my arm and I looked up into Rafe's concerned face. "Slow down. What's missing?"

"The hoodie! Her hoodie. It's gone."

I yanked my arm away because the voices clanged and roared. I backed into a corner of the kitchen and closed my eyes, slowly taking charge of my own head.

I didn't care if I mumbled out loud. "I'm Jamie Butler. I'm Amanda's daughter. I'm a retired Buffalo cop. I live in Tucson." I ran through my rosary at least three times

When I opened my eyes again, Rafe stood in the same place, wearing the same worried look. "Are you okay?"

"Sort of." Shaky, I flipped open a cabinet and pulled out two tall glasses. I filled them with ice from the refrigerator door and reached inside for sliced lemon. With both glasses full and starting to bead, I led Rafe into the living room and set the glasses on the coffee table. I lowered myself to one corner of the couch and invited him to sit on the other.

My foot jiggled on the floor, hating to waste time explaining. But Rafe wouldn't help me if I didn't confide in him.

He waited and the silence built between us while I quieted the crowd inside. He didn't say anything throughout this process. The only one I know who could rival Tara in patience with me.

Against Frank's direct orders, and not sure it was for the best, the time had come to tell Rafe the truth. I swallowed a cold flush of water, concentrated on the tang of the lemon and drew a long, deep breath. "I hear voices."

By now I'd learned his seemingly impassive face was an impressive mask for intense emotions. Right now, he might have been a mannequin. "It started when your daughter was taken?"

I studied the glass in my hand. The hoodie. I couldn't lose the only connection I had with Bethany. Mom had taken away everything else in her belief that hanging on to her possessions would cause me pain. "That's when they got bad. I've heard them all my life, as long as I can remember. Most of my life there was one voice. A loving, kind of mothering voice. Somewhere along the line she told me her name is Maggie."

I sipped, gathering my thoughts and quieting Frank's insistence that I throw the glass at Rafe. "My mother pushed me pretty hard. She loves me, but I wasn't everything she wanted."

Rafe shrugged. "Children are their own people, always."

My foot continued to jiggle, keeping time to my urgency. "Mom's father was an alcoholic and her mother never stood up to him or took charge. According to Mom, she raised herself. I never met my grandparents. They were out of Mom's life by the time I was born. I understood why she wanted so much for me. It was because she never had any attention or help growing up."

Rafe didn't comment but he looked skeptical.

I took a long drink of cold water, letting it ease the tension in my throat. My foot still vibrated. "Anyway, Maggie told me all the things Betty Crocker would tell her daughter. She said I was pretty and nice and it didn't matter if I won the medals as long as I had a good time. Most of the time, Maggie was the only voice I heard and that was no problem. Sometimes, if I got stressed, I'd hear a crowd—I don't know, maybe a dozen? They'd whisper and grumble, but nothing too awful and I mostly ignored it."

I paused, and when he didn't scoff, I continued. "After Bethany's death, Frank arrived."

Rafe hadn't touched his water. "I don't understand, what do you mean 'he arrived'?"

"I followed Mom when they told her they'd found a clue. Out to a junk yard. Rainy and muddy. Mother's Day." The hoodie. All of Bethany I had left.

"Mother's Day." He understood the significance.

Warm tears cascaded down my face and I gulped my water and rocked against the couch before I could continue.

"Frank showed up and, according to Mom, I went crazy. He ordered me to grab a broken hood ornament and stab myself. And I did. I don't remember much of the next several months. A lot of drugs. But as I slowly came back, I heard more voices than I'd ever had. Frank is the most vocal and can be mean, not so violent any more, but he has moments. I won't bore you with all the names. But there is a group I call the Chorus." *We need to go. We need to go.*

Rafe shook his head. "This is incredible."

My smile cracked my lips. "They are like wind chimes inside. They are rarely silent but often they're a soft tinkle I've come to accept. When they feel threatened or offended, they swell and when it gets really bad, they can sound like a church bell in my ears."

Remember. Remember.

"How did you get better?"

"Therapy. Lots of therapy. And Mom. She got me away from all the stress. She took care of Bethany's funeral and her things. All the messy parts of death. She found a great facility and wonderful doctors. Healing started by me having conversations with the voices. Take Frank, who wanted me to hurt myself or others. I had to learn that was his way of warning me to dangers and my fears."

Rafe's water glass ran and pooled on the table. "That's crazy. Well. Sorry. I mean—."

"No, you're right. It is crazy. I'm not, though. I understand the voices are parts of me. But they are real. As real as your voice in this room. They have weight and texture. It's not like talking to yourself. I am not *thinking* them. I am *hearing* them. With my ears."

"Are you hearing them now?"

I nodded.

He seemed curious. "What are they saying?"

Cali. The hoodie. My badge. Cali. "Frank thinks you're a moron. That's okay, because he thinks I'm a moron, too. He wants me to throw you out and is really indignant that I'm dictating his words to you now. The Chorus is about mid-to-high range now. They are still upset about the badge, the break-in, and especially the hoodie."

Peanut shrieked and cried when I mentioned the sweatshirt. She obviously wanted to be heard but I couldn't tell Rafe about her.

"How does that feel, when they...talk to you?"

"I often feel a tingling in my hands before they start in. Lots of times there's an intense pressure in my head. If I feel those sensations and I'm in public, I can take out my phone and talk to them, or even put in earbuds and it looks like I'm singing."

"What do you say?"

We have no time for questions.

"Depends. I interrupt them politely and firmly let them know our agreed-upon boundaries. And those are that unless it's an immediate or urgent matter, I'll give them time to have their say later on."

Rafe's eyes held mine, totally drawn in. "Like real people? And they cooperate?"

You need to find Cali. You need to get Bethany's hoodie.

"Like real people. Sometimes they throw their fits. Frank pops off a lot, though he doesn't really expect me to hurt myself any more. The most aggressive voices represent those feelings most needing release. So when Frank gets too noisy and insistent, I let him talk and try to reassure him that it's okay."

"What if he doesn't believe you? What if it isn't okay?"

"If I feel overwhelmed, I can soften the edges with medication. I try to avoid that as much as possible. The pills take away pieces. It may not be much of a life, but I'd like to live it." Most of the time.

I got up for more water. Rafe's ice had melted but he still hadn't had a sip. I picked his glass up.

"What about that night. When Cali went missing. Did you take pills that night?"

Frank's hilarity couldn't be contained.

No. I didn't go out that night. I didn't take Cali. I didn't hurt Kaycee. I knew this.

The ice machine chugged and clunked cubes into the glasses. When it was done I answered. "I honestly don't know. But I didn't go anywhere near the ball park."

"Do you have a witness?"

I filled the glasses and set them on the counter. "Look around. I don't have friends. My witnesses are all in my head."

I had to calm down. I led Rafe outside to the cool shade, leaving the French doors open to let in the morning air.

Along with the Chorus, Frank had some particular words to say to that. "I didn't go out that night. I'm not crazy."

"But you believe in voices that aren't real."

"They are real." Did I sound angry?

He eyed me with doubt.

"Billions of people believe in a God they can't see or hear, why wouldn't I believe in voices I do hear?"

He was silent for a long time. I curled my hand around my water glass, the cool on my palm not calming the heat inside me.

I broke the silence. "Did you run the license plate?"

He nodded. "Yeah. Belonged to some old duffer in Oro Valley. Someone stole the plate and he hadn't even realized it was missing."

I pleaded with him. "Kaycee, Cali. It's all wrapped up with Bethany's murder. We need to find Cali."

He exhaled deeply. "I might believe you, but I'm not sure anyone else will. And we've got nothing to go on. I'm going to have to take you in for formal questioning as part of the investigation."

A gasp sounded from the open door. Mom stood at the threshold, her face set in fury.

Overzealous air conditioning frosted the meeting room at the station. At least Rafe hadn't taken me to an interrogation room. I worried Mom would be off finding me a lawyer and demanding she be allowed to advise me. Maybe she bought Rafe's story about me helping the investigation. Rafe and I agreed to have me drive the Juke to make it look less like I was a suspect.

We'd been at this for an hour. Rafe questioning and me answering again and again, hoping I remembered something more.

"Okay, let's go over this again." Rafe sounded patient, though I wanted to punch something. "You say you saw the three girls at the fence talking to someone. The girls deny it. You say Shax witnessed it, but he denies it. We can't find any of the homeless people in the park to corroborate your story. You say Shax was worried about a dog. He says he doesn't have a dog. Shax says he saw you with Cali that night."

I rubbed my temples.

"You have no memory of that night after you maybe did or didn't take a sedative. Again, no witness. You have a necklace and hair ribbon. We can analyze it for DNA but that will take too long. You say it mirrors your daughter's murder case, but the evidence of that case is missing, so can't be confirmed. Your badge, which you say was stolen, was found in Cali's car. But there's no evidence of breaking and entering at your house."

I lowered my head to my crossed arms on the table. "I didn't do it."

Frank laughed.

My phone rang, surprising both of us. I looked at Rafe and he shrugged, allowing me to answer.

"Kari?"

She started in. "I don't think Grainger King did it. Doesn't make any sense. I don't know why he confessed, but whatever."

"I'm sure King didn't do it."

She chewed and I pictured her with her pencil between her teeth, as I'd seen her so many times. "I checked the timeline. The mur— incident happened not long after the early release program."

I'd forgotten about that. During the last election cycle, the polls showed a majority of constituents were disgruntled about the high cost of prisoner upkeep and felt too many prisoners were incarcerated on minor charges. Mom thought a popular move would be a sweeping early release program. It must have worked because she was reelected.

My mind raced. "Do you think it was someone I'd arrested who was released and wanted revenge?"

The pencil nibbling continued. "Could be. I'm researching your old cases to see if something jumps out. But that's going to take a while."

"This could be important. Thank you."

We hung up and I relayed the information to Rafe.

"Let me see if I can have her send us some files and we can help." He left the room.

I pushed back from the table and paced.

I saw it.

Darkness. A moment of shock in his eyes when they focus on me. Then the smile in the night. Like a ghoul.

"I need more," I pleaded with the voices.

Cuffs, the orange glow of a street light. Frosty air. Disgust that tastes like ashes I want to spit onto the cracked pavement.

The memory was so clear. I'd seen it at the grade school when the man in the blue golf shirt grinned at me. Why couldn't I place it? And why did it resurface now? *Who is shoving it at me again? Answer me!*

Rafe returned with a can of Coke in each hand. He glanced at me and froze. "What?"

"I know who's got Cali."

43

I raced toward him. "Hurry."

He didn't move. "You know? Did the voices tell you?"

We had to go. "I remembered." He studied me, still not convinced. "Please. Trust me. I know this."

Standing still while he searched my face took all my patience. Rafe slammed the Cokes on the table. "Let's go."

We ran down the corridor. We were too late. Oh God, please don't let it be too late.

He wanted to be found out. He'd given me so many clues. Exactly like he'd done with Bethany. "It's Shax. He's got Cali." I shouted as we ran toward the door.

He followed close behind me, our feet pounding the industrial linoleum. It seemed forever before we reached his cruiser and another lifetime to make it onto the street. "Lights and siren?" he asked.

Would it matter to Shax? He'd know we were coming. But not when. I shook my head. "He is playing with us. That would only make him happier."

"How do you know it's Shax? He didn't seem together enough to pull off kidnapping."

"It's a game. He's not a homeless mental case. He knows exactly what he's doing. Setting me up, telling you I'd been at the ball park that night with Cali. Lying about the guy talking to the girls. It was all a set up."

Rafe didn't look convinced. "Why would he do that?"

"He killed Bethany. He's proving he's smarter than me."

"Why you?"

Everything inside me tightened. "I don't know."

Frank said, *"Yes, you do."*

"Are you sure it's Shax?"

"The tattoos. Among all the vines are cars. Bethany was killed in a junkyard."

Rafe's forehead wrinkled. "That seems sketchy at best."

"Sure. But the thing about the dog? He said he never left her alone except this once, when he wanted time to be with someone. I had a date, the first one in years, the night Bethany was taken."

Rafe took that in.

"And he mentioned a Jaguar. You probably didn't notice the way he said it, but it had a creepy note to it. Bethany's body was found next to a Jaguar."

"And you remembered all this while I was gone?"

Why bother lying? "I didn't remember. The voices did."

Rafe didn't reply.

This was no memory because I hadn't been there. But I clearly saw Bethany sitting in front of her geometry book at the kitchen table, tapping her pencil and squinting while she envisioned the steps of the proof she never finished. The doorbell rang and she looked up, curious why someone would be at the door after ten o'clock. She was concerned someone needed help. She threw down her pencil, the chair scraped on the tile floor, and she hurried to the door. No hesitating, because someone might need her. When she tore open the door, a dark figure rushed inside and grabbed her.

For the rest, I'd have to ask Peanut. That's not something I could face.

We caromed into the parking lot in front of the picnic table laden with those who called it home. Out of the car in a flash, I rushed to the half dozen men and a couple of women sitting, laying, or standing by their motley piles of possessions. Their uniform of grimy faces and tattered clothing disguised people living lives of despair, loss, loneliness, but also joy, hope, and friendship. Human lives.

Shax wasn't among them and I dashed off, leaving Rafe to question them. Across the park, to other clumps of people, past individuals lounging in the relative cool of early afternoon under the shade of the palm trees. One man sat cross-legged and shouted to someone only he could see.

"*Crazy bastard,*" Frank said, then let loose with his cruel laughter.

At the edge of the park, moving quickly toward the street, I spotted him. Hunched into the red sweatshirt with the hood up. Bethany's hoodie. I must have shouted because he flinched and started to run.

I sprinted with speed born of rage and bottomless grief. He hadn't made it to the sidewalk, only a few steps before I tackled him.

Nothing but bones stuffed into filthy clothes and Bethany's sweatshirt, he toppled easily, almost fragile. The ground came at us hard and fast, the grass only dry threads on dirt like concrete. He cried out as I landed on top of him.

Before I could roll him over and get to my feet, Rafe stood over me. He reached down and grabbed a fistful of the back of the hoodie and as I slid off, pulled him to stand, like a lifeguard might tug a floundering kid from the shallow end.

The hood fell back. Not Shax. The cool guy, the one flirting with Cali and Megan, hunkered in front of us. No longer swaggering and confident, he had the manner of a rabbit cornered by a coyote. He shrunk into the sweatshirt.

"Take it off. Take it off now!"

Rafe helped the guy get the sweatshirt over his head and didn't take his eyes off the guy when he tossed the hoodie toward me.

I hugged it, even knowing how ridiculous it seemed.

With no overt force or threat, Rafe held the guy rooted in front of him. "What's your name?"

Eyes to the ground, he mumbled. "Huff."

"No mystery how a street name like that came about," Frank said.

Now Rafe sounded kind. "Okay, Huff. How did you get this sweatshirt?"

Huff raised his gaze slightly and scanned the park. "Shax. He gave it to me yesterday and told me to wear it in the park and wait for," he pointed at me, "her and when I saw her, to walk away with the hood up."

My heart beat in my throat and I sounded winded. "What about a couple of days ago? You were cleaned up, dressed in decent clothes, talking to the cheerleaders at the gate. Why?"

Huff cast a sly glance at me, then back to Rafe. "Shax. He hired me. Took me to his place and let me sleep there, take a shower, get some grub. Told me if I stayed sober long enough to do this job, he'd help me out, whatever I wanted."

"He had you talk to the girls when I was there?"

"It wasn't easy. We tried three different times. But when you were at the games, that little girl wasn't there or the other way. But then it happened and I did it." He sniggered and those glassy eyes shone. "Shax was good on his word. It's been a fine time since."

I wanted to grab Huff by the throat and do what the voices, those meaner than Frank, told me to do.

Rafe must have known I'd reached my limit and he took over. "Where is Shax now?"

Huff shrugged. "Don't know. Don't care. He's a spook, you know?"

I had another question. "Why? Did he tell you why he did it?"

That halfway focus drifted and a stupid smile played on Huff's face. "Yeah. Said you took everything from him and that's why he's on the street." He snorted.

Rafe clamped a hand on Huff's shoulder. "He took that girl. She is innocent and now she's hurt or dead. Do you think that's funny? Do you think it's justice?"

Huff looked stricken. "I didn't have anything to do with that."

Rafe's face hardened. "Is there anything else you remember that could help that girl?"

Huff looked at the sky. "Shax said to tell you he wasn't done. He's going to make you pay for what you did."

Desperation rose in the form of roiling waves of sound inside me. "How? What did he say?" I fought to hold back Frank's rage. "Where did he take her?"

Huff shrugged again, his whole body tugged up by his shoulders, then dropping like a bag of lead. "He said you'd know."

I didn't.

"Moron," Frank said, but he wouldn't tell me what he knew.

44

Rafe took Huff into the station. I was still a person of interest but if questioned, Rafe would say he didn't have enough evidence to hold me. Exhausted, I dropped in my Juke and headed home to think. Cali was in Shax's control somewhere and I prayed she was still alive. Shax thought I'd know where she was, so I hoped that meant he kept her alive for the game.

Early release. Someone I'd arrested. The voices cursed my stupidity. But I'd been a cop for 23 years. That's a lot of cases. So much resentment and hate.

What I knew was that I needed to retreat and calm down. Despite Frank's silence, the Chorus and dozens of voices threatened to overwhelm me. If I took some time, drank my lemon water, let myself breathe, maybe Frank or one of the others would help me.

Mom sat at the breakfast bar in front of her laptop, papers spread across the granite, manila folders piled and spilling from her leather briefcase, her Bluetooth headset plugged into her ear. She swiveled around and frowned. "You've been gone most of the day. I called the sheriff's department but they didn't give me any information."

I ignored her probing. "I'm working on a case."

It looked like she inspected a wall for chinks. "This can't be good for you. I honestly don't have the time to help you manage something that, frankly, is not your job."

I plopped in the other barstool and faced her. "We need to talk about Bethany's case."

"That's not a good idea. It will only upset you."

"I've been talking to Kari and she—."

She slapped the counter. "Kari? I didn't know you kept in touch. Oh, Honey, you shouldn't be talking to her. She's trouble."

"Is that why you transferred her away from me?"

She frowned. "Is that what she said? The truth is she wasn't a good cop and I didn't want her to bring you down. You are so loyal, even when it hurts you, so I have to look out for you."

Stunned by her casually admitting to such manipulation, I didn't answer for a moment. "The evidence box is missing."

Her eyes flared with temper. "Did Kari say that? What's she doing digging around where she doesn't belong?"

"Grainger King's file is gone. And so is the case file on Bethany."

She blew air from her lips. "That's not right. Kari is a flake. Probably doesn't know how to find files."

My hand had fisted on the counter and with effort, I relaxed it. "I don't believe Grainger King killed Bethany."

She jumped up. "Is this coming from delusions stirred up by this investigation you're involved with? King confessed to the murder."

"To you."

Her hands clasped the back of the barstool and her knuckles whitened. "Why would you doubt its veracity?"

Frank was back. He prodded and railed until I spoke too harshly. "It seems too easy. Too convenient."

"Is that what those voices are telling you? Or this Rafe person? Maybe it's a story Kari concocted because her career is crap and she blames it on me."

Her anger blew at me like napalm. The hand on the counter shook, as did the rest of my body. I needed to keep pushing, even if I lost the only person in the world who had always been there for me. "I believe Bethany's killer is still out there."

She stretched her neck as if letting go of her temper. "Oh, Honey. You're so much worse than I thought. At least I'm here in time to get you some help."

I wanted to tell her for the first time in a long time I was living. It hurt. My world felt shaky, but real. And now, when it seemed I might actually be gaining traction, she wanted to "get me help." I knew what that meant.

But what if Mom's observation of me was right? Maybe I'd slipped so far from reality I didn't even recognize it.

Her phone blasted through the room. She looked at the I.D. "It's my campaign manager. I've got to take it. We are not done here."

I stumbled out to the patio. The ground beneath me felt like silly putty and I couldn't get a deep breath. She wanted me to go back to hospital. I'd rather die.

Thoughts tumbled and smashed together, coming at me like bullets from a machine gun. Why was Mom lying about the Bethany's killer? I should have been stronger. I should have paid attention to Bethany's case.

Now Shax had Cali. But I didn't know where. Was Shax responsible for Kaycee's snake bite? I'd nearly gotten her killed. How had Shax broken into my house?

Questions, accusations. Hate. Death.

The pool shimmered from the afternoon sun, a breeze sending ripples along the surface. The rope beckoned from the cement block under the palm.

"Jump in," Frank said.

"I'm Jamie Butler. I'm Amanda's daughter. I'm a retired Buffalo cop"

It's your fault.

You'll never do right.

They will die.

Bethany smiled at me from the pool. Cool water. Sun glinted off. So sassy in her red polka dot bikini with the ruffled bottom. Fearless or trusting, she pulled her little hand from my grasp and ran on her tiny bare toes. No hesitation as she threw herself from the deck into the pool of splashing, happy children. My heart jumped to my throat as I scrambled one step behind. I pulled her from underwater, smiling, her blue eyes wide. My little Peanut. Never a doubt I'd be there to save her.

The terrifying voice inside me was back. Someone worse than Frank. The voice I'd prayed never to hear again. *"She's under there now, waiting for you."*

Frank hissed, *"You deserve to die."*

Chanting. Shouting. Pushing.

You're worthless.

Your fault.

Jump in.

The cloying smell of lilacs hit me. Was it real or imagined?

The sun burned the back of my neck, scorched the top of my head. I spoke with assurance. "It wasn't my fault. Shax is to blame."

Frank laughed.

I squeezed my eyes closed and words twisted with torture. "I'm not responsible for what he did."

Your fault.

You could have stopped it.

Jump in.

The Chorus joined in, rising in a fury. I clamped my hands

over my ears. "I know you want me to drown myself. I understand you're trying to protect me from the pain." My head felt
like Frank sank an ax through my skull.

"Jump in. Jump in."

The terrifying voice croaked close to my ear. *"You deserve to
die."* He'd been the one I couldn't say no to last time. The one
who commanded me to get the French chef knife. To place the
point to my heart. He told me the sacrifice would bring Bethany
back. I didn't believe him. But there was no resisting him.

"Jump in," he shouted. *"DO IT!"*

Standing on the edge of the pool, the bottom looked quiet,
peaceful. The blue deep and cool. They couldn't talk to me
there. No more shouting. No crowds. No guilt. No pain. Silence.

Do it.

You killed her.

Your fault.

The nylon scratched my ankle. I tied the knot, making sure
it wouldn't loosen.

Maggie's voice sounded far away, drowned by the crashing
curses and encouragement to jump. *"You aren't done."*

"What do you mean?" I croaked the question, but it was my
own voice. The rough cinderblock scraped my fingers.

She sounded a little stronger. *"Only you can save her."*

Frank growled. *"Shut up. She's never saved anyone."*

The hollow voice ordered me. *"End it now."*

The drain rippled under ten feet of crystal water. Refresh-
ing. Safe.

Peanut sobbed. She knew it was too late. Would always be
too late.

"Jamie? Are you okay?"

Clouds of voices swirled in my head and it seemed a breeze
blew, thinning and starting to clear.

"I called your cell but you didn't answer."

With a pounding head and smattering of voices, I raised my eyes. Rafe stood next to me, his khaki uniform looking heavy and hot in the sunshine.

I scanned behind him, wondering how he got past Mom.

He must have noticed my questioning glance. "Her car isn't in the driveway. I was worried, so I busted the lock and came in."

Mom was taking a call. Where would she have gone? To finish the paperwork she needed to lock me away.

"Jamie?" He brought me back. "Can I...?" He pointed to the cinderblock in my hands.

I let him take it from me, battling the surge of outrage in my head.

After setting the block down, he managed to undo the knot at my ankle.

With unsteady movement, I brushed past Rafe to the patio where I'd left my ice water. He followed me and waited while I gulped and tasted the lemon on my tongue.

Rafe kept his calm eyes on me, somehow giving me strength.

I closed the two steps to him and reached a hand to his arm. He didn't flinch, as if he knew I tested his substance. Real. Solid. Not like Frank, who continued his diatribe.

"Are they talking to you?" Rafe said. The words flowed from his mouth so I knew where they originated.

"Yes." I sounded more solid than I felt. "There's something they need to tell me."

He let my hand stay on his arm. "What is that?"

I released him and retreated to the table. After a moment, the world quit wavering as if in a heat mirage. "They are fighting about telling me."

Rafe didn't understand, that much was clear from his wrinkled brow. His dark eyes never turned away. "Can you ask them?"

My glass clunked on the finished portion of my mosaic table. "I'm trying." My head felt stuffed full of cement, with my brain struggling to find space.

The back door opened and Mom walked out. She ignored Rafe. "Honey?" Her arm snaked around my shoulders and she sounded cautious, as if I might strike. "Jamie. You need to come with me."

She sounded safe. If I went with her, the world would fade away. That's how it happened before. Mom took care of everything. She'd dealt with the ugliness, buried my baby, punished her killer, made sure I was safe.

Zoey's dead.

Cali's dead.

You'll die.

Gentle pressure against my shoulders invited me toward the patio door. Mom leaned close to my ear. "You need to rest. It's been a hard few weeks, hasn't it?"

I felt like I floated toward a soft cloud where I'd never have to lift my head.

Like a needle raking a vinyl record, Rafe's voice startled me. "Hey, where are you going?"

Mom's tone slapped him. "It'd be best if you left now."

Rafe hurried to my side. "We were talking."

Mom spoke to me in that voice like a fluffy blanket. "We'll get you something to help you calm down."

I'd wrapped myself in her comfort before. Years lost in antiseptic smells, straps, confusion. Without making a decision, my feet followed her direction toward the door.

Rafe stepped in front of the door. "Is this what you want?"

Mom stiffened, not used to someone defying her. "You don't know my daughter and you don't know me. Stay out of this."

Rafe ignored her and focused on me. "You said they had something to tell you."

Ice crystals shot from Mom. "Don't encourage that kind of delusion."

"I...." With Mom's arm around my shoulders and Rafe guarding the exit, they drew a line and there was something I needed to say.

You can't.

You won't.

You failed.

Rafe surprised me. "Who's to say it's a delusion? They talk to her."

Mom's laugh sounded like a punch. "We've had therapists like you. Telling me the voices are real. If they're real, where are the people who are talking? Look around. No one." Mom's arm felt heavy around me. "She was making progress and you came into her life and now this. We'll have to start all over again."

I stopped moving toward the door. "I'm not losing my mind."

Mom patted my shoulder. "Of course not. But you need to put some distance between you and the stress."

Rafe drew me into his gaze. "Cali. She's out there somewhere. Those voices in you—someone knows where she is. You have to help her."

Mom threw her arm out and tried to shove him from in front of the door. "Stop it. She can't handle this."

"I'm not crazy." The way they both jumped made me think I'd shouted it. I lowered my voice. "I've learned how to pay attention when they talk to me. They usually have something important to say, but it needs interpretation."

Mom glared at Rafe and hugged me closer. "The voices aren't real."

With a determined stride, I pulled away from Mom's arm. "Here's what's real. A man was released early. By you. And he killed Bethany."

Mom's jaw tightened and her eyes flashed. "Where—"

"And you found someone to blame her murder on. And conveniently, he died soon after his confession."

"What are you accusing me of?"

I pushed back the noise in my head. "You knew Grainger King didn't do it. Why did you pin it on him?"

She glared at Rafe. "Did you tell her about this? Is it you who is influencing her to revisit all the pain? You sick bastard."

Rafe's face held that emotionless expression as he addressed Mom. "Jamie doesn't need me or you to influence her. She's capable of thinking for herself."

Mom drew me into her. "You didn't see her when she broke. I was there. I picked up the pieces She's vulnerable and you have no right to take advantage of that to further your investigation."

I stepped away and glared at her. "Why, Mom?"

Behind her stony eyes, something stirred.

I pleaded. "I need to know."

Like a prize fighter, she shifted and ducked. "Now's not the time to talk about it."

"No." I surprised myself with the power. "I'm here and I want to know. Why did you do it?"

Mom softened her face. "For you. It's always been for you. I know how much you loved Bethany."

My voice cracked. "I would gladly have taken her place. I pray for it every day."

Mom nodded. "Exactly. You fell apart after we found her. You've always been delicate, needing protection. I knew how you'd grieve and the guilt you'd feel if you ever recovered enough to be aware. The suspect was long gone and I decided a quick resolution would be best for everyone."

"Not for Bethany." I sounded like cold death.

Mom kept talking in that confident way. "It would do no good to drag it out. We'd have to find him, prosecute him, long court battles. You'd never be able to get through it. So I did what I had to do. To protect you."

I shut Frank down, ignoring his point by point refutation of Mom's explanation. I didn't need him to tell me that because Bethany was a cop's daughter and granddaughter, the detectives would have found the murderer and there would have been no long court battle.

"He's killing again. You didn't protect me."

Mom appeared not to have heard me. "Grainger was happy to confess when I promised to pay his son $5,000. Trust me, anyone who would sell his integrity so cheap isn't worth worrying about."

"Is this what the special investigator is looking into?" Rafe asked. What always felt like a quiet river to me, sounded more like a rattler's warning directed at Mom. He must have been doing his own digging.

She whipped her head toward him and narrowed her eyes. "The investigation is merely a campaign tactic by a dirty opponent. I haven't done anything sheriffs before haven't done, and I've been cleaner than any of them. But they were men. They get a free pass. Of course no one believes a woman could do this job without cheating."

I pressed on. "I need to know what's in the evidence box. See the case file."

Maggie suddenly spoke from behind me. *"You have what you need, dear."*

Bethany is dead.

Zoey is dead.

Cali is dead.

I clamped my hands over my ears. "No!"

Mom leaned close. "It's all right, Honey. I'm here. Touch me. See? Those voices aren't real."

I clenched my eyes, teeth, fists, wanting to plug my ears.

One voice pushed through the crowd. Rafe. "What are they saying? Can you tell me?"

Amid the confluence of voices the quiet one repeated, *"Remember. Remember."*

And suddenly I did.

I opened my eyes to look into Rafe's. "I know where Cali is."

45

"The Boneyard." The answer came to me clear and with no doubt.

Mom sucked in a breath. "What did you say?"

Rafe studied me. "You're sure?"

I didn't want to see it but there it was.

The suffocating wet air and smell of lilacs. The chain-link gate, lined with barbed wire on top. Crumbling cinderblock garage with red paint, cracked and peeling across the front. The Boneyard. A cruel title for where Bethany's life ended.

"Shax took Cali to the Boneyard." I pushed passed Mom and yanked open the French door.

She's dead.

You're too late.

Dead. Dead.

Rafe rushed behind me. "I'll call for backup."

Mom shoved Rafe aside and grabbed my arm. "What boneyard? If those voices in your head are making you remember this, it's time to take you to the hospital."

I wrenched my arm away. "I'm fine." That didn't feel like a lie. Despite Frank's denials and the chatter of the Chorus and even The Three, I knew Shax took Cali to the Boneyard. He'd done everything but skywrite it for me.

"*Hurry,*" Maggie urged.

"Hurry," I said to Rafe, ignoring Mom's protests along with all the others.

In seconds I'd jumped into the front seat of Rafe's patrol car and he fired up the engine. Mom had given up on me and banged on the window of his side. "Unconscionable, criminal to take advantage of a mentally ill person."

Rafe's face turned immobile. He shoved the car in reverse and backed away.

Mom's eyes filled with venom. Her lips moved and her body pitched forward with the force of her yells. I couldn't hear her and turned my head away. "We can save her."

Rafe flipped on his lights and siren. "I hope so."

My foot pressed to the floor of the car as if forcing Rafe faster. We flew passed cars idling at the side of the lane. The Boneyard—the largest storage facility of disabled or decommissioned airplanes in the world—was about twenty miles from my house, skirting across the southern edge of Tucson.

The sun had already fallen beyond the western mountain range and dusty evening lengthened the shadows, dragging night along. By the time we arrived at the Boneyard it would be dark.

Rafe called his supervisor. He explained our suspicions, not mentioning the civilian he carried along in the patrol car. He listened.

"I have reliable information. We'll need to have the MPs give us permission."

The tinny response vibrated from the phone. "No proof. But we're talking about an abducted teen. Don't you think it's worth the risk if it doesn't pan out?"

He threaded his way through an intersection. "I know how

big the Boneyard is. I don't know what section. I'm working on it."

After he listened. "Just me, then. No backup. But you'll get permission for me to look around?"

I had my own conversation going on. "Shax wants me to find him. It's part of his game."

He told you.

You don't remember.

She's going to die.

"Maggie?" I called for her out loud while Rafe talked and drove. "Where is Shax hiding?"

Maggie sounded sad. *"I don't know, dear."*

Rafe pocketed his phone. He would see me talking to Maggie. "But Shax would have told me somehow."

Maggie said, *"Ask Peanut. She never forgets anything."*

My knuckles turned white on the car door. Peanut knew. She knew what Shax had done to her. She knew how I'd failed. If I let her speak she'd tell me horrible things. I wouldn't be able to forget, to forgive.

Maybe someday. But not today. I couldn't fall apart now. If Peanut's revelations sent me spiraling, as they had after discovering Bethany, I'd lose any chance of saving Cali.

I opened my eyes, not aware I'd closed them. The bleating of the sirens seemed soothing compared to the chaos in my head.

Rafe's eyes darted toward me and back to the road. "The MPs will meet us at the gate. Where are we going from there?"

Wave after wave held me under, suffocating me. "Come on. Help me."

Rafe answered. "I'm trying. Getting us in the gate wasn't easy. But you've got to think."

"I'm not talking to you." It wasn't hard to say to him and he didn't look taken aback.

"Oh." He rolled us into a sharp left, leaving Valencia after fifteen miles and heading north on Kolb. "Can you get them to tell you where Shax is? Like mental telepathy or something?"

"I wish it worked like that." We had to be traveling sixty miles an hour but it felt like a crawl.

Failed.

Your fault.

She's dead.

"No." I said it firmly. "Kaycee didn't die. Cali won't either. This is Shax's game and he'd want to keep the bait alive."

Rafe seemed uncertain. "Is that for me or...them?"

I rubbed my temples. "Them. You. I don't have the energy to sort it out. I need to figure out where he's keeping Cali."

Rafe gave me one nod. He kept quiet the last few miles until we slid to a stop outside tall chain-link gates. Headlights shown on the crisscross patterns, dividing the light into the night beyond the gates.

A Hummer pulled up in front of us on the other side of the gate. Their headlights splashed us in harsh glare and Rafe shut his down. Both doors opened and uniformed military personnel emerged from each side. With the caps pulled down I only made out one was a woman and one a man. The man unlocked the gate and the woman stepped through, coming to the driver's door.

"Evening, Officer Grijalva. Your sergeant said you need to search the grounds for a suspected kidnapping."

Rafe replied in his professional manner. "Correct. We're not sure what section—."

"B52s," I spouted it, surprising me, Rafe, and maybe the MP.

Rafe turned to me. "Are you sure?"

The MP leaned down and peered at me. "Your sergeant didn't say you had a partner."

Rafe ignored her. "What makes you think that?"

"His tattoo. He's got a new one. A B52 he showed to me."

Rafe swiveled back to the MP. "B52s. That's where he's keeping the girl."

She eyed me and hesitated. "Okay."

The aisles were wide, with the moonlight from a half moon giving scant light. Row after row of old airplanes seemed to stretch into a Twilight Zone of endless military history. A sea of metal and wings, sand and weeds. Miles and miles.

The MPs would think this was a futile errand. Maybe not too terrible on a boring night. No one could crawl into the Boneyard with a kidnapping victim. Government security and patrols would keep them out.

But Shax had managed to break into my home and steal my treasures. He'd taken Kaycee from her home and left her on the desert, maybe even knew where the rattler lived and put her in harm's way.

He knew my weaknesses. Knew I'd been hospitalized. Knew Mom had helped him get away with murder. He used everything.

Maybe he snuck under a fence. Maybe he got in during a tour. However he did, I knew Shax was here.

He's here.

She's dead.

Too late.

We climbed into the Hummer and it moved at a snail's pace, the night growing thicker around us. With our windows down, the creak of crickets, the rumbled of our engine, and the grind of the Hummer were the only outside sounds.

Inside, Frank and Maggie argued. Peanut cried. The three chanted and the Chorus whispered, moaned and kept up the roar of a crowd waiting for a rock concert.

Shax.

Shax.

Shax.

With full night, the planes were hulking dragons. The Hummer finally turned up an endless, wide passage. The desert floor made up the hard-packed road, probably covered in low green weeds during monsoon season, but a brown thatch the rest of the year. The Hummer slowed and came to a stop.

The driver turned off the ignition. He popped the glove box and pulled out a flashlight. "Anyone need a light?"

Rafe pulled the flashlight from his utility belt. The MPs had their own. I took the offered light.

We climbed out to the hot smell of desert beginning to cool off. The MPs boots crunched on the dirt lane, both with flashlights pointed to the ground. They kept their voices low, as if speaking in a cemetery after dark.

The man said, "These are the B 52s. Big planes. I guess if you think someone is hiding in one of these babies, we should take a look."

Though the woman kept her flashlight trained on the ground, she studied me. "I don't want to insult you, but since your sergeant didn't mention you, can you show me your badge?"

"I'm off-duty." It came out without guilt, as if it wasn't a lie.

She looked at my tennis shoes and shorts, my t-shirt. "This place is full of jagged metal and nails. A million ways to cut you up. I'm going to ask you to stay away from the hardware. I don't mind if you walk up and down the road here, but no going into the planes."

"I'll be careful," I said. "We can search quicker if I help."

The man shook his head. "Can't allow it. With no badge, it's pushing it for you to be out here at all. Last thing we need is for you to cut yourself, get tetanus, and go after the U.S. of A."

"She can stay with me," Rafe said.

"We can cover more ground if you let me go." The urgency in my voice might alarm them.

"No can do," the man stood firm.

Damn it. "Go on. We're wasting time arguing."

Rafe put a hand on my arm. "Search from the road and if you see something, get one of us."

"Tell him he's got a pencil dick," Frank said.

"Fine." I waved my hands to send them off.

They went in three directions, each shining a light on a desiccated pile of steel, mummified on the desert, rust slowed to a crawl, but still disintegrating bit by bit.

46

My flashlight only illuminated a few yards around me and I scanned the area. Where would he be? The lights of the other three bounced along the ground and slid over the shells of the looming mountains of planes. I turned in another direction. Keeping to the center of ground hard as concrete, I moved slowly and listened for any sound of movement.

When I spotted the flash of yellow, I knew I'd found the trail Shax laid for me. My guess is that he'd been watching, waiting for me to break away, and he'd lead me to Cali.

I picked up Cali's cheerleader top. Dirt streaked across the bright fabric. Maybe a swatch of blood. Shax's sick game led me away from the packed road and down a row of planes. Like cairns strung along a mountain trail, he left clues. A sock. A tennis shoe. Farther from the main path, through a maze of dead planes. I left the items where they lay.

Another sock. Her skirt. Isolating me from Rafe and the others. My voices cursed and rioted.

Too late.

She's dead.

You're dead.

Her shoe lay in the middle of a narrow path, pointing toward one of the planes. The seal on the door had been ripped and a sliver of weak light seeped into the darkness of the Boneyard. Pink cotton panties hung limp from a bolt.

Shax had planted the Hansel and Gretel game after we'd arrived, so I knew he watched every move. If I pulled out my phone to contact Rafe, Shax would know his time was up. If Cali still survived, he'd surely kill her then.

I had to face him alone.

The B52 rested on its belly on the ground, the wheels retracted or removed. The metal of the door still clung to the warmth of the day. It took strength to wedge my fingers into the gap between the door and ease it open.

I stepped into the belly of the metal whale. Inside, the temperature rose ten degrees. The smell of feces and urine snaked up my nose and I gagged. In midday, this place would be Hell. A candle, not more than six inches high, burned in the far corner, showing a pile of blankets.

Except it wasn't only blankets. Wisps of blonde hair swirled at the edges of the lump. A stretch of pale skin, maybe an arm or leg, spilled from the jumbled heap of blankets.

"Cali!" I ran forward, skidding on my knees.

Before I touched her, Shax materialized from the dark corner, holding a serrated hunting knife. "Officer Butler. Glad you could make it."

"You walked into his trap. You moron." Frank shouted.

"Shut up," I said to Frank.

Shax grinned, his teeth a shocking white in the dim light. "Yes. The voices. What are they telling you? To kill yourself?" He gave me a sly sneer. "Again."

I stared at him, trying to place his face. Without the Halloween prop of the false damaged teeth, he looked familiar. But how?

A garbled mess of fabric twitched in a dark corner of the plane and a weak whimper slipped across the room. By squinting into the gloom, I made out a tiny face and tangled blonde hair. "Zoey?"

She whimpered again and her glassy eyes blinked slowly.

Shax's white teeth gleamed. "Don't worry about the little one. I've been saving her. With the right dosages, she's been quiet as a mouse, waiting for her turn."

How had I let this happen? It was all my fault.

The man in the blue shirt. Shax, was the man watching me at the playground that day, the same one outside Tara's office. Probably the driver of the gray car in my neighborhood. He'd been stalking me. There was more but the memory lay hidden beneath my consciousness. Someone needed to tell me.

Satisfaction oozed from him. "Surprised I know about your voices? I've still got a medical license in New York, even though no one would ever hire me again. If you're smart and connected, it's not that hard to skirt HIPPA and find your files."

He knew. Every secret spread before him like a frog splayed for dissection.

Zoey dropped her head and closed her eyes. I prayed the drugs filling her system would block out this whole experience.

I scrambled to appear in control. "If you read my records you know I was released and declared mentally stable. I'm not about to kill myself."

He tapped the knife on his open palm. "Your records say a number of things that are only half true. Your mother is adept at manipulating official documents, because a crazy daughter wouldn't look good on Sheriff Carmichael, would it?"

I could repeat it a million times and it wouldn't make it true. "I'm not crazy."

"But you're not really sane, are you?"

Who was he? Frank and the others shouted and jostled for

my attention but I held Shax in focus. "You're crazier than I'll ever be. You killed my daughter. And now another."

He laughed. "Oh, she's no more dead than Zoey. What fun would that be? I want you to see when I take two girls for the two you took from me."

Shax had the only weapon. He held every advantage. Foolish desperation made me say, "The others are pretty far away. I won't tell them I saw you. Let me take the girls."

He tsked. "You know better than that. It wasn't easy keeping her alive and quiet. I'm not about to let that effort go to waste."

There was nothing I could do or say to stop him. If I shouted for help, he'd kill us before Rafe got here. "You don't have to do this."

"Exactly. I said those same words to you six years ago. And you know what you said?"

Six years ago. Buffalo, New York. I looked in his eyes, searched his face, and I couldn't remember. "No. What did I say?"

His mouth twisted and he used a falsetto voice as if imitating me. "'If you didn't want to be arrested, you shouldn't have done it.'"

"If I was wrong, why punish Cali and Zoey? Or Bethany? Kill me, instead."

He smirked. "You'd like that, wouldn't you? Then you could end all the pain and guilt. But you should be punished for what you stole."

"I didn't steal anything from you."

He lifted his eyebrows in scorn. "Oh? You arrested me, exposed my secrets to the world. I wasn't hurting anyone. And you ruined me."

"How does that make it okay for you to murder innocent people?" Reasoning with him wouldn't make him change his mind, but it might give Rafe time to find us, or give me opportunity to make a plan.

"You don't remember me, do you?" He seemed disappointed.

If I said no, it might enrage that ego he so clearly fed. "Sure, I do."

Tap, tap, tap. The knife slapped into his palm. The reek of the plane made me shudder and my stomach lurched. He taunted me. "Someone inside your head knows."

Peanut. But I can't ask her.

Shax bent over and whisked the blanket back, revealing a naked, blood-smeared Cali. She lay on her stomach, her blonde hair tangled and matted, hiding her face. "Wake up, darling."

Shax grabbed an arm and jerked her up. A muffled scream escaped from her. He yanked her over and she landed on her back. A soaked and grimy bandana gag cut into the sides of her mouth, tied snug around her face. He'd beaten her face and the skin under both eyes ranged in color from deep purple to spoiled meat yellow. Bruises lined her arms and legs.

Cali opened her eyes, revealing dark, dilated pupils. Her glassy stare, full of terror, made me think she was confused about where, and why, and who. But she knew pain.

"Remind you of anything?" Shax asked.

The moaning came from my throat. I raised my eyes to Shax. "Why are you doing this?"

He leaned over and placed the sharp tip of the knife on Cali's flat belly and pressed, drawing a bead of blood. She writhed and choked against the gag.

Zoey whimpered again.

I lunged for him and with a quick thrust, he rammed the knife toward me. It tore through my shorts into the side of my thigh, missing the artery. He didn't strike deep but it burned, the serrated edge shredding my skin.

"You stay over there, Officer Butler." Shax held up the

bloody knife. "I can kill you now, and maybe that's what you prefer. But I think you'd rather stay alive and look for a chance to save them."

Frank coiled and rattled inside me. The rest stayed quiet, except Peanut's sobbing.

"Tell me. What do you remember about me?" He smiled with perfect white teeth.

Nothing. I remembered nothing. There was noise in my head and the flames of Frank's hatred licked at me.

Shax pressed the knife to Cali's left breast and drew blood. She shrieked, a horrible sound clogged by the gag.

"Think about it. Six years ago. Late night. Parking lot."

It could be anything. Anyone. Maggie spoke through the haze of voices. *"Ask her. Ask Peanut. She knows."*

Shax ran the blade across Cali's breast bone. She sobbed and fought but her movements were feeble.

"No. Stop!" I shouted at him.

He grinned and held the knife in front of his face. "I want you to remember who I was so you can see what you did to me. So you know at the end of the day, this is all your fault."

Maggie finally spoke. *"Ask her, dear. She knows."*

If I spoke to Peanut, it would kill me.

Shax's blade bit into Cali's right side, sending a trickle of blood to the blanket. She turned her eyes to me, pleading, crying, grunting around the gag.

"Peanut keeps the secrets, dear. You have to ask."

My sobs echoed in the plane's belly. At the end of the day. At the end of the day. Shax repeated that. Who else said that?

"Tell me." I cried. "Peanut, talk to me."

She sniffed. In a small voice, so quiet I barely heard her, she began. Shax, Zoey, Cali, the horror of the plane's interior faded. I dropped to my knees, no longer feeling the wound in my thigh.

Peanut started in halting words but as I let her talk she grew stronger. I don't know how long it went on. She told me everything and I remembered.

Frost hangs in the air, making a hazy circle around the orange street-light that casts enough shadow to see the telephone and cable wires crisscrossed through the alley.

All I see at first is a man, head back in his Lexus. Then a young boy pops from the back and leans over the seat, watching something on the floor of the driver's side. The man jerks into the seat, then he too, looks to the floor.

The little girl shimmies from the floor between his legs and scrambles to the back seat.

No child should be awake at three a.m. A girl her age should be tucked into bed, her flannel pajamas protecting her against the night chill, the glowing warmth of a nightlight holding back scary dreams. Not out on a frosty night, naked on the floor of a monster's car.

Frank finally interrupted. *"Enough!"*

I opened my eyes, still on my knees. Everyone shouted in my head, Frank loudest of all.

Shax stood in front of me. Cali lay bleeding to his side and I didn't see that he'd done any more damage while I'd been away. He studied me. "I never get tired of watching schizophrenics interact with their various personalities."

"You should know better, Dr. Wainright. Not all voice hearers have split personalities. Some of us function quite well. Might even seem normal."

His face broke into a wide grin. "You know me. Amazing. One of the personalities told you."

I placed my hands on the floor and pushed to my feet, favoring the injured leg. "She told me a lot of things. But I remembered most of it."

"So you know how you ruined my life?"

"I know you're the worst scum that walked the planet. Child

pornography. Exploiting children not even old enough to see an R rated movie."

He bristled. "Puritan. Those kids loved it. They got paid good money. Got attention. And it felt good to them."

I nearly gagged. "It doesn't feel good. It's a living horror."

His eyebrows shot up. "Sounds like experience talking."

"You deserved to go to jail. You should be rotting there still."

He slapped the knife into his palm again. "But I'm not. Released early for good behavior. By Sheriff Carmichael, who needed tax cuts to win the election."

Growing rage bubbled like hot tar.

He sneered at me. "Because of you, I lost my wife and my daughters. Once you exposed me, they had to leave. We were a loving family. My daughters were in private school, excelling, probably going to be accepted at all the Ivy Leagues. My practice was thriving. But no one wants to see a psychiatrist who's been convicted of child molesting. So," he snapped the fingers of one hand, "poof. It's all gone. Thanks to you."

"I didn't do those horrible things to children. You did."

"I'm not a man without resources, though. Way too smart for you or your mother or that wetback cop. You're wondering how I got into your house? The keycode isn't hard to figure out from a parked car and a set of high powered binoculars."

My head pounded and I couldn't concentrate on his explanation.

Another wet crimson line jumped from his knife point as he ran it along Cali's bicep. This time she didn't move. "Getting that little girl to come to me was clever. Your quiet neighborhood where everyone retreats behind their doors in the heat of the day was a blessing to me. I slipped in the front door, told her the baby birds needed her help. She came with me easily, and no one heard her scream when I grabbed her."

I fought to keep my hands from my ears.

"If you looked behind you on your run, you might have seen me trailing you. Of course, the bushes and cactus hid me well enough. How you manage to run that far in this heat is admirable. You know rattle snakes only venture in about a hundred and fifty feet radius their whole lives? A little rope around her feet kept her in place long enough for me to roust that thing."

"She's alive. Doing quite well." I manage a taunt. "You won't succeed here, either. The MPs and cops are out there. If I found you so quickly, they will, too."

He blew that off. "You found me because I drew you here. I didn't leave bread crumbs for them. I picked a place they'll never search."

Frank bellowed and I held him back by the thinnest thread. "You're not that smart, Shax."

"You can call me Doctor now that we have no secrets between us."

Frank shouted and pushed.

"I wanted you to watch Bethany scream and beg me not to hurt her. It would have given me so much satisfaction to see your face as I raped her, hear her anguish, watch the life drain from her eyes. But I miscalculated. I killed her too soon."

My ears filled with the confusion in my brain. I didn't want to hear any more.

"Then you lost your mind. That was even a bigger disappointment. You broke down so you didn't have to suffer the guilt of what you did."

"I didn't do it. You did." The voice coming from my throat deepened and took on a gravely quality.

He bent over and traced a thin line down the top of Cali's left thigh with the point of his knife. She whimpered. Her eyes were closed and her breathing shallow. "Your mother whisked you away and I spent a long time tracking you. She wanted to be sure to tuck you so far from Buffalo you couldn't taint her reputation."

Frank pushed harder.

"If you'd have left me alone, I wouldn't have to punish you. Bethany, that sweet girl, would be, what, nineteen now? She'd be in college. And Cali would get to see the sun rise tomorrow. All of this is your fault."

The roaring in my head made it impossible for me to answer.

Shax poked the tip of the knife in the skin just under Cali's left ear. Her eyes flew open and a guttural scream soaked into the gag. Her legs and arms twitched, as if she didn't have strength to fight more.

He looked up at me, glee shining in his eyes. "Death by a thousand cuts and we're only on about six hundred now. Of course with Bethany, I only got to five hundred or so. But she had some of your mother's spirit and fought much harder. She didn't want to die."

Frank exploded. Out of my head, into my whole body. He roared with a voice that vibrated the metal walls of the plane. My muscles burned with his hatred, fueling a primal urge to kill.

"No!" I screamed it with all my strength. My head felt as if it burst with bits of bone and brain exploding into the plane. Before I could face Shax, I had to defeat Frank.

My hands clamped over my ears and I squeezed my eyes closed. "No!" I shouted again, not able to form words and instead using everything within me to push Frank back. Not with the rage of death, but with the strength of love.

I held him back but the roar and pressure in my head made it hard to breathe or focus my eyes. I needed Frank but I couldn't let him take over or I might never come back.

Shax threw back his head and laughed, a high-pitched cackle. "Fascinating."

Cali opened her eyes, lost and terrified, they pleaded with me.

The voice thundering from my throat was Frank, but it was me who burst from the floor. I hit Shax full force in his chest, driving him backward where we crashed to the ground. My years as a cop and his small size gave me a chance. I pushed up and straddled Shax's chest.

Shax held his knife and slashed wildly.

Blood flew as I grabbed for the weapon and the serrated edge ripped my palm. I pulled my left arm back and popped it forward, punching Shax squarely in the nose. The crunch of cartilage and warm spurt of blood made Frank bellow for more. I clamped my mind closed.

Shax screamed and arced his knife with no real aim. His eyes lost focus in his panic.

The knife struck me in my right bicep but Frank beat against my brain.

Kill. Kill. Kill.

I ratcheted back and punched again, this time smashing into Shax's jaw with a crack.

The pain must have snapped something in Shax and his face hardened with determination. This time when he thrust the knife, he had a clear target.

The knife headed toward my jugular and I twisted to the left, my knee slipping from the ground. The knife punctured skin and muscle just below my collarbone, sending fire through me. Frank howled.

Kill. Kill. Kill.

Shax bucked and knocked me to the ground. Air rushed from my lungs as Shax landed on my chest. The knife flashed in the scant candlelight. High above, then arcing down. I jerked enough the ragged edge tore at the side of my neck.

Again, Frank let out a savage shriek and I summoned the strength of the multitude to hold him back. Frank roared and surged and I didn't know if I could keep him locked inside much longer. I grabbed the blade, screaming at the pain as it tore through my hand.

I wrenched it out of Shax's grasp. He rolled off me and jumped to his feet, panting and eyeing me. "Are you going to kill me?"

Blood streamed from my hand, thigh, chest and maybe a few other places. I concentrated on the pain to keep from listening to Frank's blood lust. A desire to kill so strong I was afraid it would obliterate everything else.

Shax backed to the wall. His eyes suddenly darted to the door propped against the opening. He held up both hands. "They're here. You were right. I guess I didn't hide well enough after all."

KILL HIM!

Frank wanted Shax's blood. His only reason for being was to make that blood flow, hard and hot. I shifted the knife from my right hand to my left and wiped blood from my palm to my shorts. Frank was left handed. With the knife firmly in hand, Frank urged me to advance on a trembling Shax.

Kill. Kill. Kill.

Shax once again flicked his eyes to the door. "Wait. See? You don't have to do this. They're here."

"Jamie!" Rafe's shouts sounded from outside the door.

Now! Kill!

The knife seemed to breathe and Frank's passion threatened. I wanted to shove the blade into Shax's heart, feel it sink deep, hear his cry of agony, watch his life ebb as he'd watched Bethany.

Do it! Now!

All I had to do is let Frank take over. Shax deserved to die.

"Don't kill me." Shax fell to his knees and begged.

Kill. Kill. Kill.

I couldn't take the chance he'd slip the system and be on the loose again. The world would be better off without him. It would be easy to finish him now. All I had to do was let Frank have his way one more time.

But I couldn't hide from myself any longer.

"Hurry," I shouted to Rafe. "In here."

47

Rafe and the MPs burst into the plane. Shouts, confusion, noise, both inside my head and out. Rafe grabbed me by the shoulders at the same time the MPs rushed Shax and had him tackled to the floor before I dropped the knife.

"Cali." I pulled away from Rafe and threw myself to the ground next to her. I tugged a filthy blanket to cover her. "It's okay." I crooned, even though I knew it would be a long time before it would be okay for her again. "I'm here. You're safe."

A radio cracked behind me and the woman MP ordered an ambulance. She knelt next to Zoey and took her in her arms and whispered comforting words.

Rafe used his cell and called for backup.

The other MP cuffed Shax and shoved him toward the door.

Shax ranted about his innocence and that I was the one hurting Cali and Zoey. He yelled I was trying to kill him.

The tiny candle flame only gave muted light but the male MP donned a headlamp and set flashlights around. He screwed up his face. "Holy crap, it smells awful in here."

Rafe disappeared, probably to help guard Shax.

The sirens sounded in the distance and Cali wept, like a weak kitten crying for her mother's warmth.

I pulled her close and rocked her, telling her over and over that she was safe and I wouldn't leave her. The voices inside of me quieted as we waited for the ambulance.

When the EMTs arrived, I stepped back only long enough to let them attend to her and load her on a stretcher. The woman MP carried Zoey, cuddling her and refusing to relinquish her to a stretcher. I followed one step behind as they lifted her from the plane into the cool night air. The girls were carried to two waiting ambulances.

Rafe stood in a crowd of uniformed officers surrounded by three patrol cars with pulsing blue and red lights. He jogged to my side and laid a gentle hand on my arm. "You're hurt. You need to get cleaned up and bandaged."

Blood oozed from my hand and at his mention, I felt the burning along my collarbone. Dried and sticky blood covered my leg where it had spilled from my thigh. "I'll get it done at the hospital."

The MP climbed into one ambulance with Zoey. I kept following Cali until one of the EMTs held her hand up.

"I'm sorry, ma'am. You need to wait for the next unit. They'll treat you and take you to the hospital. You can see her then."

Cali opened her eyes and focused on me.

I levered the woman's arm down. "I'm not leaving her."

Something about the way I said it made her pause. She looked down at Cali, then back at me. "Fine."

Rafe watched me climb into the back of the ambulance. "I'll be there soon."

48

The next day, Rafe drove me home from the hospital. I'd recovered quickly once they pumped me full of fluids and dressed the wounds, but they kept me overnight and through much of the next day. I was grateful for Rafe's backup when I insisted they put me in the same room with Cali. I'm not sure they'd have allowed it without his charm.

I wandered the hall outside Zoey's room. Family and friends packed the small space and I felt she was in the most loving care possible.

Mom had hurried to the hospital, but after a few hours, I'd urged her to wait for me at home. She was annoyed with my attention to Cali and obviously put out by Rafe's presence, so she agreed to stock up on groceries and keep the house clean for my return.

I spent most of the time sitting by Cali's bed and talking to her whenever she was awake. Her mother had spoken to her on the phone and said she wouldn't be able to get a plane back to Tucson for a few more days. Clearly, Cali's mother didn't see the need to cut her vacation short to nurse her daughter. I wanted to throttle Kandy, but Frank had nothing to say.

When Cali slept and while Rafe watched TV set on low volume, I'd closed my eyes and worked through everything Peanut told me

"Are you feeling okay?" Rafe asked for the hundredth time, pulling me back to the rumble of the car's tires on the road.

"The stitches sting. This baseball glove of a hand is going to be a pain in the butt, but, yeah, I'm fine."

"That's not really what I was asking."

"Oh." I slipped my arm under the chest belt and tugged it away from the bandages on my collarbone. The bright sunshine colors of the Mexican bird of paradise waved from the median and the orange flags of the ocotillo cactus gave me something to focus on. "They're back. Most of them."

"Not all?"

Tara was going to have a field day with this. "Frank hasn't said a word."

After Mom left, I'd had some time to talk to Rafe. I'd told him about Benjamin Wainright, the prominent psychiatrist whom I'd arrested for child molestation. Then I tried to explain about Frank and what happened in the plane belly.

Rafe turned into my neighborhood. "Is Frank gone forever?"

I slumped into my seat, only half remembering the blood-lust and the desire to kill. "I can't be sure."

That scant smiled slipped onto his face.

Not what I expected. "What's so funny?"

"I picture Frank as big and green. He's the Hulk and you're this mild-mannered Bruce Banner."

A smile forced itself onto my face, then fled. "Except he's not the Hulk. Frank is me." The cloud dipped lower on my head and I said, "What would you think of me working with troubled kids?"

Rafe let out a chuckle. "'Cause you were so good with Megan?"

"Okay, maybe I have a prejudice against entitled brats with helicopter mothers, but I think I can help kids. Like Cali."

He glanced at me and his face softened. "I think you'd be terrific. I know of a mentoring program that could use you."

We drove closer to my house. Sherilyn's front door opened and a rainbow of Mylar and ribbon burst onto the yard. Rafe braked while little feet raced toward the street.

I tensed. Sherilyn needed to be more careful with those kids.

Cheyenne held the strings of two balloons in one hand and jumped up and down, shouting and waving. Kaycee clutched a balloon string in each hand and stood patiently on the curb. Sherilyn, in cutoffs and tank top, carried Jackson on her hip, a ribbon tied around his arm and the balloon bobbing overhead.

Barely above an idle, Rafe inched into the driveway and the whole family swarmed my car door. They only backed up enough to allow me to open it. Keeping my grunts and groans to myself, I favored the least injured arms and legs to push and pull myself to stand.

"We baked you a cake!" Cheyenne shouted.

Kaycee threw her arms around my legs and the stitches in my thigh bit me, but it still felt good. In her passion, she accidentally let go of her balloons and they sailed away. She watched them float into the sky, tears accumulating in her wide blue eyes.

Cheyenne tsked. "I told you we should tie them to your arm. Here, you can have one of mine."

Sherilyn grinned at me. "It's been like this since Kaycee came home from the hospital. I 'spose she'll get tired of being nice eventually, but I'll take it for now."

Rafe made it from his side the car and slipped an arm around my waist. For once, the feel of someone close to me didn't make me want to scream. I wound my arm around him and leaned in, letting him take weight from my bad leg.

Mom stepped out the front door and hurried down the walk. She scowled at Rafe. "I told you to rent a wheelchair. I should have gone myself."

I squeezed Rafe closer. "He had one but I made him take it back. I'll heal faster if I exercise the muscles."

She made a move to take Rafe's place but he tucked me closer.

I stopped my slow progress and looked up at him. "Can you help Sherilyn and the kids with the cake and all the pictures I'm sure they've painted for me? Give me a few minutes to talk to Mom."

His passive face and intense eyes told me he didn't like it. I nudged him away and limped toward Mom.

She wrapped her arm around the small of my back and I flung my arm over her shoulder. Cheyenne and Kaycee raced toward the street.

Sherilyn issued a shrill whistle that made Mom and I both jump. We turned to see Cheyenne and Kaycee standing like soldiers on alert, their feet on the curb. Dempsey's white Lincoln cruised down the road and pulled into their driveway. We all waited while Mr. and Mrs. Dempsey lumbered out and hurried toward us.

"Don't you look like something the cat dragged in," Mr. Dempsey said.

Mrs. Dempsey batted at him. "Oh bosh. Don't listen to him." She stepped forward and kissed my cheek. "You're beautiful. And my, what a hero! First you save little Kaycee and then those poor, poor girls."

Mom's arm turned to stone. Her smile looked strained. "She really ought to get some rest. Thank you for your concern."

I twisted around. "Sherilyn, there's enough cake for everyone isn't there?"

Cheyenne jumped up and down. "Yay! We have Skittles, too!"

Mrs. Dempsey brightened. "A party! I've got some sparkling grape juice left over from Christmas." She grabbed Mr. Dempsey's arm and tugged him across the gravel yard to their house.

Sherilyn released the girls to dash across the street. She hollered at the Dempsey's. "Grab your suits. We'll meet at Jamie's in fifteen minutes for a pool party."

Not all the voices in my head were happy about the coming invasion, but even the most rattled took it better than Mom appeared to. "That's not a good idea. Give us—"

My upheld hand stopped her. "I want them to come over. But we need to talk first."

She helped me limp inside and I directed her to the back-yard and asked for a glass of ice water with lemon.

She brought it out and set it on the half-finished mosaic table next to my chair.

After a sip I said, "The real reason I wanted Rafe to bring me home instead of you was to give me time to make a phone call."

"I hope it was to Tara. I talked to her as well and we agreed you should definitely go to the spa in Palm Springs, maybe longer than I'd thought at first."

I held my hand up, the white of the bandage flashing like the warning of a deer's tail. "I called the retirement board this morning."

She froze.

"My records are clean. With accumulated personal leave and union benefits from my breakdown, I retired legitimately. You didn't pull any strings."

She stared at the desert sky above the cinderblock fence.

"You lied to me. Was it a matter of controlling me?"

She still didn't answer.

I took a swig and let it cool my throat while I gathered my courage. "I made another call."

She glared at me. "Let me guess. Not to Tara."

"I talked to the special investigator this morning."

Her face paled. "Why?"

Sweat beaded along my back and I leaned forward to let the air flow. "There is this voice."

She exhaled. "Not that again."

"Her name is Peanut. Remember how we used to call Bethany that?"

She flinched. "She was so tiny and that blonde hair, so sweet."

I tried not to think about it. "When I started therapy, I began to address the voices. Little by little I talked to most of them."

Mom rolled her eyes.

"But not to Peanut."

Mom stood up. "I'm not going to listen to this fantasy about a made-up person."

"Please. Sit down."

She stared at me, clearly debating, and I held her gaze. In a slow movement she lowered herself to her chair.

"I couldn't bring myself to talk to her. Of course, I thought Peanut was Bethany and she'd blame me for leaving her alone that night. She'd tell me things I couldn't remember from the scene, and I knew I'd break."

Mom's eyes filled with tears, so unlike her. "Bethany isn't a ghost in your head. That's your disease. It isn't real."

I wiped the tears dribbling off my chin. "I finally talked to Peanut. My little girl. And it made me stronger."

Mom shook her head, the tears refusing to fall. "I'm going to call Tara. She'll prescribe something to help you calm down."

I blinked and gathered strength. "I've felt guilty and begged to die. I abandon Bethany and her death is my fault and I knew she'd hate me."

Mom jumped up and rushed toward the door. "This is ridiculous."

I raised my voice so she couldn't run from it. "I realize Peanut is my mind's version of my daughter." I stopped myself from adding that I wasn't crazy. "But she didn't blame me." I choked around the lump in my throat. "She told me she loves me. No matter what. Unconditionally."

She raised her gaze above my head, as if tuning me out.

"Something you and Dad never did."

"Oh, please. Are you complaining about being a victim?"

I gulped my water to calm myself. "I've stopped defending you. Peanut reminded me of the neglect. The evenings and weekends I spent alone. All the school events you never attended. The disappointment and lectures when I didn't perform."

She looked disgusted. "You've always been weak. If I had been soft it would have ruined you."

"I was a child."

Her lip turned up. "I learned early to rely on myself. You needed to learn to take care of yourself." Mom advanced toward me. "I did what I thought was best for you."

Relief kissed each word. "The voices started early. First Maggie, the mother. She loved me, was kind to me. Forgave all my faults. Was never disappointed in me."

"You can't blame me for your mental illness."

"I needed someone who cared and you and Dad weren't there."

"You have no idea what it was like for women then. Even now, we have to fight for every advancement. Your career was easy because I was there to pave the way for you."

"It was never about me. You knew Benjamin Wainright killed Bethany."

"That's ridiculous."

"If you'd let them investigate, they'd have discovered you let him out on your early release program. You'd be to blame and might not get reelected."

She grabbed the door knob. "I don't have to listen to this."

My control slipped and I yelled at her. "She'd be alive today if you hadn't chased your career so hard."

She whirled around. "It was your fault, not mine." She advanced on me. "You never taught her how to take care of herself. It was you who left her alone and you who didn't drive home the lessons to never open the door for a stranger."

There was no sign of forced entry. Why had she opened the door?

The look on Mom's face was one I'd seen before when an officer had screwed up and made her look bad. Her face could go from the patient, caring mentor to a raging Alpha wolf ready to rip apart a weak pack member. "When she called I told her to lock the doors and windows, pull the shades. She would have been fine if she'd done what I said."

My head roared and it took a second to clear. "She called you?"

Her look of disdain didn't bother me. "You were on a date. Always putting your relationship with a man ahead of what's really important."

I ignored her lie. "She called you? Why?"

Mom's lip curled. "Because she was afraid. She thought she heard noises outside. She was fifteen and had a wild imagination. I thought she got herself spooked. If she'd have done what I said—"

My voice shook. "She called and you did nothing?"

Tears finally tumbled from her eyes. "She was always timid

and scared, like you. If I indulged either of you by running every time you cried, I'd never get anything else done. How did I know this time was different?"

I couldn't distinguish the voices as they wailed. "And you covered it up."

"You were so fragile. If you knew all of this, you'd have fallen apart. I had to keep it from you. To protect you."

Despite what she'd told me my whole life, I realized now, I was no more fragile than Bethany was timid. It was all lies. My throat ached with screams I suppressed. "It wasn't for me. It was never for me."

One angry swipe took care of her tears. "Everything I ever did was for you. I worked hard, found opportunities, and scrambled after them. All to show you a role model of a strong woman. Someone you could look up to and emulate. You could have followed in my footsteps and even surpassed me. All you wanted was to put in your time and go home to your family. Like a typical woman."

My voice was small. "I loved being a mother."

"You could have been so much more."

I sat back and drained the last of my water, the slivers of ice slipping to the bottom as I set it down. "You're going to have to leave."

She choked. "What?"

"Cali is being released tomorrow morning and she needs your bedroom."

She looked shocked. "That's ridiculous. You won't even commit to getting a dog. You can barely take care of yourself."

There was no point in arguing. I stared at her in silence.

Her body snapped. "Fine. Enjoy your special party with your new friends. We'll talk more later."

"No." There might have been an echo of her in that word. "We won't talk for a while. Maybe never. I told the investigator about the missing evidence, which Kari will confirm. She knows about you bribing Grainger and the payout to his son. When they hear I'm going to testify, other county officers will come forward."

Now her jaw dropped open. She slammed it closed and spewed at me. "After I spent my whole life sacrificing for you."

I held up my bandaged hand. "No more."

She started to protest.

"Leave."

She paled and stared at me.

"Now." Using my good hand, I pushed myself to stand and limped past her, through the open French doors and into the house.

The doorbell rang and little fists pounded. Through the thin walls came Cheyenne's muffled shouts, "Let us in!"

It was long past time for me to do just that.

LOVE READING MYSTERIES & THRILLERS?

Never miss a new release! Sign up to receive exclusive updates from author Shannon Baker and the SRP Mystery & Thriller Team.

Join today at Shannon-Baker.com

YOU MIGHT ALSO ENJOY...

The Desert Behind Me

Echoes in the Sand

The Nora Abbott Series

Height of Deception

Skies of Fire

Canyon of Lies

The Kate Fox Series

Stripped Bare

Dark Signal

Bitter Rain

Never miss a new release! Sign up to receive exclusive updates from author Shannon Baker and the SRP Mystery & Thriller Team.

Shannon-Baker.com/Newsletter

Echoes in the Sand

A fresh murder in Arizona throws a family into chaos, and unravels a decades-old mystery.

It's been twenty years since the accident. A nighttime car crash on a desert road that left her parents dead and her sister disabled.

Now a law enforcement officer with the Arizona Rangers, Michaela Sanchez has tried to get over the guilt she feels. She's tried to move on.

But when her brother is charged with the murder of a local activist, echoes of her family's tragic night come crashing back.

Bound to her siblings by the shared scars of loss, Michaela will do everything in her power to prove her brother's innocence. But as she investigates, Michaela unearths shocking information. A new version of events that makes her question everything she thought she knew about her family's tragedy.

What really happened the night of the accident, years ago? Could her brother really have committed murder? If not, then who did?

Now Michaela is certain of only one thing. To get to the truth, she must confront the secrets of her family's past.

Get your copy today at Shannon-Baker.com

ACKNOWLEDGMENTS

I've said it before and I'll whine about it again, writing books is hard. At least it is for me. If it weren't for the love and support of others, I'd never get to The End. Without fail and for everything I've ever written, including newsletters, my biggest thanks is to Janet Fogg. She pushes, prods, proofs, inspires, and expects better things from me.

To my clever and hard-working agent, Jill Marsal, a huge debt of gratitude for thoughtful reading and for finding this book a good home. Thank you to Terri Bischoff, and editor with a gentle touch and a keen eye.

To the amazing team at Severn River Publishing, Andrew, Amber, and Keris, as well as all the talented craftspeople they've gathered, I couldn't be more grateful. You've welcomed me and my stories into the fold and it's a nice place to be.

Eleanor Longden's TED Talk about hearing voices grabbed me by the heart. During research for this book, I heard so many wrenching stories, as well as some with humor, and many inspiring journeys. I was surprised to find out how many people hear voices. For all of these people, I hope I addressed the subject with fairness, accuracy, and compassion. I don't know the road you travel but thank you for courageously sharing your truth.

I tip my hat, as always, to Rocky Mountain Fiction Writers. This group is splitting at the seams with generous, talented, smart, savvy, and unbelievably supportive writers. Every danged one of you. Thank you.

And to my phenomenal daughters, Joslyn and Erin, who teach me, inspire me, tickle me, and keep me on my toes. People say writing books is like having children, but I disagree. There is nothing as special as you in my life.

Thank you to Dave. For so much. Always.

ABOUT THE AUTHOR

Shannon Baker lives on the edge of the desert in Tucson with her crazy Weimaraner and her favorite human. Baker spent 20 years in the Nebraska Sandhills, where cattle outnumber people by more than 50:1. She lived in Flagstaff for several years and worked for the Grand Canyon Trust, a hotbed of environmentalists who, usually, don't resort to murder. She is the proud recipient of the Rocky Mountain Fiction Writers 2014 and 2017-18 Writer of the Year Award.

A lover of the great outdoors, she can be found backpacking, traipsing to the bottom of the Grand Canyon, skiing mountains and plains, kayaking lakes, river running, hiking, cycling, and scuba diving whenever she gets a chance. Arizona sunsets notwithstanding, Baker is, and always will be a Nebraska Husker. Go Big Red.

You can find Shannon online at www.Shannon-Baker.com, and connect with her on Facebook at AuthorShannonBaker or Instagram at ShannonBaker5328.

CPSIA information can be obtained
at www.ICGtesting.com
Printed in the USA
LVHW110343171019
634411LV00005B/585/P